The Inheritance

by
Morgan K. Wyatt

Published by Sleeping Dragon

www.morgankwyatt.com
www.facebook.com/AuthorMorganKWyatt

Books by Morgan K Wyatt

Anthologies

The Hope Chest

The Lake House

Sunkissed: Effusions of Summer

Fiction

The Inheritance

Seeking Shelter

Non-fiction

Dating After Forty-eight

Suspicious Circumstances Series

Love or Deception

He Loves Me Not

Soul Mate Series

The Soul Mate Search

The Love Talisman

Chapter One

THE GEESE, HONKING as they flew overhead, woke her. Melody blinked a few times trying to bring the room into focus in the weak morning sunlight. The familiar dark furniture abutted the walls, leaving a slender walkway to the door and closet. The tang of pine-scented cleaner hung in the air. Old Roy's house. Technically, it was half hers now—hers and some neglectful nephew who allowed his uncle to die without even a goodbye.

Melody had spent hours listening to her patient reminisce about his nephew, Levi. The stories drew an image of a confused, often awkward boy who tested the man's wits while working his way into his heart. Roy's tone of voice and every wistful expression demonstrated fondness, even pride in Levi. She didn't know why.

Pushing herself out of bed, she headed to the kitchen to make coffee. Roy had never used a coffee maker with a programmable timer. Still, she was glad for the unexpected bounty of Roy's house and all its furnishings. Her former roommate Linda's decision to marry stripped their shared apartment of anything movable.

The night before the extreme cleaning, she and Linda argued about what belonged to whom. Anything they bought together, Linda claimed because she needed it more. Her reasoning made no sense, but instead of debating it half the night, Melody chose sleep over arguing. After an unusually long day, she arrived back to a locked apartment. When she unlocked the door, the empty room had her clutching her cell phone ready to call the police.

An ugly rocker chair from Linda's grandmother squatted in the corner, half a dozen fashion magazines lay open on the floor, and a broken vacuum were the only things left in the living room. Panic kept her close to the door with her hand on the knob, ready to flee if the robber showed himself, but a bright pink sticky note clung to the nearby wall. Notes stuck to random surfaces had served as Linda's calling card. She'd papered the apartment with reminders of things she needed Melody to do, including emptying the dishwasher and taking out the garbage.

Suspicion replaced fear as she strode over to the wall and jerked off the slip. Her eyes scanned the short note. *I only took what was mine. L*

Her fingers fisted around the note. Yeah, only took what was hers. She would have hauled off the appliances if they hadn't belonged to the apartment complex. A quick search revealed Melody still had a bed, clothes, toiletries, and whatever Linda didn't want or was broken, useless, or both.

As a hospice nurse, besides providing palliative care, she had to keep her patients' spirits up, but her bitter resentment toward her roommate trickled out. Roy pulled the entire story from her as she fixed his lunch the next day. While most hospice nurses never cooked for the patients, Melody chose to. It helped both her and Roy have some semblance of a life. His body made the inevitable slide toward a pre-death state in becoming an unreliable stranger. Before, with other patients, she witnessed their friends and close family visits dry up like a creek during a drought. Roy, on the other hand, often refused visits because his frail body and wonky memory embarrassed him. He told her once he didn't want his friends to see what he'd become, a shell of a man wearing adult diapers and not enough wit to follow a conversation.

Her muddled rant about Linda leaving suddenly resulted in Roy offering her his extra room. The man had winked at her and told her she could be his private nurse instead of the battleax CNA the agency had sent. The opportunity served as a pot of gold in the completely dreary scenario. Her insertion into Roy's life went against the agency's policy against personal involvement. For a short time, Roy was her workload, which suited her fine.

Walking around the lake, taking photos, swapping stories, just sitting together in the evenings made it real, almost family. Sometimes, she pretended Roy was her uncle. Still, she should have tried harder to get Roy's friends to visit, despite his wishes. Of all the friends and associates who never showed, none of them was as bad as Levi. The man never even wrote his dying relative a letter.

With the coffee started, she opened the mail that exhaustion had prevented her from looking at last night. One envelope with a lawyer's address on it caught her attention. Grabbing a butter knife, she sliced it open and scanned the contents. The absentee Levi's response to his uncle's death was to sue her for sole possession of the house and boat.

The letter fluttered to the floor as she growled, "I'll see you in court."

Melody picked up the letter. The day, which had started only minutes before, turned gloomy despite the sunlight flooding the living room. Clutching the letter, she collapsed onto the plastic-shrouded plaid couch and stared out the window at the narrow road winding past the house. Old Roy believed in getting the most mileage out of everything. The upholstered furniture sported plastic slipcovers while the tables wore pads to protect their surfaces. The practical furniture served its purpose without too much attention to its basic lines and faded brown plaid material.

Often, she wondered for whom he was preserving his 1950s furniture. She assumed the missing nephew merited the furnishings. Not once had she ever considered it was for her. Still, Roy had plied her with personal questions about her future prospects and gentlemen friends. No doubt, when the man discovered she had no sweetheart or family, he felt obliged to make provisions for her, an old school male who believed women needed protection.

She pulled her nightgown up under her legs to prevent them from sticking to the plastic. The usual thing would be to strip off the plastic, but something stopped her. Even though she'd lived in the house for over a month, it still didn't feel like home. She unfolded the letter and reread it. Still the same, it hadn't changed because she needed it to. *Damn.* Her body flopped back on the couch, adhering to the plastic with a slight smacking sound.

The unexpected bounty of the house and boat happened when she most needed it. Her luck tended to run to bill payments lost in the mail, which resulted in overdue charges. Even though she inherited the house, she expected the arrival of the soft-spoken lawyer every day, explaining it had all been a mistake, the reason behind why she never removed the plastic. Her left hand worried the stiff covering as she contemplated where she'd go. If possession was nine-tenths of the law, then she wasn't leaving. The high-handed Levi would find out she wasn't a pushover.

I have more right than he does. Sure, I'm not blood, but I was there when Roy needed someone.

Running a restless hand through her hair, Melody sighed deeply. It was Sunday. One of the few times she got an actual weekend off. Her free days disappeared under errands, laundry, and a stint at the animal shelter. The physical activity of bathing and walking the animals made her feel useful. It also undid some of the stress from dealing with mortality on a daily basis. Most patients were similar to

Roy and made their departures with dignity. A few considered her the angel of death and treated her with a mixture of horror and contempt, often cringing when she came near.

That's why a pet would come in handy. A pet would greet her with enthusiasm after a long day. She even had one in mind. A tan mutt about the size of a beagle, but with the long body of a basset, would be the one. He came through the dog drop window for cowardly owners who avoided any interaction with shelter staff as they deserted their pets. Melody nicknamed the dog Charmer because he stole her heart.

The pound kept the dog despite his age and lack of bloodlines after she suggested she might take him. The concept of commitment, however, troubled her, even to a canine. A good row across the lake would calm her mind.

Dressed in cutoff shorts and a faded college T-shirt, Melody headed down toward the dock. A man's silhouette against the morning light drew her eye. His ramrod posture eliminated him as a neighbor. As she drew closer, she admired how his T-shirt stretched across his defined chest.

He turned, possibly hearing her footsteps on the wooden dock. Their eyes met for a few brief seconds as she scanned his face. Since she already examined his body from behind, she kept her eyes above the shoulders. Close cut hair, a firm, determined chin, and well-defined lips that tilted up at her approach. *Nice.* He stood about six inches taller than her five feet and nine inches. He wasn't anyone she recognized from the area. A strange man between her and the boat should present a danger, but no alarm sounded in her head. Could it be his smile reassured her?

The man's grin grew and warmed, showing interest, which surprised Melody. Men didn't typically pay attention to her. Not that she could consider herself an expert on men since most of the ones she dealt with were at least sixty-five.

Still, the words of her last date haunted her, words her date never meant for her to overhear. Linda had fixed her up with a friend of her fiancé. The four of them went out to dinner. She and Linda were returning from the restroom when she heard his damning words.

"Melody is bigger than I like my women."

Her new outfit became an extravagant splurge. In no way could she have pretended she wasn't five nine and a curvy size fourteen. On dates, she usually wore flats because men typically obsessed over their own height. The rest of the night had been uncomfortable with her pretending she hadn't heard. Fortunately, there was no second date.

A rich baritone voice brought her back to the present. "Nice morning, isn't it? The lake is smooth, making it perfect for an early morning row." He nodded in the direction of the rowboat.

Melody automatically smiled back. "Yes." The one word escaped her lips as her mind tried to translate what he meant. Was he going to row Roy's boat across the lake? Did he invite her? The idea of sharing the close quarters of the vessel tempted her until she looked straight into his eyes. Her hand covered her racing heart. It couldn't be, but she recognized the slate color. Her breath hitched, testifying to his appeal, but if he knew who she really was, he'd toss her overboard.

Turning up his smile a notch, he explained, "I was going out for a row and would welcome company."

The idea tantalized Melody, but she knew better than to climb into the boat with Levi McDaniels.

Melody looked at his outstretched hand and took a step back even though something inside her urged her to take his hand. She would have if he were someone else. Levi would push her out of the boat if he knew her name though he'd have a hard time doing so. Being an active, robust female, as Roy like to call her whenever she swung him up out of his wheelchair, had advantages. Playing football with the neighborhood boys when she was younger not only made her tough but also willing to use any underhanded methods to secure the ball. A boy who cried foul when she bested him ended up ridiculed by his teammates. The brighter fellows soon learned to avoid her sharp elbows, gouging fingers, and troublesome knees.

Levi's eyebrows winged upward at her refusal. His outstretched hand fell abruptly by his side.

Regret weighed down her shoulders, despite knowing his identity. An attractive man on the right side of forty flirting with her was not an everyday occurrence. Biting her bottom lip, she tried to think of an excuse. "Can't today. I need to go pick up my dog."

Disbelief flickered in his eyes, but he chose not to call her on it. "Okay. If you change your mind, you have a rain check." His lips tugged up again, crinkling his tanned skin attractively around his eyes.

Her traitorous heart gave a little jump, despite knowing nothing could happen between the two of them. It was better that she didn't spin fantasies in her mind, ones that made excuses for his neglect of his uncle. A trip across the water would give him time to work his charm on her. She'd be offering the house and rowboat with both hands. No sir, she needed it more than he did.

His voice interrupted her thoughts. "What's your name?"

She kept walking, pretending not to hear.

LEVI WATCHED THE woman stride away with a sigh. He enjoyed watching her rounded hips climb the path, but what was the use? Apparently, she wanted nothing to do with him. Turning to stare at the water, he watched the early morning light slide across the lake. Shoving both hands in his pockets, he pondered her gentle rejection.

He'd never earned a reputation as a ladies' man, which he just amply demonstrated.

Leaning down near the edge of the dock, he grabbed the rope tethering the rowboat to the pier and pulled it closer. He might as well go for a row. Nothing else was going to happen this morning. He awkwardly lowered himself to the dock keeping his left leg out straight. His mysterious woman didn't even know the war had turned him into a cripple, but she still passed on him. Putting all his weight on his real leg, he eased himself into the boat. Some of the amputees at the rehab assured him his new leg would soon be easier to use than his remaining one, but he doubted it.

What was he thinking, flirting with a woman? It would only last until she got a glance at the straps attaching his new leg to his thigh. Then, she'd disappear with some mumbled excuse about looking for her dog or something. The thought surprised a harsh bark of laughter. Well, no matter. She'd already used that one.

The rope came loose from the pier after he flicked the rope a couple of times, releasing it from its hook. His left hand steadied his balance as he reached for an oar. Slick, cool wood rested under his fingers, the slats he and his uncle bent together to create the vessel. He never appreciated what he had then. Wisdom always came too late.

The time he and Roy shared working on the boat meant more to him in retrospect than it did at the time, even though it meant a great deal then. Life had dealt harshly with him or so he thought, leaving him with an uncle he barely knew while taking his parents. He heaped his anger at the world on his only remaining relative. Instead of becoming angry or distant, his uncle taught him what he knew about reading the waves, sailing, even making a boat the old-fashioned way as opposed to buying one of the factory-made fiberglass shells.

His hand caressed the side of the boat. Sweat, determination, and love went into the vessel. It hadn't been a fast build. His impatience must have chafed on Roy, but all he would do was murmur how things worth doing took time. Two years had passed before they completed the project.

Levi had resented school because it took him away from working on the boat. He didn't make too many friends at his new school at first. The large chip weighing down his shoulder had him looking for fights he quickly found as a new kid. Old Roy knew what was going on. Instead of lectures on staying out of trouble, he taught him to fight with quick, dirty moves his relative learned on dangerous shores where the American fleet was not always welcomed. Eventually, Levi became someone to avoid. Then he developed friends or at least guys who decided it was better to be his pal as opposed to a potential punching bag. Girls were a different matter, though. As a tall, thin, combative male, he was not a chick magnet. In that regard, not much had changed.

A few hard pulls on the oars sent him in the direction of the small wooded island. It wasn't much, just enough spindly pine trees to hide a boy. His sanctuary looked small and sparse close-up. He imagined Roy could have spotted him through the skinny tree trunks. No wonder the man never asked where he'd been.

A few houses dotted the shore. He wondered which one housed his mystery woman. As well as he could remember, most of the residents were old. She might be visiting. His masculine instinct made him aware of attractive single females in his vicinity. A quick glance at her left hand confirmed she sported no wedding band. Her eyes flared with awareness when he turned. No mistaking it, and yet her interest cooled suddenly, which made no sense. Why was he bothering to think of her? She'd made her opinion clear.

He replayed the meeting in his head. Perhaps he was too forward in asking her to go for a boat ride. She didn't know him, which explained her hesitation and questionable excuse. Once he settled in at the house, he might meet her again. A snort escaped him as he realized what he was doing, planning an impromptu meeting that would somehow lead to a happily ever after or at least a mildly happy right now. Yeah, right.

No woman had much use for only a partial man. A fellow patient at the rehab center told him women were crazy about wounded warriors, as the center referred to their patients. Women felt it was their patriotic duty to welcome them home. His roommate expected a heartier welcome than he did. Even if Levi's lack of welcome was a foregone conclusion, it didn't mean he liked it.

The island grew larger as the boat's nose slipped into a shallow, gravelly area serving as a beach. His intention hadn't been to visit the island, but here he was. He stepped out of the boat into the chilly water to pull the rowboat ashore. The first time he visited his island sanctuary alone, he'd made the mistake of leaving the boat among the rocks, imagining that it'd stay like a trained dog. After a brief exploration of the place, his heart sank when he'd sighted the rowboat drifting back to the pier, similar to a horse returning to its barn.

With no chance of the boat disappearing on the small lake, he remembered the despair he underwent knowing Roy would have to rescue him from the spit of land. At the time, he cursed himself and the island for causing his dilemma. He'd expected Roy to row across the lake, irritated that he'd taken his brother's child. The remembered pain stabbed at him as painful as a broken glass splinter wedged into his already bruised body. His uncle never raised his voice or even argued, except for the last time, their only real disagreement.

His mind had the discourtesy of replaying their acrimonious parting, causing his pace to quicken. His prosthesis slipped on a damp stone on the ground, causing him to pitch forward. A quick grab at a nearby sapling slowed his descent.

"Hell!" The word popped out as his body landed heavily. "That's what I get for rushing around. Roy warned me an impulsive action often led to regret." Levi sighed, picked up the stone near his hip and threw it. He enjoyed the sun's rays. There was no real heat in the sunlight, but it beat sitting in a hospital bed.

"You were right. I should have listened."

He could have called his uncle anytime during his enlistment, but he didn't. Pride kept him from making the call. If he'd contacted Roy, then he'd have asked about how he was doing. The Army itself wasn't too bad. The strict discipline, the routine, even knowing what to expect on most days, gave him a feeling of stability and belonging. It gave him a purpose when Angelique left him, taking his enlistment bonus with her. Roy had warned him the dark-eyed beauty bore him no love. He'd shouted that Roy was a lonely, bitter old man that no woman chose and that he didn't know a thing about real love.

Wincing, he remembered the shock on his uncle's face. He could have hit him with a two by four and not done as much damage. Roy had managed to say, "You're wrong," before turning away.

At the time, Levi thought Roy meant he was crazy for marrying Angelique. Yeah, Levi would admit his uncle was right. A letter from an anonymous friend tipped him off. Angelique ran through his pay the way a sailor did liquor on a three-day liberty while he awaited orders in a foreign hellhole. That part wasn't unexpected. Besides, he wanted to take care of his wife. He liked the idea of someone waiting for him to return. He'd idealized the woman, giving her traits she didn't possess.

As the only civilian in the recruitment office, Angelique had access to enlistee information. Roy insisted she knew who got the better enlistment bonus. Levi's hefty bonus for enrolling in explosive ordinance job specification could have inspired her sudden love for a man five years her junior. The fact she took off with another man using his enlistment bonus only confirmed Roy's theory.

If it wasn't bad enough, it took him a while to stop his pay going into their joint bank account and handling legal matters from overseas was hard. His uncle would have helped if he'd asked, but pride stopped him.

An anonymous typewritten letter alerted him to the real situation. He assumed it came from Roy because of the heavy imprint from each keystroke. He didn't know anyone else who still owned a typewriter. The letter only confirmed his original suspicion that his wife didn't care overly much for him. The other men received letters and cards. Boxes of stale cookies were ambrosia to the homesick men. He received two letters, one from Angelique at the beginning of his deployment. In it, she reminded him she needed all his pay for bills. The other was from the anonymous friend.

Time to get up and stop feeling sorry for himself. The tree that slowed his fall also served as a brace, helping him regain his footing. Birds scattered, squawking in alarm as he came nearer, indicating a nearby nest. Somewhere on the island, he had buried his time capsule. For some reason he couldn't quite remember, he was afraid his parents would vanish from his history. His uncle helped him to assemble the memorial, finding old, faded pictures of his parents when they were dating, photos Levi had never seen until then.

The urge to see those photos propelled him over the terrain, staring at the scattered rocks. His marker was a ring of stones with two lines through it in a Druidic symbol, apropos to nothing other than being a sign. No such sign existed that he could see. What did he expect? Years had passed. Wind and water would have moved the rocks, not to mention other young boys who took advantage of his refuge.

Time to get back. He couldn't miss the meeting with his uncle's lawyer, especially since he had to eject an interloper. His eyes focused on the ground, watching for troublesome tree roots and slick rocks. Off to his left, a half circle of stones rested under a scraggly evergreen branch. That was it. He knew it on an instinctual level. It would only take a few seconds to uncover his childhood treasure.

Looking about, he found a broken limb to employ as a digging tool. The can wouldn't be too far down. The day Roy rowed him out to the island to bury his capsule was early on in their relationship. He didn't know his taciturn relative well then, and Levi believed then his uncle's lack of chatter coincided with his appearance. He'd scampered out of the boat, anxious to be away from the silent man, so different from his talkative father. His uncle had waited in the borrowed dinghy as Levi dug the shallow hole.

Several stabs at the sandy ground stirred up the soil. On the eighth try, a metallic thud rewarded his jab. Excitement bubbled through his body, causing him to paw at the dirt with his bare hands, earning a scratch from an embedded rock in the process. Eager digging revealed the rusty popcorn tin Roy had insisted on to encase his memory project. His attempts to pry the lid off failed due to the waterproof caulk sealing the top. He'd have to take it with him before he could open it.

Images of the woman who'd managed to weasel her way into his uncle's affections grew as he carried the tin to the boat. The woman took the form of a fiftyish gold digger whose best years were behind her. Her hair would be unnaturally bright and her voice rough from chain smoking. Her exterior might be different from Angelique's, but inside both existed cold, calculating bitches who knew how to squeeze the most out of a trusting male.

In his mind's eye, he saw the tired, blonde haired woman flattering his ill uncle with promises she never planned to fulfill. His steps automatically quickened as he drew closer to the boat. No way he could miss this meeting. Getting the harpy out of the house would be the first thing he'd do. No doubt, she'd already decorated it with black velvet paintings and neon pink flamingos. Roy adorned his house with an eye to the practical by replacing whatever broke with what was cheapest. With all the transitions, Levi had experienced recently, the familiar, no matter how old or ragged would be welcomed.

Chapter Two

MELODY SAT IN the animal shelter lot staring at the empty parking spaces. No one was here, not that she expected it. Sunday was the only day the shelter officially closed. Saturday ruled as their best day with resigned parents arriving with eager children in tow. Often, those same families returned two or three weeks later with their adopted pet, apologetic expressions, and weak excuses. Most people didn't understand the unique needs of a shelter animal.

Taking a pet was an equivalent to adopting a foster child. The children often tested the foster parents by showing their worse behavior, expecting rejection. She'd been guilty of such herself. Her childhood rivaled the fictional Little Orphan Annie's, except no Daddy Warbucks ever arrived. She spent more time with her social worker than her fosters. She could identify with a boomerang puppy. Her returns had resulted from her alleged moodiness and tantrums. The people who took her for the money she'd bring quickly asked for a different child.

"This one is too spoiled," was the complaint of one short-lived foster mom.

Spoiling involved someone loving you and giving you whatever your heart desired. Not her mom. Her mother showed up once while she stayed with her first foster family. The memory arrived with silent tears as she mentally replayed the drama.

Her mother showed with a doll, sweets, and promises. Melody had considered her mother beautiful in her sparkly top and fake eyelashes. Her teeth had flashed white against her artificially tanned skin as she promised how they'd be together soon. Her mother's latest boyfriend had tapped the horn as he waited in the car.

As they drove off in a cloud of oil-rich smoke, her foster mother, Barbara, had commented to her husband. "That whore's promises are as false as her eyelashes. All show no substance. She doesn't even love the child."

A red rage overcame Melody. The woman's words had stripped away the warmth and happiness she'd experienced over her mother's visit. What happened next depended on whom was talking. Barbara claimed she'd attacked her like a wild animal when they took her back.

A thick fog enveloped that part of her memory, making it hard to recall. How much harm could a four-year-old do? Barbara's words did a lot more damage to a hurting child. Cruel or not, the words proved to be true. It was the last time she saw her mother. She worked her way through different families, landing with the Collins family when she was twelve.

They kept her until she was eighteen, saw her through high school, and helped her to find her first apartment. In most ways, they were her only family. The invitation she sent them for her nursing school graduation earned her a small note. No check or congratulations, not even a card, only a terse message declaring they'd done their Christian duty, and it was time for her to move on. Move on she did.

A movement caught Melody's eye as Mary steered her car into a nearby spot. The white-haired woman bounced out of the car with more energy than one would expect from someone her age. Melody opened her car door. Mary met her before she could even get out.

"What are you doing here? It's Sunday. We're not even open." Her broad grin announced her happiness in seeing her, even if it was unexpected.

Melody didn't want to admit she came out of loneliness. She needed something to love, even if it was only a canine others gave up. "I thought I'd give you a hand taking care of the animals."

Mary cocked her head seeing through her flimsy excuse but chose not to call her on it. "I could use the help. My back isn't what it used to be."

Melody flashed a weak smile and followed the woman to the building door. Was she getting the dog since she implied she had a dog to Levi McDaniels? Eventually, they'd meet face to face. If she didn't have a dog, it would just make her look like a liar. Besides, a dog would make her appear more settled in the house, less likely to move out.

Mary searched through her huge ring of keys for the needed one. "This isn't the only shelter I visit. I'll make two more stops before I head home."

The woman's devotion to the welfare of orphaned pets impressed Melody. "Goodness, Mary, maybe they need to canonize you. You could be the patron saint of abandoned pets."

A hearty laugh broke over the rattle of the keys. "Saint Mary? That'll be the day. I'm only here because I have no husband or family to fuss over. The critters are my family. I love each one as much as I can."

With no husband, no family, no one to spend time with over the weekend, Mary sounded like her. No wonder they both were spending their Sunday morning with rejected canines and felines. Melody chewed on her bottom lip. Would she end up like Mary? Better yet, how did such a sweetheart end up alone?

Mary nodded in the direction of the pens where a small potbellied pig snuffled his excitement at their entry. "Some rich lady driving an expensive SUV dropped the fellow off. Told me she was tired of it. Decided she wanted peacocks."

How could people abandon their pets so abruptly? Why should it surprise her when she'd been the victim of abandonment by her mother and half a dozen foster parents who decided she wouldn't suit? What hurt was when people decided to keep the other foster children. Why was she the one who had to go?

Mary gathered the food dishes while Melody lugged in a fifty-pound bag of dog kibble. She ripped the bag open and generously doled out the food.

"Being awfully free with the food, aren't you, girlie?" Mary teased her, wiggling her eyebrows.

She shook the pans to even out the kibble. "Maybe I am. For some, it might be their last meal." Saturday was the last-ditch attempt for some animals to find a home. An adult mixed breed dogs' only chance, came when an individual wandered into the shelter, who didn't mind the gray in the dog's muzzle. Unfortunately, it didn't happen often. Monday was kill day.

Grabbing two of the filled dishes, Mary carried them to a nearby pen. "You're so right. A few found homes yesterday."

"Charmer?" Afraid the dog she invested all her affection on went home with someone else, her heart skipped a beat.

Mary snorted. "Good heavens, no. You're the only person who likes the cantankerous beast. Besides being old and a mongrel, he has a temperamental disposition."

Her eyes scanned the kennels looking for the dog in question. Charmer gazed at her with devoted eyes and gave a hearty thump with his overlong tail. "He's just had a hard time. His grumpy facade is just an act."

Mary brushed past her to feed the other dogs. "Believe what you want. I'd be glad to see another dog placed. You have a place in your heart for hard luck cases."

Things could be worse, she reminded herself whenever she got down and wondered if she'd spend her whole life alone. "Mary, have you ever been in love?"

"Good Lord, child, what woman hasn't? I had fallen in love half dozen times before I turned twenty-one." The woman grabbed two more bowls and stooped to place them in the kennels.

Melody continued to fill the containers, trying to recall if she had ever been in love. There were boys she'd liked in high school, but they'd never even noticed her. She went out with Kevin about a dozen times but wasn't too heartbroken when he dumped her for someone else. At the time, she wondered why she wasn't more upset.

"Did any of the men actually mean anything to you?" She realized she was prying. Her knowledge of love came from movies, songs, and books, which she knew were fiction, painting life as people would like it to be. The families she stayed with were not models of loving behavior, usually just the opposite.

The Collins family kept her the longest. There had never been an affectionate gesture between the couple. With that kind of modeling, she figured she'd be better off with a dog than a man.

Using the kennel bars to pull herself up, Mary rested against one of the larger enclosures while a dog with some visible traces of Great Dane licked her hand. Her brow knitted as her eyes flicked upward, remembering. "There was one man who held my heart."

"What happened?" Mary's remark was about as close to love as Melody had ever been. She discounted her roommate's experience. All her roommate ever wanted to do was to get married and finally convinced a man to marry her. They never struck her as a love-dovey couple, despite the fact Linda bought matching outfits for them to wear on their honeymoon.

Mary blinked a few times and cleared her throat. She whispered the words, making Melody draw closer to hear. "I told him to go. Turned him loose. I didn't need any service boy making me into a young widow."

Tears slid down her withered cheeks. Mary used the back of her hand to wipe them away.

It didn't take a mind reader to see that the memories made her friend sad. "Did you love him?" It was hard for her to grasp loving someone, then casting them away like a pair of worn-out shoes.

Inhaling deeply, Mary shook her head. "People always think the young don't know their minds and hearts and need guidance in the ways of the world. My mother was no exception. The Vietnam War had just started up. My sweetheart was going for a tour of duty. I understood this was what he had to do, even though I was frightened about him being in harm's way."

Melody guided Mary to a chair. The robust woman had taken on a decidedly fragile air, making Melody wonder if the sturdiness served as a front. "Did he cheat on you? Why did you break up?"

Mary coughed and worked hard to clear her throat. Recognizing her struggle, Melody located a bottle of water in the staff fridge. The woman took a few sips and then threw her a grateful smile. "Thanks, sweetie. It's hard to believe fifty years have passed since I told my only love I did not love him."

Love appeared to be such a fleeting, rare commodity. "Why did you do that?"

"I often ask myself the same question, especially when I see an elderly couple crossing the street holding hands. I think it could have been us. We'd have grandchildren now to spoil. Instead, I fuss over these hounds."

Melody covered Mary's hand with her own. "The hounds need you." It hurt to see her friend's wavy gray hair falling into her tear-shrouded eyes. Her curiosity wanted Mary to finish her story, but Melody wouldn't ask.

Finishing off the water bottle, Mary slammed it against the table with vigor, missing their clasped hands. "I was a fool, you see. My mother was a widow. My father died in the Korean conflict. All I ever heard was how hard it was to be a widow and how she never had a man to do for her. When we started to date, she liked him until the time he enlisted. Then she had nothing good to say. All she did was predict doom and gloom. She hounded me day and night until I broke up with him."

The woman jerked her hand back, buried her face in her hands, and sobbed violently. Melody knelt beside her friend and wrapped her arm around her shoulders as Mary grieved. Her cries lasted a few more minutes, fading into hiccupping sobs. Mary sat up and managed a watery smile. "You'd think I'd be cried out by now. I keep thinking about the look on his face, the only man I ever loved. I broke his heart, threw it on the ground, and stomped on it. What good did it do me?"

What sounded like a rhetorical question was certainly one Melody couldn't answer. Her experience with love and loss all involved made for television movies, which managed to resolve all issues in under two hours. No words of wisdom to offer, not even a hackneyed platitude came to mind. Instead, she settled for a trio of light pats on the back.

Not getting an answer, she grasped Melody's hands. "Promise me something."

Her manner was so emphatic Melody knew she dared not ignore the woman's request. "Anything." She meant the words. If she could accomplish whatever Mary asked, then she'd do it.

Mary's eyes glowed as she spoke. "Never give up on love. Too few people ever truly fall in love. Most think they do, but realize later, they were mistaken. Love is a grand adventure, not for the timid, but well worth taking the chance on. No matter what. My mother convinced me to give him up because he could have died, and I'd end up a widow like her. It could have happened. If it had, I would have had a grand adventure. Sure, I would have lost my soul mate, but for a brief part of my life, I would have actually loved, wildly and generously. I gave it up to be safe." Mary let go of Melody's hands to gesture to the concrete brick walls.

LEVI CARRIED THE popcorn tin under his arm as he climbed to the dock. His legal errand caused him to grind his teeth. Soon, the law would do its job, and he'd be back in the home he remembered. Heaven knows Angelique never made a home for him. The two of them lived in her tiny apartment once they announced their engagement, right after he and Roy exchanged their final angry words.

There were so many clues in the cramped apartment. Things were not as they seemed. Takeout cartons littered the counter, and bare walls reflected her lack of domesticity or unwillingness to settle in one place. Of course, he either didn't see it at the time or refused to, lost in the sexual haze Angelique affected.

All through his training, he believed Angelique would be waiting, although her impatient response to his calls should have served as a hint. No doubt he'd interrupted her partying by calling, hoping for some sign of support and love. Instead, he got the brush-off. She'd mumbled a few words about it being a bad time and calling back later. Of course, she didn't call back. It wouldn't have mattered. He had his suspicions. Angelique showed enough smarts to show up at his graduation with an overly made-up girlfriend. For a little less than forty-eight hours, he paraded around the base with his gorgeous wife on his arm. That and one more visit, when he was at Fort Lee was the last he saw of Angelique.

In retrospect, she probably winked at other men when his back was turned, setting up the next fool. In her own way, she served him well, teaching him that women merely used men. The remembered betrayal firmed his determination. The time had come to get one of his ex-wife's ilk, Nurse Melody, out of his house and hitting the road with a little assistance from him. The car door swung shut with a little more vigor than he intended. No reason to take his frustration out on the car. Besides, he needed it to last a couple more years.

His foot rested heavily on the gas pedal, allowing him get to the lawyer's office on time. The solemn man met him at the door. His expression didn't bode well.

"Well, Levi, I could have saved you a trip." The man waved him into the office.

Levi knew the lawyer's name from the paperwork, and something familiar about the man tugged at him. Had they met before? Difficult to remember. After his fight with his uncle and the realization Angelique abandoned him, he did his best not to think about his past. The explosion rattled his head good, making ordinary memories elusive. Visiting the places from his teens and early adulthood revived scenes he'd forgotten. He shook the older man's proffered hand.

"I hope you're wrong, Mister uh…" He stalled on his name.

"Douglas." The man prompted and added a hearty pump to the handshake. "Take a seat, Levi."

The austere office held a battered oak desk, a few wooden chairs, and gunmetal gray filing cabinets and didn't give the impression that Mr. Douglas was a prosperous lawyer. Could be the will wasn't as airtight as he thought. "Can I examine the will?"

Douglas worked his way back to his desk with slow steps. "Of course, you can. I figured as much." He flipped a manila folder open. "I'd do the same myself."

Levi stood to take the document. The first thing he noticed was Uncle Roy's shaky signature at the bottom of the page. When had his uncle become so frail? Guilt assaulted him unexpectedly with the suddenness of a pop-up storm, as he considered his Uncle Roy dying without anyone beside him.

Pride kept him from returning his uncle's anxious calls when he first left the house. Angelique ladled on the charm and continued to do so until the wedding. To be more exact, she kept hugging, kissing, and petting him, treating him like an overfed poodle until his first bonus check came. The Army didn't give you all the money right off. It had at one time, but several potential soldiers vanished with the money. Now they dribbled it out in payments. The first bonus check came after basic. Another one appeared in the checking account about the time he'd served six months in Afghanistan. It coincided with the anonymous letter he received and Angelique's exit from town. Once he tried to investigate what was going on with his wife and money, she must have realized her days were few.

His scarred hand pinned the will to the worn desk. The lawyer cleared his throat, indirectly reminding him he was still there. He should say something. The man expected it. What was he ranting about before he saw his uncle's signature looking so thin and frail? It was the handwriting of an old man. Someone on his last legs as opposed to the strong, vibrant uncle he remembered.

Roy was never shy about saying what he thought. As a teenager, Levi had been harder than most to raise. Still, his uncle never lifted a hand or his voice to Levi until the last argument. Roy's discipline, although it took several convoluted turns, was fair.

Levi picked up the will feeling the weight of the heavy stock paper in his hand. Typed in bold font were the details of how he and someone named Melody Gibbons would share everything equally, including the house and boat. Just maybe this was Uncle Roy's final attempt to discipline him beyond the grave. What point was he trying to make?

Flourishing the paper, he asked. "Is this solid? I already had my lawyer send a letter contesting Melody Gibbons' claim."

The older man shook his head and sighed deeply. "I wish you hadn't done that. It's going to make things sticky when you meet today."

Meet today? Evidently, he hadn't heard the old lawyer right. Roy's attorney even suggesting a meeting on a weekend surprised him, but now he suggested a jaunt to the house. Maybe he thought to serve as a mediator between the two of them. "It's Sunday. Why would we meet today?"

The old man raised his bushy brows, allowing a twinkle to show in his faded blue eyes. "I'm well aware it's Sunday. I had to force myself to get dressed in something more professional than sweat-pants. Melody Gibbons works long hours as a hospice nurse. She happens to be off this Sunday." He grabbed a pen to roll between his hands. "Who's your lawyer?"

"Dillard, James. I tried to find my old lawyer, the one who handled the divorce, Malachi Weiss, but couldn't find him. Weird."

"Malachi Weiss was your lawyer? He's been dead a good six months. Heart attack." Douglas shook his head and dropped the pen. "Good man. I took over his existing cases recently just to tie up loose ends for his widow. Well, we should get going."

A tingling sensation, the type he had felt before the monster jumped out during a horror movie, shot through him. His lawyer dying couldn't be positive. Still, there was a good chance the divorce was finalized before his death. All he needed was the official paper-work.

His attention shifted to the home usurper he would meet in a matter of minutes. Works long hours? Well, *that* part didn't sound much like Angelique. As soon as they married, she'd quit her job. His uncle's inheritance of a rowboat, a modest home, and all the dated furniture inside wouldn't support a person, either. Half of everything belonged to him so she couldn't sell it, anyway.

A jabbing pain shot through his leg, causing him to stumble toward a chair. Damn, he hated being an invalid. Collapsing into the swivel desk chair, he turned it toward the wall to avoid scrutiny. His fingers massaged the area above where his leg ended, even though the phantom pain went much lower. The physical therapist explained that discomfort in a missing limb was normal since the nerves still sent messages to the brain. Somehow, they missed the memo.

The ache lessened under his ministration while the thought of visiting Melody didn't seem as horrendous as it first did. After all, he survived the loss of both parents, Angelique's betrayal, his uncle's death, and coming out of the war a damaged man. What could Melody Gibbons do to him?

Not exactly a cheery thought, but it bucked him up some. He inhaled deeply as he leaned into the chair's curved wooden back. "Okay, I'm ready."

The lawyer's voice boomed closer to his ear than expected. "Good, I'll drive."

Apparently, the man took advantage of his absorption to step closer and peer over his shoulder to see if the cripple would need a nine-one-one call. Ever since he returned, everyone looked at him in a similar fashion or just looked away, except for the woman at the dock. She saw him as an attractive man, judging by the momentary flare of interest in her eyes. Of course, the flicker went away as she made some lame excuse about a dog to escape.

"Let's go, son." The smiling man jingled his keys. "It's time you children met and cleared up some of your misconceptions."

He wanted to object to the child label, but instead pushed up out of the chair. Did the man think he was incapable of driving? "I drove here myself."

"I know." The man nodded his gray head as he swung the door open. "If I drive, it gives us time to talk. It also eliminates your escape if you want to leave in a huff. By the way, you can call me Oliver. Most people do."

Oliver. He tried out the name in his head. Yes, he did remember his uncle talking about him, something about fishing. "You and my uncle were fishing buddies?"

"Guilty." Oliver moved enough to allow Levi room to maneuver out to the sidewalk before turning to lock the door. He looked up with a grin. "It might be better to call us beer drinking buddies because we never caught much fish."

Levi forced out a chuckle, trying to quell his apprehension at the same time. Finally, he was going to meet the woman who caused so much festering resentment. Oliver present in his official capacity could help smooth things out. "Ms. Gibbons agreed to this Sunday meeting?"

Oliver stood by a large, late model sedan, making Levi question his previous belief about the man's lack of professional expertise. A sharp chirp from the key fob unlocked the passenger door. Oliver walked around the front of the car to reach the driver's side. His reply drifted over his shoulder. "Oh, I never actually made an appointment for a visit, just inquired if she'd be home for a call. The doorbell will notify her we've arrived."

Great. He slid across the smooth, leather seat and slammed the door. The man reminded him of his Uncle Roy more and more, from trapping him in the car to talk to showing up for an unexpected visit. Both were techniques his uncle used in the past. Several *discussions* occurred as his uncle drove him somewhere.

Talk might be the wrong word. His uncle would have some story about a friend, who bore a remarkable resemblance to Levi. The friend usually came to a bad end. In some of the tales, the friend reformed his ways. After the stories, Levi refused to talk, but he did think about them, even moderating his actions sometimes.

Oliver started the car and switched off the radio before speaking. "Let's look at things from Melody's view." *Let's not*, he wanted to say, but he remained silent. It was déjà vu. "Melody sees you as a greedy, uncaring jerk."

"Hey!" His objection hung in the air. Oliver didn't sugarcoat anything. "Why am I a jerk?"

Oliver eased the sedan into traffic, making two right turns before answering. Silence was a legal trick, allowing him time to squirm.

"Did you call your uncle? Even send him a quick email the whole time you were deployed?"

Oh great. Another lawyer trick, asking questions when he knew the answer. "No, but not once did he contact me and say, 'I have cancer and I'm dying.'"

"True," Oliver agreed. "We both know it wasn't his way to manipulate you to get some attention."

The lawyer's words mirrored his thoughts. "No, it wasn't. I wish it had been, though, because I would have called. I wouldn't have held on to the anger over something he was right about."

"That's life for you. Watch your words carefully because you never know when they will be your last ones. We're here."

The familiar house loomed in front of him. The door opened, and a hound appeared, rending the air with a long bay. Following close behind, holding the leash, was the woman he met at the dock. "It's her."

The words slipped out of his mouth without intention as his eyes devoured her. There really was a dog.

Oliver chuckled. "You've already met Melody, then?"

Chapter Three

CHARMER'S ONLY MOVEMENTS at the shelter included standing to greet her with a vigorous tail wag and shuffling to the food bowl. Melody snapped on the lead, expecting a leisurely walk around the lake. The dog's sudden lunge for the open door surprised her. Scampering to grab the vanishing leash before it disappeared, the sound of car doors slamming checked her speed.

A long canine bay alerted her she might have unexpected guests. *Great.* She wasn't dressed for company. A sudden tug sent her stumbling out into the yard. The elderly dog barked so hard his front legs came off the ground. Melody tightened the lead to prevent Charmer from escaping.

She looked up to see two men standing beside a luxury sedan. Roy's lawyer approached her with a happy expression and an outstretched hand. "Afternoon, Melody, I should have called."

Mustering up a smile to hide her surprise, she barely heard the other man say. "The woman at the dock."

The half-whispered words shifted her attention. The tall, broad-shouldered man half leaned against the car as his eyes roamed over her. *Levi McDaniels.* She bit her bottom lip. No, it couldn't be. Time is what she needed to prepare, to know how to act, and to devise the right thing to say.

Charmer took the opportunity to rest after his unexpected show of energy. A slight breeze rustled tree leaves while the late afternoon sun warmed her back. Apparently, nature didn't get the memo to stop everything. Her body did, as she struggled to draw a breath, wondering if she'd somehow forgotten how. *In and out, that's it. Just breathe.* Her mental instructions helped some.

His eyes reached her face. The gray eyes were, unfortunately, still as attractive as she remembered, though they were not to be trusted, she reminded herself, especially when her pulse jumped. *Just a man, that's all he is,* she'd convinced herself when her evil angel whispered into her ear about his rugged allure.

He was an attractive man, and a young one, too. When was the last time she had met a man under sixty-five? If she didn't count her former roommate's fiancé and jerky friend, it had been months. It could be the reason behind her over-reaction to a man who was her nemesis. *He's the enemy. Overlook the excellent packaging, the firm jaw, the ripped arms, and the attitude. He's trouble with a capital 'T'. Don't even let him get near the front door.*

Charmer's ears went up, hearing something, and then he dashed in the direction of Levi. The leash slipped out of Melody's hands as her canine loped across the yard. Would he welcome the man with a lopsided doggy grin or roll over on his back for a belly rub? With her luck, Charmer would deliver the house key. Then again, maybe the lawyer already had. Her eyes drifted over to the attorney, hoping Mr. Douglas would enlighten her about the nature of the visit, although she had her suspicions.

Levi's voice had her attention whipping back to the man. "Hey, what's the stupid dog doing?"

Her dog balanced on three legs while he hiked the fourth, thoroughly drenching Levi's leg. Worried he might hurt her dog, she rushed forward, knelt beside the dog, and wrapped her arms protectively around his body. "Please don't hurt him. He's old and already has enough trouble walking with his arthritis." Her eyes searched Levi's face. Would he take out his anger on her instead?

A rueful look crossed his face. Raising one eyebrow, he asked, "What do you think I am, a monster?" *Don't answer.* She even sucked in her lips in to prevent a spontaneous reply. Levi put both hands on the car and slowly moved to a kneeling position. He placed his hand on Charmer's head and stroked it. "I know what it's like old fellow, not being able to move around as well as you'd like."

The part of her resolved to hate him melted a little when he talked to her dog. The lawyer stepped to where the three of them squatted. His gaze went to Melody, and then to Levi. "Well now, seeing how well the two of you are getting along, I think it's time to talk about setting up housekeeping together."

The hand stroking Charmer casually brushed hers, causing her to lose her balance and fall on her rear. At least she wasn't standing, but it didn't stop her face from coloring. Was it what the lawyer said, or his touch that knocked her off her feet?

Mr. Douglas held out his hand to help her up. Levi, on the other side of Charmer, didn't even hide his smile. If he were any type of gentleman, he'd at least offer to help her. Instead of taking the proffered hand, she scrambled up on her own. She had spent most of her life doing things on her own. It certainly wasn't the time to start depending on others.

A minivan pulled into the nearby neighbor's driveway, spilling out what looked like an entire miniature sized soccer team and one tired father. The man held up a hand, and Melody waved. Charmer managed a robust bark, causing the man to stop and turn.

"You got a dog? When did that happen?"

Levi snorted and stared up at her from his crouched position beside the canine in question. The last thing she wanted to confess was she'd rushed out to get Charmer as to not get caught in a lie. Her voice cracked on her reply. "Recently."

Levi snorted again. Amazing how the man could convey disbelief and maybe even humor at her discomfort in one sound.

He offered her the end of the leash. "I'm getting up. I thought you might want to hold onto this wild one, especially being so unfamiliar with him and all."

Her fingers brushed his as she grabbed the leash. The slight touch sent a tiny jolt of electricity through her fingers and up her arm. *It means nothing. It's more likely his sarcasm slimed me.*

Keeping her eyes on Charmer, she waited for the hound to make a sudden move. Besides being uncaring jerks, there had to be a reason his family got rid of him. He'd already demonstrated his lack of social graces. What else might he do? Her attention was on her dog, but she didn't miss the cane that appeared in Levi's hand. Well, it explained a lot, including why he was stateside.

The cane gave her a momentary pause. Was she wrong to want the house? Who was she to keep the dwelling Levi deserved as the only surviving relative. Not only was Levi the heir, but a wounded veteran on top of it. She had no choice but to give it up.

A sense of loss settled on her like a thick, wet blanket. Disappointed, her fingers tightened around Charmer's leash before he'd showed another reason why he ended up at the shelter. From her slightly bent position, she observed Levi using the car and his cane to push himself upright. The struggle wasn't only between an unwilling leg and gravity, but his pride entered into it. His gray eyes grew glacial when he noticed her watching him.

"Yeah, I'm a cripple all right. Not so attractive anymore, am I?"

Blood rushed up to her face, coloring it an unbecoming red, she was sure. Apparently, he'd noticed her interest before, making everything worse. Soon she wouldn't have the snug, little house on the hill. It didn't matter if she found him attractive or not. He may even have found the idea laughable. Apparently, she didn't fit the current idea of beauty. A couple hundred years ago, she'd have had it made when a man needed a strong woman who could work beside him and give him sons. *Face it*. She was born in the wrong century, one stuck in the middle of the current crop of anorexic females with too high heels and too much makeup.

Her impromptu self-pity party caused her to miss some of his words. The glowering man leaning against the car didn't think any woman would find him handsome because of his leg. The thought was unbelievable. Her eyes roamed over him, affirming her initial observation. Oh my, he was very nice, bum leg and all.

Noticing her stare, he leaned back against the car as he adjusted his stance. "Did you get a good look? What did you see?"

The words came out on their own without her reflecting on them. "I see a handsome, rugged man. Maybe he has a bum leg, maybe he has an artificial one, but it doesn't stop him from being attractive. The only unattractive feature is his sucky attitude."

Levi's eyebrows shot up, and his mouth twisted with what was no doubt another negative comment, but then he stopped and laughed. Oliver joined in the laughter, which relieved Melody. Maybe she'd been wrong to say it, but it didn't seem like anyone was taking it too badly.

Charmer kept pulling at the leash, anxious to get away. Wrapping the lead around her hand twice, she tugged him in the direction of the house. "I guess ya'all might as well come in. I wasn't expecting company, but no reason to hash out our personal business in public."

Her shoulders hunched with the knowledge of what she was about to do. She could be grateful there always seemed to be plenty of jobs for hospice nurses at least. Apartment life would be harder this time since she had a taste for what it was like to live in her own house. Apartments didn't usually allow dogs, either.

Charmer's unexpected balk caused her to stumble forward, stopping her descent by her grip on the screen door frame. The canine in question stared in Levi's direction. *Great*, it looked like everything went to the man. Grabbing the door handle, she swung it open. Roy's plastic shrouded furniture still crowded the room, but there was part of her here, too.

A small vase of brightly colored daisies sat on the end table. A black and white shot she'd taken of the lake sat on the far wall in a cheap frame she'd purchased at the dollar store. Her slippers peeked out from under the couch. The book she started rested open faced on the sofa where she abandoned it to take Charmer out. They were tiny things. Most people might not even notice the steps she hadn't taken knowing this day might come, and it had.

Might as well get it over with, she thought as she tugged the reluctant dog behind her into the kitchen. She could be civil about the whole thing. No reason to be ugly about it. If foster care taught her one thing, it was you never allowed your genuine feelings to show. The leash slipped from her fingers as multiple scenarios played through her mind, featuring uncomfortable social workers from her past who had escorted her to their car. How odd that she remembered the worker's distress over another failed placement. At the time, she thought it was somehow her fault. The social worker failed to see most people were unprepared for the difficulty of foster children.

The men's footsteps thudded on the hardwood floor along with the tap of the cane. "Melody, do you want us to meet in the kitchen?" She recognized the lawyer's voice and glanced at the kitchen table with some breakfast dishes along with a discarded newspaper. "Sure, the kitchen works. I'll make some coffee." The dishes ended up in the sink, and she tucked the paper under the counter before running a dishrag over the table.

Oliver Douglas entered with a smile and pulled out a chair. "Coffee would be appreciated. My wife calls it the devil's brew since she started a caffeine-free health kick. I try not to drink it in front of her. Removing temptation."

Melody turned back to the counter to rinse out the coffee pot before she started a fresh batch. It also allowed her not to watch Levi prepare himself to sit. It would wound any man's pride, having to struggle with a leg that wouldn't cooperate, but in a man so young, it must be worse. The tightness of his shoulders and his general demeanor let her know his injury was a permanent one.

The plastic coffee can lid popped off under her fingers releasing the potent aroma. The coffee scent reminded her of wrapping her cold hands around a warm cup on countless mornings. For a second, it made her forget the wounded warrior at her table. She didn't see any real choice. To fight him for the house would be, well, un-American. Besides, he already had a lawyer. Was it Mr. Douglas?

The silver-haired lawyer hummed under his breath as he arranged papers on the table. At least someone was happy. He could be contemplating the coffee or getting the business done with and returning home. At least he had a home. *Stop that. It isn't anything you haven't been through before.*

It would be hard to imagine the friendly lawyer penning the stern missive she'd received. Besides, she didn't recognize the name on the letter, only the title, attorney at law underneath. Grabbing a dented tray, which proclaimed the wonders of the Grand Canyon, she arranged cups and spoons on it. She never thought she'd have any use for it when she picked it up at the thrift shop.

"Uhm, I don't have any sugar, but I do have artificial sweetener." She put a couple of packets of the substitute on the tray.

The lawyer stopped rustling the papers and smiled up at her. "Perfect. I need to lose a few pounds anyhow." Her eyes moved over to Levi.

"I like mine black." The words came out abruptly, rather like the man. Just as well, since she didn't own any creamer. She bobbed her head in acknowledgment, but it didn't matter because he wasn't looking at her. *Well, be that way. I'll show you who the better man is. I mean woman.*

She took out a small plate and arranged on it the cookies she had bought as an indulgence for herself. Similar to the lawyer, she could stand to lose a few pounds. Might as well share the calories, and it would help Levi feel small when she signed over the house.

The scene took shape in her mind as the wounded veteran realized what a truly unselfish person she was. Of course, he'd apologize for his uncharitable thoughts toward her. Maybe even shed a tear or two. A glance at his stony face made her consider the shedding of grateful tears as going a bit too far. Part of her objected strongly to her current course of action, the part which never had a home.

She carried the tray to the table as the coffee made its final gurgle. Taking the cups and saucers, she placed one in front of each man and another for herself.

A sense of wonder filled Levi's voice as she turned her back to him to grab the pot. "Good Lord, I never expected to see these dishes again. Don't know how many times I sat at this table with Uncle Roy drinking coffee out of these cups. Sometimes, he'd apologize for serving me coffee. Even as a confirmed bachelor, the man never cooked. We'd usually have coffee and cold cereal every morning. Sometimes, on the weekend, he'd complement the morning meal with a side of donut holes."

Real affection flavored his words. Melody kept her back turned to fight the tears forming in her eyes. He'd loved his uncle. It didn't explain why he hadn't come around when Roy fell sick, but it made him a little less of a jerk than she initially thought.

Using one hand, she wiped away any betraying moisture and

inhaled deeply. If she started bawling, it wouldn't help. The sound of children's voices drew her gaze to the window. A parade of children ran across the lawn heading for the lake. She'd miss being there. At first, she thought it was how normal people lived. Now, she wondered if it was how extraordinary people live, surrounded by love and nature.

Coffee pot in hand, she filled each cup as she steeled herself to do what she must. Setting the pot back on the pad, she slid into her seat. The men were sampling their coffee as she cleared her throat.

"Well, ah, I'd like just to get it over with. I am willing to sign the house over to Levi seeing as he's the last relative and, um, he needs it. I only hope you might consider taking Charmer since most apartments don't allow dogs."

Okay, she'd done it. Made her noble little speech, but she was feeling anything but noble. Angry, resentful, sad, rather like the first time she'd been put out of a foster home after her beautiful mother flitted in to see her and was gone just as fast.

Levi slammed his coffee cup down, sloshing the contents over the side. Wiping his damp hand on his pants, he remarked, "I'm amenable to your suggestion, but don't go being a martyr about it. I'll buy out your share."

Her back went stiff at *martyr*. Didn't anyone notice her saint-like behavior? His lips remained in a firm line, not exactly the reaction she expected. A little more joy would be nice. Didn't he realize she was giving him everything?

"Not so fast." Oliver Douglas made sure to catch both of their eyes before continuing. He tapped the paper in front of him. "It appears neither one of you listen very well. According to the will, there will be no buying or selling until you both reside in the house together for one full year. I already told you," he glanced at Levi, "the will cannot be broken."

The comment restored hope to her depleted soul. A year would give her a chance to make other plans. Who knows? Maybe she could buy Levi out. Not all at once, but she could get a loan using the house as collateral. She'd lived with plenty of people in her life. Levi would be a better roommate than most of them.

"Aw, shit!" The man swore and slapped his hand on the table. "What else can go wrong?"

Her excitement died a little. Perhaps he wouldn't be a great roommate, but she'd had worse. Time would tell.

Instead of soothing words or quoting legal jargon, Oliver picked up his cup and sipped it slowly. Finally, he replaced it in his saucer. Clearing his throat, he gained both their attention. "I expect the two of you feel like Roy McDaniels did you wrong, but he didn't. He was a man who had a great deal of hardship and loss in his life. I am proud to have been his friend. I imagine the two of you are feeling sorry for yourselves, so stop it right now. You're alive and have a future, which is a hell of a lot more than Roy has. He loved you both dearly. What he wanted was to give you both a home. Initially, I tried to discourage him from making the two of you co-heirs, but he wouldn't listen to me."

He shook his head slowly, remembering. "He wanted the two of you to meet and even thought you would be friends. I explained anyone would hesitate at sharing a home. Roy finally agreed to the clause stating that after a year if things didn't work, one could buy the other out. That part was my doing. The rest was all Roy. The way I see it, you both need a home. Plenty of people share lodgings, and it doesn't cost you anything. A couple of months ago neither of you had a house. Now you both have lakefront property. After a year, you can sell the house and split the proceeds. Is it such a hardship, really?"

Levi hung his head. It was hard to say if he was ashamed or de-spondent. Part of her was thrilled to be able to remain in the house.

Still, it would be difficult living with a sullen, sexy man. She would have to wear more clothes around the house. Did Roy actually think to match the two of them? If he did, she could have explained why it wouldn't work.

"Okay." She volunteered her agreement since it didn't look like Levi was talking. "I am sure we can work out some ground rules so the two of us can co-inhabit the house."

Oliver grinned. "It's why I'm here. I thought it would be easier to do with an impartial third party."

It was hard to know how fair the lawyer was. She knew he was representing Roy's interest as opposed to what she or Levi wanted.

Levi sighed, and then raised his head. "You knocked me down more than a few pegs. I suspect Uncle Roy gave you lessons."

Oliver snorted at the assertion. "Who do you think taught him?" He gestured for Levi to continue talking.

He blinked once, slowly turning his head to face Melody. "I was too reactive, always one of my worst faults. If Roy trusted you, then he had a reason. With two bedrooms, I am sure we can work out a livable arrangement." He gave a nod and tried to smile. Too bad his eyes didn't know what was happening. They remained distant, but it was a start.

Oliver reshuffled the papers, pulling out a sheet already printed with a roommate agreement with bulleted blank sections. Clicking his pen, he put it beside the first one. "Let's start with the bedrooms. Melody, what room are you using?"

All the talk about bedrooms epitomized the word awkward, but there was no help for it. After all, it was the only practical way to deal with things. "I'm staying in the same room I used as Roy's nurse. It was easier that way, which means the bigger bedroom is open for Levi."

Truthfully, she could not bring herself to move into Roy's room.

The small second bedroom suited her, especially since she'd made changes in the room.

Her sullen roommate, instead of being surprised at her generosity in yielding the larger room, stared at her. "You're sleeping in my room? In my bed?"

"Yes." What else could she say? It made her a bit like Goldilocks. She could give it up if it bothered him, but the twin bed would be too small for him now. A twinge of guilt hit her as she recalled she took down all the posters. Angry that the prodigal nephew never visited his dying uncle, she tossed them. Call it her one act of aggression. "Do you want it back?"

His shoulders went up with a shrug. "No big deal. Just a comment. You keep it."

Oliver's pen scratched across the paper. "That's settled. We need guidelines for the use of public rooms such as the living room, kitchen, and bathroom."

The urge to say she'd not use the rooms died in her mouth when she realized the sheer stupidity of it. Not go to the bathroom? Hardly, since there was only one. She'd needed the kitchen, too. Even if she were only passing through, she'd still go through the kitchen to reach the living room.

They both agreed to the suggestions the lawyer put forth for combined use. She wasn't sure if she could abide by the time schedules. The idea was to keep the two of them from bumping into each other. With her job, she was gone the majority of the day. Charmer leaned against her leg under the table reminding her of the new responsibility she'd forgotten.

"Um, how will you feel about Charmer in the house when I'm at work?" His actions made her think he liked the dog even after he urinated on him. Jumping up, she knocked her chair back as she lunged for the paper towel roll. "For your jeans," she mumbled, pushing the paper roll in his direction.

He took the towels with an easy acceptance. "Thanks. As for Charmer, I'd welcome the company. It might give us both a chance to work on our manners."

Old stone face actually made a joke. Was her mouth hanging open? She hoped not. "Yeah." *Wait, that didn't sound right.* "I meant Charmer could work on his manners."

Levi gave a short laugh. "I know what you meant."

Oliver looked back down at the papers, hiding a budding smile. "Okay, you two. We need to plan on how you'll handle entertaining friends and future dates."

Would she come home to a tie on the doorknob indicating entertainment of the mattress variety was in session? Walking past the two of them cuddled on the couch would be awkward enough, but what if she went to her room only to hear the bedsprings groaning in the room next to her? She'd managed with Linda and could do the same with a man.

Levi harrumphed his opinion, reminding her of his uncle. They even sounded alike. His snort made it hard to know if it translated to no dates.

"No worries about me. I won't be entertaining." It sounded pitiful even to her ears. After her last failed date, the idea of dating didn't appeal. Everyone she met in the hospice field already had friends and family to occupy them. Currently, Mary and Charmer were the extent of her social life.

"Same here. Besides, I'm still working on the details of a divorce started in a war zone." Levi added. "If I should run into some old friends, we could meet in a restaurant or someplace else."

Oliver looked at his cup meaningfully, and then up at her with a smile. Taking a hint, she stood to get the coffee pot.

"Nevertheless, we should have some guidelines. No other person will be permitted to move into the house during the year." He wrote swiftly and murmured his thanks as she filled his cup. "This doesn't mean you can't have guests, but you need to contain them to the private areas so as not to discomfit the other inhabitant. You cannot allow a person to stay two nights in a row, which would imply a form of co-habitation."

Still no problem existed on her part. The few men friends she'd had didn't want to stay the entire night. Truthfully, none rated true love. Most didn't even rate the term 'relationship'. "Not happening."

Levi's fingers were on a cookie but stilled with her words. "Are you telling me what I can do? I might meet a woman who would take pity on me."

"Seriously, you're starting that crap again? With your attitude, you'll meet up with someone who will treat you like a charity case. Decent women would value you without two strong legs. I was talking about myself, Mr. I-Jump-to-Conclusions. There won't be any overnight dates in my case." Her skin heated at the awkward dissection of her non-existent love life. It would be wonderful if they moved on to something else, like paying the utilities.

His fingers wrapped around the cookie, and he took it to his mouth. Chewing, he appeared to consider her words. "You're not one of those prudes who don't believe in sex before marriage."

Her esophagus spasmed with his casual comment, making it hard to breathe. She closed her eyes and mentally counted. A trick she had taught herself to ease her nerves. Counting always worked for her, if it was counting her steps or the ceiling tiles in the gynecologist's office, just as long as she had something to count. Still holding the coffee pot, she turned her back to him. Her pinkie grazed the burner pad as she replaced the pot. "Ouch." The man not only had her stumbling around the place but burning herself with all his raw masculinity, too.

"Ouch? What kind of answer is that?" Levi leaned his chair back, locked his hands behind his head and smirked, although he'd probably call it a grin.

Exhaling deeply, she decided to put things on the table. There was no reason to have this silly cat and mouse game going on. "Ouch is what you say when you burn yourself."

"It's not what I'd say." The man smirked at her.

"Yes, I know. Let's make it plain. You don't have to worry about me dragging home men to keep in my bedroom. I am well aware I'm not attractive."

The clatter of the chair legs hit the floor. "What the hell are you talking about? Most men would give their eye teeth for a woman like you. You're tall, curvy, and have the most gorgeous hair. It is clear that you give as much as you take. What's not to like?"

What did he say? Did she hear him right? Her fingers touched her face as she suspected her mouth was open. His words made no sense. They certainly didn't jive with her last date's comments.

"This gets more interesting by the minute," Oliver commented while watching the two of them.

"I'm not sure what to say. The last date I went on the man mentioned I was too large to be attractive. I assumed other men thought likewise." Melody gripped the counter behind her back in case another verbal volley hit her, knocking her off her set of accepted beliefs.

Levi's gray eyes warmed as he smiled. "Melody, you don't get out much."

"No lie there," she readily agreed. This ground she knew. Her knees firmed up a bit, less shaky than before. How could she ease into her chair, making it look natural? Standing at the counter made her feel on display. The voices of the children coming back from the lake sent Charmer into a series of half-hearted barks, enough of a distraction for her to sit down and fold her hands in her lap.

"This date of yours, was he a little on the small side?"

The question had her trying to remember. He hadn't been overly tall—a little on the scrawny side—or wide across the shoulders and chest as Levi was. "I think so. He never noticed my new outfit, my hair, or how hard I worked on my makeup, just how big I was."

Oliver put his age-spotted hand over hers. "It hurts me to hear you talk like this. You remind me so much of my wife when she was young. Let me tell you, she's the prettiest thing I ever set eyes on. She still is."

What a sweet thing to say. Her eyes grew suspiciously damp. She didn't necessarily believe his words, but still it was nice to know a man still deeply in love with his wife.

"I know the type." Levi nodded his head hearing a conversation only he was privy to.

Charmer nudged her leg. Her fingers scratched his head, not quite familiar with what he might want, not knowing the dog well enough to know his non-verbal cues. Instead, she asked, "What type?"

Crossing his arms, Levi looked in her direction, then back at Oliver. "Men who are unsure of their masculinity like small, dainty women. They don't know how to be a man. As far as masculinity, all they have is superior size and different plumbing. A doll-like woman makes him feel like a man, but it doesn't make him one, more like a boy playing with his sister's Barbies."

A man who needed a small dainty woman was a man not sure of his own masculinity? Yes, that did sound like her date. The man would probably marry a diminutive woman who would run him ragged. The thought made her smile. If she got out more, she might meet someone who was secure in his masculinity. Her first challenge would be to figure out how she'd encounter such a man.

"Good analogy." Oliver agreed, gesturing to the paper with his pen. "Let's finish this so I can get home to my loving spouse, and you can get your car and gear to move in."

Move in? The words startled her. Good thing she was sitting down. Oliver confused her smile for acceptance of her current state. Oh well, it could be worse.

"I am certainly glad to see you're no longer opposed to Levi moving in." The chairs scratching across the linoleum brought her out of her reverie. Standing, Oliver pushed the papers across to her. "If you're good with the guidelines, sign here."

Taking the proffered pen, she signed the paper. She handed the pen to Levi wondering if he'd balk, but he didn't. He signed right under her signature.

"Okay, children. I'll have Amelie type this up when she arrives on Monday. For now, this is the temporary agreement. I can make a copy for you at the office, and Levi can bring it with him when he returns." Oliver capped his pen, securing it in his shirt pocket. He gathered up the papers and put them back in his case.

The three of them walked to the door together. She watched them head to the car. Oliver had his hands in his pockets, whistling while he walked. Levi kept his back ramrod straight and tried to use his cane as little as possible, attempting to prove he didn't need it. When they both turned to open the car doors, she waved automatically, comparable to bidding old friends goodbye.

"I'll be back around six." Levi's voice carried easily.

The man was probably used to yelling over gunfire. Not knowing how to reply, she waved and tried to stretch her lips into a smile. *He'd be back at six.* Only a few more hours before her life changed again. The only thing certain was nothing ever remained the same.

Chapter Four

THE EMPTY COFFEE cups on the table called to her. Starting the dishwater in the sink, she picked them up. A quick glance around the kitchen spotted a pile of junk mail on the counter along with Charmer's open bag of dog food half-spilled. When did she do that?

The bathroom needed cleaning, too. A quick wipe of the sink basin should remove all her long hairs. Removal of her makeup and feminine hygiene items was necessary. Sure, they had to live together, but they didn't need to be intimate. Truthfully, she never had to share living quarters with an attractive male close to her age.

Would he be a slob? The image of her picking up dirty socks and underwear came to mind. *Not doing it.* She'd sweep it all into a corner if it came to that. Melody always thought of herself as a neat person. Her tidiness came from a combination of rootlessness and not having anything.

Things held you down, she learned early in life. Even the doll she clung to as the last tangible reminder of her mother disappeared in one of her moves. Another child claimed it. The foster mother didn't know, but the child certainly had. It was one reason Melody didn't put much stock in things. Her sudden obsession with holding onto the house and rowboat surprised her.

She rinsed the cups with the designs half rubbed off from use, thinking of Levi's reaction to them. Though of little value, the cups held a shared history. The heavy stoneware came from a discount store or even a yard sale. Levi saw them as a touchstone to long conversations with his uncle.

Toweling the cup dry, she held it a moment. What would it be like to have something tangible from someone you loved? She never knew her father, and she was forgetting her mother. She wasn't even sure if she had other relatives. She'd always assumed not because she figured social services would have hunted them down. Was someone out there who would love her?

As a foster child, she dreamed of a mysterious relative who'd whisk her away. The relative would have been traveling abroad or been a spy, possible explanations she'd come up with as to why he or she hadn't put in an appearance as the years passed. Most kids had illusions their parents weren't their parents, hoping to be an heir to a small kingdom or a love child of a notorious celebrity. All she ever wanted was a place to belong.

Charmer gave a sharp yip, startling her. She dropped the cup. It hit the hard counter with a thump, breaking into several pieces. The jagged edges of the shards mocked her as she stared at the mess. *This mess demonstrates why I have no one. I destroy everything I touch. Mother told me she loved me, but it was just too hard to have me around.*

Tears made it difficult to see. She blinked to clear her eyes only to have other tears replace the previous ones. Everything made her cry today. What was wrong with her? It was only a cup. Stumbling to the table, she pulled out a chair. Yeah, it was a cup, but it was a memory for Levi, which she destroyed. It made her little better than the child who stole her doll. She didn't mean to do it.

While Levi talked about sitting and talking with Roy at the kitchen table, she'd remembered doing the same. The relaxed conversations, the shared breakfasts, and part of her wanted to believe she was part of the McDaniels family. Maybe a cousin they lost track of, but she knew better. Roy wasn't the type to allow a relative go into the foster care system. Levi served as proof.

The reminiscing made her feel less special. Until then, she didn't realize she'd developed a scenario where she was a special part of Roy's life as opposed to simply being his hospice nurse. Still, she had to be special. He left his estate to her jointly. Could it be he knew it would take Levi time to get back from the service, and she was just a caretaker? That would explain the year clause.

The tears kept falling. Picking up a napkin, she wiped her eyes with the rough paper. Yeah, that was it. Caretaker. Generally, she oversaw people as they slipped from this life into the next. This time her job was to keep the house and all its contents safe until the real owner took possession. Eventually, she'd leave, but not without receiving payment for her share, which was much better than anything she'd received from previous clients.

One elderly woman gave her a lovely ruby and pearl ring. Unfortunately, her daughter threatened to report it as theft. Keeping it really wasn't worth taking the chance. Besides, there was family history with the ring, meaning something to the daughter.

Death often brought out the worst in the people. Not so much the dying, who accepted their limited life span with both grace and regret. Many times, the families, with their power struggles over controlling care of the ailing family member along with last-ditch efforts to ensure a place in the will, sickened her. Some families started bickering about property before the ambulance arrived to transport the deceased. A few bold relatives came into the home and removed whatever they wanted, putting her in a difficult situation since she had to report everything taken to the agency, proving she hadn't stolen it. If cherry picking their inheritance while their relative lay dying wasn't enough, a few insisted she lied about their sticky fingers. Luckily, their characters remained the same over the years, which meant their unethical behavior surprised no one.

Roy's passing was easier than most since he tied up things in a box with a legal bow. Sure, having co-heirs with a year clause was a peculiar box, but Roy didn't do anything without a reason.

Remembering the kind man and his down-to-earth practicality, she stopped crying. He'd tell her there were other cups. One cup wasn't any better than the others were. She'd try to explain, but he would dismiss her explanation and tell her he was thinking of tossing the cups anyhow.

She blew her nose hard, making a honking sound that startled Charmer into barking again. Using the wadded-up napkin, she gave her eyes a final wipe. Too many things to do before Levi arrived. She had no time to sit around crying over a broken cup or feeling sorry for herself. It is what it is. Clean up the cup mess, remove her stuff from the bathroom, and prep Roy's room. The last item on the list made her heart drop.

After his death, she cleaned the room from top to bottom, even changing the sheets, but she hadn't been in the room since. All his clothes and various labeled boxes crowded the closet. Even his reading glasses rested on top a tower of books on the bedside table as if Roy had only stepped out for a moment.

Since it would be the harder room to clean, she decided to start there first. Grasping the door handle, she opened the door. Drawn shades shut out the daylight, and a musty, unused smell floated out of the room. It had been weeks since she last opened the door. Charmer wiggled around her to get his nose to the floor.

The canine left footprints in the dust demonstrating the room needed cleaning in the worst way. Melody watched as the dog make a circuit around the room sniffing the bed, the wheelchair, and the toilet chair. It would be best to remove those last two items. No need for Levi to think of his Uncle Roy as a frail man whose privacy departed with the arrival of the commode chair.

Visitation dwindled when the terminal label attached to someone. Excuses ranged from the tired refrain they wanted to remember them as they were to being busy at work. Personally, she suspected many of them were afraid of catching what her patient had. Those of a similar age saw their own mortality in their friend or relative's decline. Survivor's guilt made them ashamed they were healthy while their friend died. Not visiting served as a coping mechanism.

Charmer's overlong ears went up in a questioning manner. Part of her expected to see Roy's ghost seated in bed. Nothing. Animals were supposed to be aware of spirits. The basset-mix didn't pick up anything besides dust. Time to get to work and stop being fanciful about ghosts and other nonsense.

Determined, long strides brought her to the first window where she raised the shade and opened the window. The sunlight and fresh air made the room a little less of a shrine. She opened the second window, hoping a cross breeze could eliminate the unused smell. Music might enliven the atmosphere.

A small radio/CD player combo sat on a crowded dresser. Roy had a fondness for music, especially Elvis Presley. He told her about dancing with his sweetheart before he went to war, how they danced to the ballad, *It's Now or Never.* The fact he never married made her think the lover went with never. What a shame. The way he worried about both her and Levi indicated a caring nature and thoughtful husband material.

She plopped down on the bed, sending up a small cloud of dust. Who knew a room could get so dusty in a couple of months? No help for it, she'd have to wash the coverlet, too. In only a few minutes, she had the bed stripped, exposing the plastic sheet underneath. It would have to go. Despite her thrifty ways, she knew Roy would appreciate her destroying any reminders of his failing body. That settled it. The chairs were going into the garage. The toilet chair first because it stripped a person's dignity the most.

The music swelled around her making the onerous task light-hearted. Levi could go through all the boxes since she hadn't. It would have been an invasion of privacy. No one else had ever expected her to close up their house once they passed. Grabbing the large plastic and aluminum commode chair, she wheeled it around the corner of the bed. It stuck between the closet and the end of the bed frame. Rolling over the mattress, she tried pulling it from the other side.

Grabbing hold of the aluminum frame, she tugged, trying to break it clear of space she had involuntarily wedged it in. "You have to fit, you stupid chair. How did you get in here in the first place?"

The agency had delivered the equipment. At the time, she'd made a point of taking Roy out for a walk as two hefty men unloaded the items. It had been her experience that people grew melancholy seeing symbols of their slipping health.

Still, it was an awkward chair. She gave it a vicious tug. "Damn chair."

A voice said close to her ear. "Maybe I could help?"

She let go of her grip on the chair and fell backward, tumbling into a body. They both fell to the floor with a solid thump. Melody pretended not to hear his muttered curse. Seriously, could it get any worse? For a second, she rested against his warm, masculine body, enjoying the solid feel, even the scent of sun-warmed male. Remembering her position, she scrambled to her hands and knees and pushed up to stand.

Levi lay sprawled on the floor with a menacing frown. Charmer licking his face only exacerbated the situation. He pushed the words out through gritted teeth. "Could you get the dog away from me?"

She clapped her hands together with no effect. Well, it did work for some dogs, but not this one. "Charmer, no, no."

The dog stopped long enough to look at her, and then continued delivering sloppy canine kisses. This wasn't working out well.

Levi pushed up to his elbows, removing his face from Charmer's administrations. "I see you have the dog trained." His sarcastic tone negated the words.

His tone stung, even though his words were accurate. She had no apparent control over her dog. Just when she was trying to like him a bit and think better of him, he had to go make some crack like that. She held her hand out to him, knowing it would be hard for him to get upright quickly.

Levi ignored the hand and used the footboard of the bed to pull himself up. His refusal served as another mark against him. It irked her. "What were you doing sneaking around the house and scaring me?" There was no way she was admitting she first thought he was a ghost.

"Sneaking around?" Both eyebrows shot up, as he balanced himself on both legs. "First, I wasn't sneaking around. You had the music blasting. When you weren't singing, you were cursing the chair."

Her face reddened. His description made her sound like the fool. "I was cleaning up the room for you. I wanted to get rid of all the signs of your uncle being an invalid. Stupid chair," she stopped to glare at it, "won't fit through the opening."

Levi looked at the chair, gave it a hard kick sending it backward, freeing it from its trap. He wrapped his fingers around the metal arms and swung it over the end of the bed with little or no effort. It was certainly easier and faster than her determination to pull the chair through a too small passage.

"That's how they did it." She marveled aloud wondering why she hadn't considered this. "Thanks." Placing her hands on the chair back, she pushed it through the door and headed toward the garage.

"Where are you headed for with that chair?" Levi followed behind her.

"The garage," she answered without looking back at him. It made it easier, considering her earlier fall. The man must believe her to be a cross between clumsy and crazy.

LEVI WATCHED HER determined stride as she pushed the chair. She wouldn't even look at him when she talked. She couldn't stand the thought he wasn't a whole man, even if she declared his manners were the only thing wrong with him. Of course, she was a nurse, and they said stuff like that. All the time he spent recovering and learning to use his new leg, a few of the nurses pretended to flirt with him in nothing more than a game they invented to improve a soldier's morale.

After all, he hadn't attracted women when he had two healthy legs unless he had a fat enlistment bonus to go with it. After high school, he'd hung out in Wilsonville trying to figure out what to do with his life. He'd picked up a job working with a local mechanic with hopes of saving up enough money to rent an apartment. Roy's idea of subtle included leaving brochures for trade schools and junior college all over the house. At the time, he figured his relative had enough of housing him. His original plan of rooming with his sometime friend fell through when his friend's girlfriend moved in instead of him.

Roy had never mentioned anything about his moving out but had told him he was grateful for the company. Levi never considered Roy might be telling the truth. He didn't want to, especially after butting heads with him over his late-night partying. Angelique happened right about the time he needed a push. What he needed was to move, not get married and fight in a war on the other side of the world.

A grimace crossed his face as he thought about his money-grubbing ex-wife. Whatever happened to her? He had started the paperwork for the divorce but being blown to kingdom come wiped the thought from his mind. He should check on that, not because he'd start dating as he implied to Melody, but because the last thing he needed was Angelique showing up. His life was complicated enough.

His eyes followed Melody's hips as she pushed the chair in front of her. The woman certainly packed a pair of shorts. He hadn't minded the feel of her on him either. His lips tilted up, breaking into a smile. What bothered him was he should have caught her as opposed to falling beneath her like a domino.

The physical therapist emphasized that his prosthetic leg was even stronger than a human leg. Once he learned to balance himself, it would hold him up. However, the issue of gravity challenged females had never come up in discussion. All the same, he didn't want people fetching and caring for him. His pace increased as he hurried behind Melody.

The garage door stood open, exposing the tools in their outlined places on the pegboard. As a teen, he found the outlines silly, but now he could see the usefulness of such a system. Countless hours had gone into constructing the boat inside those four walls. Along with the camaraderie of working on a project together, he gained some insights into his taciturn uncle, along with lectures on the importance of caring for tools properly. No wonder his uncle could spot a missing screwdriver. Either it was out of place or missing since a quick scan of the outlines told the story.

The redhead with enough attitude to challenge any drill sergeant kept ramming the offending chair into a corner. Unable to figure out what she was doing, he was willing to bet half the aggression the chair bore was for him. Yeah, he'd messed up her plan by showing up if she planned to sell the house by default when he didn't. There was a good chance he wouldn't have returned if the message had never caught up with him. When it had, he'd been in a coma, unaware of the doctors trying to save his life or his uncle across the sea losing his.

Even though the service prided itself on keeping service people in contact with families, his message had taken a circuitous route. The friendly nurse who worried about his melancholia may have decided not to give it to him. At the time, waking up proved to be more than he could handle most days. After already starting the divorce proceedings, he overheard a conversation confirming he'd done the right thing. Two nurses, who thought he was asleep, mentioned Angelique's name along with the fact she'd only asked if she were the beneficiary. Hot acid had curled up his throat at the words. He made sure to keep his eyes closed and his breathing even to not give himself away. The tiny snippet of conversation fueled his determination to survive if only to deprive Angelique of any death benefits.

The nurse who cursed Angelique was the same one who told him he'd find someone who would appreciate his real worth. *Yeah, right.* He didn't believe the nurse's assertion he'd find someone then or now. Damn, what a fool he was. He'd spent almost an entire year training and still believed Angelique would be there for him when he received leave despite her infrequent phone calls. Most of the guys in his units received care packages from their loved ones and the occasional weekend visit from their sweethearts. Angelique came to Fort Lee in the summer on her way to Virginia Beach with her cousin, Brittany, on a weird visit.

Brittany talked to him more than Angelique ever did. Bodie, his battle buddy, mistook Brittany for his wife. He snagged a short liberty due to Angelique's appearance that allowed the three of them off base privileges. A quick dinner at a local seafood place took most of their time. Her expensive sports car made it difficult for the three adults to fit, but they'd managed. When he asked about the car, Angelique claimed it was Brittany's. Too bad her cousin hadn't got the memo. Her open mouth and wide eyes announced everything as a lie. Grateful for the visit, Levi had tabled the subject.

Melody amused him with her stubbornness and determination to do things her way. She could be an opportunist, but she wasn't anything close to Angelique's ilk. Before he surprised her, she was getting the room ready for him. The fact she wanted to shield him from the details of his uncle's decay surprised him with consideration he hadn't expected.

Most people would want him to know how much they did. They'd throw in some guilt nails, too, speeches about how they were there caring for the ailing uncle while he wasn't. They would definitely mention his uncle crying out for him in his final moments. Roy could be just as bullheaded as he was which canceled out the idea of any deathbed forgiveness scenes.

Stepping deeper into the garage, he moved closer to Melody, feeling the weight of the memories. "What are you doing?"

A sharp screech and a jump announced her startle. The good news was she didn't fall on him again. Charmer barked in response. Melody slowly turned around, pushing a tendril of hair behind her ear. "Oh, you scared me."

A shadow hung over the corner where Melody stood, making it hard to determine her expression. Flustered might be the best description since her right hand rested on her chest, holding her heart in place.

"I was…" she started, shrugged her shoulders and tried again. "I was attempting to make it less noticeable. Roy took a lot of pride in his garage. He wouldn't appreciate a chair like this right in the middle of it."

A thought occurred to him as she spoke. All the tools were in place in their numbered outlines. There was a key for the tool placement, but after a while, he didn't use it. The woodworking tools were expensive, but they were all there. She could have sold them or lent them out to friends, but she hadn't. It looked like she was trying to preserve the house exactly the way Roy liked it. "You do know Roy isn't coming back? He's not going to check to see if the garage is in tip-top shape."

Her sigh penetrated his skin like the summer sun going past the initial layer and resting underneath. His hand rubbed his aching neck. He carried his troubles in his neck and back, according to the physical therapist.

"Yes, you're right." She covered her face with both hands for a heartbeat, and then dropped them. "I'm not sure what I am supposed to do, so I kept doing what I did when Roy was alive, except for the caring for him, of course."

"No wild parties, skinny dipping, or orgies on the front lawn?" he asked, knowing the answer, but her shocked expression amused him.

Her hand fluttered back up to her heart. "Good heavens, where would you get that idea? As a hospice nurse, I've several patients. Most of the time, I'm gone."

If they weren't running into each other all the time, it would make life easier. Apparently, all he did was scare the daylights out of her. Half the time she looked like a deer caught in the headlights. The other times she reminded him more of a cornered wildcat, an angry one, making him wonder if she had a guilty conscience. "Why'd you get a dog, then?"

Her soft footsteps came closer, but when he thought she would stop and talk, she kept walking. He turned, followed silently as she headed into the house. What was up with that? Less than a minute later, she returned with the dog in question dancing at the end of the leash.

"I had to go get him before he annoyed the neighbors with his barking."

The thin excuse served as her explanation for her rude behavior. It might be all he got. "Taking Fido for a walk?"

"His name is Charmer, and yes, I am." She gave the leash a tug and headed in the direction of the lake, but Charmer sat staring at him. "C'mon, Charmer."

For whatever reason, the dog liked him. It was ironic, really. "Tell you what, I'll get my cane and walk with you."

Her reaction, complete with pursed lips, made it hard for him to hold back a hoot of laughter. Her refusal stayed behind her teeth the same as his. Manners and her dog wouldn't let her. If this whole situation weren't such a screw-up, it would be funny. His cane was just inside the living room door. Opening the door, he reached in and held it open keeping his eyes on Melody. Even if she made a break for it and opted for a solitary stroll, she'd still see him later. Living in the same house had a tendency to ruin dramatic walkaways or slammed doors.

Cane in hand, he brandished it. He only resorted to the cane when the terrain was uncertain. The physical therapist wanted him to get one of those three-legged things, saying it would be safer. He might as well wear a yellow warning tape. Instead of *Do Not Cross* stamped on it, *Handicapped* would decorate the banner. Maybe even one of those circle emblems with legs inside it and a big slash across it. No thank you. He wasn't even thirty. Whatever years he had left, he wanted to live full out instead of hobbling around as if ninety. As it was, the lowering sun behind the trees threw out long shadows, heralding the approach of the evening. He'd need to watch the ground carefully. Sometimes shadows hid holes or uneven ground.

Charmer stood once he caught up with them. That had burned, he imagined since Melody had recently adopted the dog. There would be no dog prize trophies in Charmer's present or future. There was no way of telling how many different breeds went into the dog. The long body, floppy ears, and mournful face were basset hound. The rest could be a half dozen breeds with his wiry coat and speckled pattern. The gray muzzle and stiff movements indicated advanced years. What type of person picked an elderly mutt with no evidence of obedience training? As far as he could tell, the dog had no redeeming features.

Charmer chose that moment to look up at him adoringly with a wide-mouthed doggy grin. Okay, maybe one feature. "Why'd you pick Charmer out of all the dogs you could have had?"

"He would have been gassed tomorrow. People have no interest in adult dogs, especially old ones."

She said the words matter-of-factly without any sentimentality, making him think the way she lived her life, considering death was an everyday thing to her. "Um, were you with my uncle when he died?"

"Yes," she replied but didn't offer anything else.

Yeah, it would be as hard getting information from her as it had been with his uncle. Despite spending his teenage years with the man, he didn't know all that much about his reticent relative. The question was on the tip of his tongue to ask if his uncle ever talked about him, but he stopped it. It would be better not to know. He could have savagely cursed him with his dying breath.

"Did he die at home?"

"Yes."

Oh great, another lengthy answer, but she surprised him by looking at him and continuing. "If you are wondering if he died in the bed you'll be sleeping in tonight, the answer is no. He rented one of those easy lift chairs so he could get out of it on his own. Independence was paramount to him."

Levi nodded, keeping eye contact. They were at the stairs to the lake. He gestured for her to go ahead. The stairs would be easier than rambling down the hill, but he'd prefer not to have her see him manage the stairs in case he stumbled.

Charmer took the lead while she negotiated the sloping terrain behind the canine. The view was a very fine behind, another reason he let her go ahead. There were things he might not be able to do, but he could still appreciate a nicely rounded pair of hips.

Her voice drifted over her shoulder, softer for facing away from him. "He died in the lift chair. The place he rented it from came and retrieved it."

"Makes sense. Roy was always a frugal one." He understood the logic in renting a chair for a short time, and a pang of guilt still twisted his gut. His uncle would value being able to do for himself as long as possible. The bachelor was not in the habit of depending on anyone else. It must have hurt to have a hospice nurse rooming with him.

The feminine ponytail bobbed and swayed in front of him as Melody and Charmer negotiated the hill. No doubt his uncle appreciated an attractive woman fussing over him, too. What man wouldn't? At least Roy didn't die alone. His cane dug into the dirt with a little more force than necessary when he realized he owed Melody some respect for being there when he couldn't.

The stairs beckoned him with a promise of an easier walk while the other two plowed down the knoll. Melody's voice floated on the wind as she sang to the dog, something old-fashioned about a valley and a true love. Her lilting voice touched something he thought long dormant. No, it couldn't be. *Get that thought out of your head soldier. That type of thinking leads to danger.*

With the same words his field sergeant used to train him, he lectured himself. One foot was on the wooden platform leading to the steps. A breeze slid across the lake bringing coolness and a mist as it wafted up the slope. The familiar landscape comforted him, but it didn't clear his head as he hoped. Instead, his eyes drifted over to where Melody waited as Charmer investigated a fallen branch before baptizing it.

For Pete's sake, he was only in his twenties. Was he going to spend the rest of his life watching other people live? The thought caused him to step off the platform and scramble after the disappearing pair. Luckily, she didn't look back to see his ignoble half slide down the hill. His cane and a convenient sapling slowed his descent. His pride remained intact since he managed to stay upright.

Chapter Five

CHARMER DECIDED HE'D walked enough and settled in a flat, mossy spot as an impromptu bed. Melody tugged on the leash. "C'mon, boy. You can't just stop walking. You have to go back up the hill."

In answer, the dog rested his head on his paws. Not getting any response, Melody eased down beside the dog on the spongy greenery, dropped the leash, and stretched out her long legs. The stop would give Levi time to catch up with them. Leaves crunching and pebbles rattling signaled his descent down the hill. *Don't look.* Her fingers plucked at a nearby wildflower. Twirling the tiny flower between her fingers, she pretended contemplation until Levi's shadow touched her.

"Dog already tuckered out?" An audible gasp indicated his exertion level, too.

Melody leaned back on her arms to look up at him. From her position, he went on forever, rather like a tall tree. The sun's angle lengthened his shadow, allowing it to cover her. It felt intimate. Shaking the strange thought off, she answered, "Apparently."

Charmer, knowing he was the dog in question, lifted one eyelid, gave a tail thump, and closed his eye again. It didn't look like the dog planned to go anywhere. His failure to bark or growl didn't say much for his guard dog skills, but then again, they both knew Levi was behind them. Strangely, the bitter veteran somehow magically endeared himself to the headstrong mutt.

Just my luck. I adopted the dog on death row, and he prefers someone else to me. The story of my life. Her sigh was audible, attracting Levi's attention.

He nodded, indicating the ground next to her. "Mind if I sit?"

Several replies raced through her head with the major one being concerned about him getting back up. Would it be worse to watch him struggle to his feet or to help him? Levi wouldn't accept her help with gratitude, either. A colleague who did physical therapy with some of the patients emphasized an attitude of self-sufficiency. At times, she thought it was a harsh stance, but time had proven that patients who managed to do things on their own had a better outlook.

"Suit yourself." Melody tried for a casual smile, hoping it signaled both a carefree attitude and a certain flippancy she never possessed. Levi's beetled eyebrows assured her she'd achieved neither.

Using his cane as a tripod, he kept his artificial leg straight as he lowered himself to the ground beside her. His biceps bulged as he concentrated the majority of his weight onto the slender rod. Her eyes went to the tip of the cane buried into the loamy ground.

Thank goodness for that. If it had been on a rock, it could have slipped. Concern and experience working with patients whose bodies had failed them caused the words to slip out without thinking about the consequences.

"Your prosthetic leg bends, too, and can carry your weight."

His body a mere inch or two above the ground dropped as his swiveled to pin her with a glacial glare. "Do you think I don't know how to use my own body?"

His former stare practically oozed warmth compared to the present one, but his irritability could be a symptom of Post-Traumatic

Stress Syndrome. Even knowing that, her instinct urged her to grab Charmer's leash and leave. Her fingers tightened around the lead. Two problems with that response started with the dog not moving. She couldn't afford to engage in dramatics and expect to live in a small house with Levi. Logically, the man deserved a pass, considering he'd just left a war zone.

Breathing in deeply, she tabled her anger. How would she feel if she'd lost a leg, her family, and her place in the world? Her lips pulled to one side as she considered. Well, she'd already lost the family, but as for the rest, she'd be mad at the whole world.

"Thinking about telling me to go to hell, but holding it back because you're too nice of a person?" Levi asked as he eased himself into a prone position, lacing his fingers behind his head. His upward gaze met the interwoven tree branches, sporting leaves tinged with color hinting at autumn.

His words caused her to laugh before saying, "No, I was trying to think how I would feel if I were in your position."

His head rolled in her direction, and his eyebrows shot up. "Really? What did you come up with?"

Sucking in her lips, she'd debated what to say or better yet, how much to say.

"C'mon, Melody, out with it. I can see the wheels turning in your head. Maybe I should watch my words so as not to offend the crippled roommate. Did anyone ever tell you that you'd be a lousy poker player?"

There was yet another vote against her entering the world of competitive gambling. Even though his words weren't comforting, his voice held a degree of warmth, even playfulness.

"Yes, everyone tells me I'd be lousy at gambling. As for how I'd feel," she hesitated slightly until he nodded. "I'd be as mad as all get out. Aware I'd lost my place in the world after struggling so hard to get one."

A long, low whistle rent the air, causing Charmer's ears to go up slightly. "Mad as all get out, huh? I figured you for the feisty type back in the kitchen." His playful tone turned introspective as he continued. "Lost my place in the world?"

Her hand covered her heart. He hadn't considered this yet. Maybe he was too concerned about learning to walk, and then finding out about his uncle was enough to keep him busy. Leave it to her to make the man feel even worse about his present state.

"My place in the world," he repeated the words looking out over the lake and not at her. It could be that he wasn't even talking to her.

Could she recall her words? Silence would be her best bet. So far, every time she'd opened her mouth, her foot became wedged inside.

Levi shook his head as he continued to gaze off into the distance. His voice came out softer than before. Melody was unsure if he even remembered her sitting beside him. He drifted off to his own little world where outspoken females were not welcome. "I guess you're talking about the military. Funny, I can't remember why I signed up now. Went down to the recruiter with no particular plans, then I found myself signed up to locate and defuse bombs. Apparently, my high score on the ASVAB, good vision, and muscle mass decided my MOS."

Goodness, people wanted to do that. "It must have been dangerous." *Whoa, way to state the obvious.*

"It was and wasn't. It used to be a lot more dangerous than it is now. I heard once that all the early explosive ordinance personnel had was a long stick." He grabbed his cane and waved it over the ground to demonstrate. "Needless to say, many men were lost with this method."

The cane fell from his fingers as he continued. "Bomb specialists went out first with heavy armor to shield them before the actual troops came through. Sometimes they met their end due to a buried explosive, but more than likely it was the enemy picking them off from a hidden location."

He rubbed his hand over his face wiping away the memories. "Eventually bomb defusing vehicles provided more protection. They used one called the Minotaur over in Afghanistan. Now they even have a remote one, some modified Bobcat bulldozer. Even though it's been invented, it's a decade or more away from being used."

Melody bit her lower lip, wondering if she should say anything, especially since his initial anger had dissipated. Her curiosity got the better of her. "Um, did your accident happen when you were driving one of those bomb defusing machines?"

He laughed, sounding neither amused nor happy. "You'd think. It would make sense. Being inside an enclosure made me restless. I figured a walk would help. It was a Sunday, and I went outside the fence surrounding the fort, mere feet from safety. My crew and I continuously swept the area every morning for bombs, but there must have been one very fearless or ambitious individual who planted one in daylight."

Her muscles tightened, picturing a restless Levi deciding to take a walk outside the fence. It must be hard to live in a hostile environment, away from everything familiar, realizing at any time you could be seconds away from a painful death.

"I made a stupid decision. No one tried to stop me, figuring as I did that it was safe. Preoccupied or feeling cocky, one or the other caused me to step on the tripwire and blow myself sky high."

The words came out of his mouth so casually. Melody even refused to imagine the explosion and the horror of it. Soldiers in combat had to be calm and couldn't get upset about every explosion, every attack, every death, or they would be no good in battle. "Thank God, you're alive." The words came out breathy. An impartial observer might be fooled into thinking she had some investment in the taciturn man beside her.

"Yeah, alive." His lips pulled down indicating his ambivalence with the situation. "I only had one job. To neutralize explosives and I failed."

Melody's heart tripped a little. There had to be something she could say to make him feel better about his life. "Um, your work finding bombs is dangerous. If it weren't, you wouldn't have received such a big bonus check for signing on."

His head came up fast, and Melody found herself the focus of two angry, gray eyes. The expression 'if looks could kill' could have originated with someone on the other end of a glacial glare from Levi McDaniels. It didn't take a mind reader to figure out he was royally pissed—again. Breaking the stare, she fondled Charmer's long ears and wondered if the pooch was up to leaving. Now would be a great time to do so.

Children's shouts drifted through the silence, reminding her there would be witnesses to any scene. Dropping one hand, she wrapped her fingers around the leash, prepared to flee, not that she thought he'd hurt her. No one so forgiving of Charmer could be a threat. Rocking forward, she managed to move into a half-squatting position before Levi's hand landed on her bare thigh.

"Sit down. I'd like to know how you know about my big bonus." He bit the words out, giving the impression he didn't trust himself to open his mouth fully. His hand remained on her leg, warm and exerting enough force to stop her ill thought out exit.

Dropping back to the ground, she stared at his hand until he removed it. The large, red handprint she expected to see on her leg was missing. She could have sworn his hand seared into her skin. It must have been her imagination. A breeze wafted off the lake, cooling her heated skin and face.

At least, she knew what not to say. "It was something your Uncle Roy said, not to me actually. It was more to himself. As cancer progressed, he talked more and more to himself. I'd walk into a room, and he'd be having a conversation. Roy usually stopped when he saw me."

Levi blinked, his laser gaze softening some. He moved his jaw slightly, mulling over something before asking, "What exactly were his words?"

Her nostrils flared a little, realizing each remembered word would dig a deeper hole. It was bad enough to have an involuntary room-mate who hated her being there. Worse, she found herself attracted to him. Now, he thought she'd been nosing around in his personal affairs, but she hadn't, despite wondering what kind of person would abandon a lovable old man.

"It wasn't a conversation. I was picking up clothes to do laundry when I walked by Roy sitting in the living room in his lift chair. He wasn't talking to me but mumbling to himself. Something about everything went to hell in a handbasket once you got the big bonus for defusing bombs."

One of Levi's eyebrows arched. "He didn't say anything else about me or Angelique?"

A quick search of her memory didn't bring up any mention of Angelique. "He told me you two made the rowboat together. It made him proud. I asked about you, and all he said was that you left. I thought I could contact you to let you know your uncle was sick, but he refused to give out any more information. I didn't even know you had the same last name. Who's Angelique?"

"Never mind. Not worth talking about, trust me." Levi half growled the words and cast a sideways glance at Melody. "Still feel like running from me?"

The man read her well. The wind rattled overhead tree branches, sending two leaves fluttering down to the ground between them. Her initial response was to deny her spoiled attempt to leave, but unfortunately, he'd know it for the lie it was.

Shrugging her shoulders, she admitted, "I doubt I would have made it far with a dog that seems determined to stay by your side more than mine."

His laughter surprised her and apparently Charmer, who sat up. The canine's baffled expression could have been hers. Levi's face lit up when he laughed, chasing away the lurking shadows. The man could have been a heartbreaker with a little smoothness.

His laughter faded as he wiped suspicious moisture from underneath one eye. "Melody Gibbons, you've made me laugh more in the last twenty-four hours than I have in the entire year. It's going to be an unusual experience living with you."

"What's so funny?" She had been the butt of jokes before. She just wanted to know the reason why.

"You and your hard luck dog. You go rescue the mutt who should be eternally grateful to you, but he attaches to me, another stray. Burns your butt, doesn't it?" He grinned unapologetically at her, exposing a crooked bottom tooth.

Yeah, he was right, but damn if she'd let on he was. "Could be Charmer knows you need love and attention more than I do." She waited for him to deny the claim, but instead he stroked the dog's head.

"You could be right." The words sat there between them as Levi continued to stroke the dog.

It was hard to believe such self-awareness could come from the man beside her. No way had she expected such a response. Her intention had been to irritate, even though experience taught her not to rile up her roommate. In the end, they have to share the same kitchen, bathroom, even the washer and dryer.

A sideway glance revealed his hand still caressing Charmer's head. It could be that he wasn't even talking to her, but to the dog. It didn't make the words any less true. Using her hand as a shield, she rubbed it over her face, using the opportunity to observe Levi through her fingers.

Yeah, he had had a rough life, maybe even tougher than hers. If a person had their real parents, or at least one of them, and the parent was halfway normal, then their lives were at least better than hers. Sometimes she wondered if she had made some cosmic mistake in another life to merit her current one. Whenever she threw a pity party, her thoughts tended to run that way. The only way she could leave the party was to realize what she had. Maybe she wasn't a doctor, but she had a good job. She would never be a stick thin model, but she was strong, healthy, and had two legs. In that department, she had one over on Levi. There was no reason for her to start her life over, which appeared to be the situation for her roommate.

A tiny window in her heart opened, allowing compassion to rush out and encompass the hurting man next to her. A poster in the social services office came to mind. On it, a defiant child looked up at the camera. The script on it stating the child who acted the least lovable needed love the most summed up the adult Levi. The poster could be him as a teenager, too. It could have been her when you got right down to it.

Something inside her chest began to unfold like an opening rosebud. Levi spoke, but she didn't catch the words, too absorbed in the unfamiliar feelings flooding her body. Sure, she cared about her patients and their struggle to accept their mortality. Her unconditional love she saved for those who could do her heart no harm, like Charmer.

"Pardon me?" Redness suffused her face, having to ask him to repeat his words. It could have been another revealing statement. Each word would have cost him plenty. Melody turned her head and locked her gaze on his lips to make sure she didn't miss a word.

At one of her foster placements, the natural siblings excelled at tormenting her. They would launch their attacks by silently mouthing their plans to each other, assuming she couldn't read lips. At first, she couldn't. She learned fast though not quickly enough to prevent her move to a new home, but she didn't mind leaving.

A small scar off to the right of his lips tugged at her imagination. Had he cut himself when he first attempted to shave? Focus, she reminded herself as she watched and heard the words at the same time.

"I'm heading back to take a look around and see what you've done to the house, especially my room." He didn't wait for a reply, but instead rolled to his good leg and maneuvered himself into a kneeling position. Pushing down on his cane, he stood with a lot less trouble than previously.

His unexpected words silenced her and froze whatever was blooming in her as efficiently as a spring frost. Charmer lurched to his feet and tried to follow the man. "Oh no you don't." She grabbed the leash before the dog took more than a few more steps. "Males."

They never did what they were supposed to do. This included her dog, pulling in the direction Levi went and whimpering slightly. For whatever reason, the canine preferred Levi. She dropped the leash and allowed him to lumber after the object of his affections.

The setting sun silhouetted Levi. *Damn, even as a shadow he looked good.* It didn't matter that jerky words came out of his mouth every time he opened it. Once he got to the house, he'd stick his head into her room, which used to be his room. The thought caused her to jump up and run after him.

Sure, she had removed his adolescent posters of rock bands, fast cars, and models falling out of their microscopic swimsuits. The walls wore a more flattering peach color thanks to her hard work. She even sprung for feminine curtains and a bedspread set. If he were hell bent on revisiting his adolescent years, he wouldn't find them there.

A bird's cackling call sounded like laughter as she scrambled up the hill. It was always easier going down. Besides, she'd never attempted to run up the hill before. A stitch developed in her side, and she wedged her fingers into the offending part of her body.

It was her room. The only part of the house she claimed for her own. While Roy was alive, she didn't worry about him entering her room. He was a man who respected boundaries, unlike his nephew. Well, unlike most people. It shouldn't have surprised her to discover her foster parents went through her room on a regular basis. Worse, the other foster children or natural children did so, too. Instead of looking for drugs or weapons, as she assumed the parents did, the children stole the few things she had of value. One even took her diary and enjoyed quoting passages aloud.

As an adult, she hoped to leave that type of behavior behind. Her former roommate wasn't much better, taking the majority of the furnishings with her, despite not owning them. The woman would have taken her clothes and shoes if they had fit. It only reinforced Melody's obsessive need to have her own space.

A final push had her on flat land and a few steps away from Levi, who was in the act of picking up Charmer's leash. Using his distraction, she surged past him. The screen door slammed behind her as she ran to her room and pulled the door closed. Her breath came in gulps as she leaned back against the door waiting for Levi's approach.

The sound of him talking drifted through the screen door. The tone was warm, even affectionate. She assumed he was talking to the dog. Mary liked to say you could judge a man by how he treated a dog, a creature that could do nothing for him in the eyes of the world. The door opening and closing, plus the jingle of the dog's tags, let her know both were inside.

Her arms spread wide across the door, assuring no would enter her room without going through her first. Charmer was the first to discover her. He sniffed at her feet. Had he forgotten her with his sudden love for the usurper? His spotted head lifted as he regarded her with a dubious look before trotting away.

Even my dog thinks I'm crazy. Spread eagle against her door didn't make a case for emotional stability. God, she looked ridiculous. Before she could change position, Levi wandered into view. His eyebrows shot up.

"I realize I've been out of circulation for a while, but is this an attempt to invite me into your bedroom?"

What? He thought she was trying to be enticing. Okay, maybe her position could be misinterpreted. Still, why did he always have to jump to the wrong conclusion? Temper tinged her words. "No, quite the opposite. I'm preventing you from entering my room."

The left side of this mouth tipped up indicating amusement. "Do you have a meth lab in there?"

"Certainly not." The fact he thought such a thing insulted her. "Anyone with the least bit of sense would have it in the garage." The other side of his lips tipped up confirming the fact she amused him.

Using a knuckle, he rubbed the skin between his eyes, half-hiding his expression. "The way I see it, I own half of your room, which means I should have access to it."

Oh, no, she didn't like where this conversation was going. It was foster family dynamics all over again. The difference was she legally owned half of everything, too. "Well..." She stopped hoping for an inspired zinger. None came.

She darted passed him into Roy's room and jumped onto the bed and rolled around on it. "How do you feel now? I own half this bed, too. Think I'll take the middle." She rolled across the bed, kicking and wiggling, waiting for him to protest. Nothing. Not a word.

She stopped to look up to see if he'd even followed her into the room. His hands gripped the door sill while his eyes focused on her. His mouth was the slightest bit open ready to speak, but he said nothing. The cane leaning against the doorway fell, launching Levi into action. It only took him two steps before he fell on the bed beside her.

His outstretched arms prevented him from landing on her, but it was close. What now? She was transfixed, similar to how a rabbit must feel when a hawk's shadow crossed its path. His face moved closer. If she were someone else, someone petite and beautiful, then the slightly glazed expression on his face would make sense. His face moved closer, filling her vision as he leaned toward her.

"I want you to know you brought this on yourself." He had whispered the words before his lips touched hers.

She couldn't believe it. He was kissing her, Melody Gibbons, hospice nurse. The thought made her smile and moved into his kiss. Her fingers slipped over his close-cropped hair to cup his head and encourage him to continue. The lingering sunlight shot through the window in a colorful blaze, covering the both of them.

THE KISS ENDED too soon before she even had a chance to appreciate it properly.

Levi leaned back on one arm while making a slow perusal of her body and leaving behind a tingling path. "You're welcome to the middle section anytime you want. I'd be more than glad to have you there."

They weren't the words a romantic hero might speak, but they still made her heart sing. His next words, however, stopped the song.

"Keep in mind you're tempting a man who's been too long without a woman. Seeing your luscious form rolling across my bed mimicking ecstasy was too much for me. Instinct dictated that I join you." A lazy smile turned up his lips. For once, he relaxed as he rolled onto his back.

Melody sat up stiffening with each word. *Too long without a woman? Instinct?* He might as well say any woman would do. She scooted off the bed and walked silently out of his room to hers. What was she thinking? His words stabbed at her similar to tiny needles breaking through her hormone-laced fog. Of course, she hadn't been thinking at all. Her body kicked into sexual overdrive thinking Levi actually desired her. Maybe she should have commented *same here* since she'd been too long without a man. As a comeback, it lacked any bite, especially because it only made her seem more pathetic.

"Melody, wait."

She ignored his plea and continued to her room. Was there a tiny bit of remorse in his voice? It's what she wanted to hear, but in truth, the slight upward swing of his tone covered suppressed laughter.

Once in her room, she slammed the door. For a few seconds, it made her feel a tiny bit better. She collapsed into the slipper chair and sighed heavily.

Great. This is another fine mess I've gotten myself into.

Chapter Six

ASLIGHT SCRATCHING at her door alerted her to the location of Charmer. A thought crossed her mind to keep her fickle canine on the other side of the door. Another whimper prompted her to open it instead. The dog pushed his nose into her hand. Maybe he did know who needed him more.

Her fingers caressed his ears as she replayed the mortifying scene in her head. Oh, she kissed him back all right. Enjoyed the feel of his firm lips on hers and even hoped for more than a moment as she encouraged the kiss. Then, the man spoke and ruined it all.

Sighing again, she managed to make it to her bed before collapsing. The dog rubbed against her legs. So far, Charmer demonstrated an inability to jump on furniture. He was either trained, had excellent manners or his age kept him down. Her fingers reached to scratch his head. Even knowing it would set a precedent, she slid off the bed and wrestled the sizable hound onto her bed. The way things were going, he'd be the only male in her bed.

The conversation flashed through her mind, but this time the words *fine form* stuck out. There was no reason for him to say that unless he meant it. Levi didn't strike her as a man who doled out casual compliments. In the heat of the moment, he'd be unable to sort through a series of expressions. If he could, then he'd have chosen something better than 'too long without a woman'.

Charmer's ears went up slightly before he jumped off the bed to stand at the door. Levi was on the other side, she had no doubt. The dog was a regular Levi detector. Her lips pulled down in a frown waiting for whatever lame apology the man might cobble together. Silence. Charmer's scratching at the door indicated his presence on the other side. If the canine had thumbs, he'd swing the door open. Could it be the dog heard something else? Melody leaned against the pillows and looked up at discolored spots on the ceiling that could benefit from some paint.

The slight tap of the cane moving away from her door, she almost missed. The hard door slam levitated her off the bed. *What right did he have to be mad? She hadn't told him any man would do.* An urge to tell him exactly that had her sitting up in bed with her legs dangling over the side. A breeze ruffled her curtains and reminded her how she'd opened the windows to air out the bedroom. Could be the wind gave an extra push to the door.

Sighing deeply, she fell back on the bed. If she was going to survive living with Levi, she needed an outlet, preferably a sexual one. *God, she sounded worse than a man did.* Still, it wasn't her plan to spend the rest of her life alone. There had to be some man who'd see her good traits and love her. An idea had her reaching for her laptop that she kept under her bed.

After her last disastrous date, she decided against dating, not exactly forever, but at least the immediate future. Moving in with Roy kept her busy, too. It made her feel like she had a family. Her current schedule consisted of a series of people she visited who either lived with their parents or had home health care workers living with them already. Most families preferred a home health care aide since medical insurance seldom paid for the expense of a live-in nurse.

Staring at the computer screen, she waited for the familiar operating system logo to show. The computer chimed, indicating it was ready. Melody's fingers hovered above the keys. What should she type? There were dozens of online dating sites and a variety that catered to niche dating. There was one for Jews, Christians, and those over fifty. Unfortunately, there wasn't one for lonely hospice nurses. Remembering the name of one that conducted a test, she decided on it.

Most men would avoid a test. Only those interested in finding someone would subject themselves to one. The site appeared complete with smiling, perfect couples. Goodness, every couple could be a pair of fashion models. Did she even fit in? Well, she was single.

The banner informed her that her first ten days were free. With nothing to lose, she could try ten days. Melody answered nonsensical test questions, such as would she rather go to the moon or dance in Swan Lake? She didn't want to do either, but that wasn't one of the choices. Her eyes might be on the screen, but her ears focused on the room next door. Outside of the door slamming, she hadn't heard anything. Was Levi all right? What she thought was the door slamming could have been him falling.

She should look. *No, don't do it. The man was stubborn, but not stupid. He'd call for help if he needed it.* Turning back to the quiz, she perused the next question. Would she rather live in the mountains, in the city, or by a lake? This one she could answer honestly. It didn't seem like much of a test, but rather a series of likes. No doubt, they tried to find people who liked the same thing. It made sense. As the bar at the top of the screen indicated she was ninety percent finished, a shiver of excitement coursed down Melody's back. It was possible she could meet someone. The site introduction stated there were currently more single adults than married ones. It would be natural that some of those singles were looking for love and just maybe someone like her. Even a few might be located close to Wilsonville.

After about one hundred plus questions later, she reached the end of the section. *Couldn't accuse them of not being thorough.* The sound of the television alerted her that Levi was in the living room. How did he get by her without her hearing him? He wasn't on the floor writhing in agony, which was a good thing. Her shoulders relaxed as she scrolled down to the next section.

It read DESIRED CHARACTERISTICS. A person could list everything from religion to height. Most of the boxes had to do with appearance. Her top teeth clamped down on her bottom lip. *Did she have any right to specify any likes when she was so upset about how her previous date treated her?* She passed over most of that, except for age. It would be nice to have someone close to her age.

With her luck, some geezer would see she was a nurse and hope to marry her to get out of paying for nursing services. *C'mon, she wouldn't be so foolish to fall for that. Then again, she wouldn't be alone and would belong to someone.* Melody cursed softly as she continued to scroll down and check off desired characteristics. Down to earth sounded good. Check. Sense of humor was a must. Check. Easygoing, another desired trait she'd like in her future date. Honesty seemed good, too. She bypassed items like handsome, athletic, tattooed, and good dancer. A person who wanted too much often ended up with nothing at all.

A bolded message at the bottom warned that being too particular would result in fewer matches. Well, at least she and the dating site agreed on one thing.

The next section was photos. Oh God, she hated photos. A couple of years ago, she purchased a camera when she thought she might take up scrapbooking. That didn't work out well since she never did anything worth preserving, and she had a hard time asking people to take her photo. Roy had taken a few snapshots of her around the lake and in the rowboat. The man prided himself on his photography.

All she needed was the memory chip from her camera. Overjoyed about the unexpected bounty of the house, she'd taken several photos of the lake and the house from different angles. Where did she leave the camera? Mentally, she retraced her route only to realize the camera was in the living room. Great. *I can do this. I walk into the room all casual and grab the camera and leave. It's my house as much as it is his.*

Mind made up, she stood, much to the delight of Charmer, who'd kept vigil by the door. The hound led the way with his tail wagging. *Act casual.* She attempted to wipe all emotion off her face, but she wasn't sure if she had. The man could have fallen asleep watching television. She'd slip in and grab the camera from the end table.

Instead of slumbering, Levi bent over something in his hand. It was hard to tell what it was, but it consumed his attention. Just maybe she could still grab her camera without him noticing. Her eyes flicked to where her camera—wasn't. *Where was it?* The bottom of her stomach dropped. Melody knew what he had in his hands.

Charmer bumped up against Levi's leg begging for attention. "Hello, fellow." He looked up in time to catch Melody attempting to slither out of the room. "Hey, where are you going?"

Back to hide didn't seem like the best reply. She settled for a shrug.

Making no comment about her non-reply, Levi held up the digital camera. Mischievousness sparkled in his eyes. "Look what I found, Uncle Roy's camera."

Now was the time to correct him, but she chose not to. It was better to see what he might say.

"Uncle Roy didn't have a lot of hobbies, but photography was one he had picked up before I left." His glance went back to the camera. "I don't recognize the camera, but he must have bought it later."

Melody nodded, compounding the misimpression. *All she needed to do was get the camera from him.* "Yes, he liked to take photos. Even asked me to pose for shots." That sounded awkward.

"I saw them. They're good."

The photos would give her something to put on her profile if she could get the camera away from Levi. "Wow, I'd like to see them. Even download them to my computer."

He raised an eyebrow as he handed the camera to her. "Go ahead. I think you'll be surprised at how he made you look so natural and relaxed."

She snatched the camera from him. *What was that supposed to mean?* Pivoting sharply, she marched back to her room leaving the traitorous Charmer.

Levi's voice followed her. "I especially like the one with you in the boat, but the close up with the trees behind you is great, too. If I saw those two photos on a dating profile, it would definitely pique my interest."

How did he know? "What are you, a peeping Tom? How did you know what I was doing?"

She yelled her questions, not caring that they were insulting or that frustration coated every word. Putting the camera in her room, she stomped back to the living room and fisted her hands on her hips. If he could do the death stare, then she could, too. Lowering her chin, she tried to imagine fire shooting out her eyes and smoke seeping out of her nostrils. If done right, only smoking ashes would inhabit the chair.

A grinning Levi had the nerve to wink at her. *Did he actually wink at her?* "I didn't know. I was taking a wild guess knowing what I know. You're single. You admitted to the esteemed lawyer and myself you weren't seeing anyone. Obviously, you're sexually frustrated."

A gasp had escaped her mouth before her hand could stop it. "I can't believe you just said that." *Could it get any worse?*

"I could hear you pounding away on your laptop. I wondered if you might be filling out a dating profile. I'd understand and all. The thought of a partial man like myself isn't that attractive."

She rolled her eyes at his words. "You're not going down that path again. Plenty of women would find you attractive if you'd give them half a chance. Instead, you make up their minds for them."

"Listen to you. I bet you do the same thing. Sure, there are men who are jerks out there like the last loser you dated. Sometimes, they just might be overwhelmed because you're such a strong woman." The smile vanished from his face as he edged up to the end of his seat.

His words confused her, making it hard to tell what he might do. "I don't often pick my dates up, so I doubt they know just how strong I am."

He waved one hand in the air mimicking erasing his previous words. "That's not what I meant. It seems like you have it all together. You have a career, a pet, an interest in photography, and you know what you're going to do with your life."

Her mouth dropped open when he mentioned photography. *The skunk knew it was her camera all along, and he still looked at the photos.*

Levi smirked. "You have your name on it in silver permanent marker."

A remnant of living with Linda, who often picked up things and claimed they were hers. Luckily, Linda had no interest in cameras or was unaware that Melody had one. "You knew." She managed to hiss the words a little late as far as replies went. Enough! There was no talking to him. The sooner she got her profile up, the better. Turning, she gave him her back allowing him to know the conversation was finished.

Levi kept talking, showing he was unaware that the conversation had ended. "Go on. Make your profile if that will help you forget about your inappropriate attraction to me. Hell, I'm hot for you, and I won't deny it. You'd be more honest if you'd acknowledge your attraction. Roy raised me to be enough of a gentleman that I'll wait for a sign from you."

The words made her legs react more like wet noodles than bones and muscles. The only thing that kept her upright was leaning against the wall. He wanted her or did he want any woman? Her breath caught, and she fought the desire to turn and look at him. *What expression was on his face? Was it calculating, fierce, lover-like?* She placed a hand against the wall anchoring her in place and preventing herself from turning.

His voice came again, seductive, and close. "I won't make it easy. In fact, just the opposite."

He was behind her. How did he move without her hearing him, without Charmer setting up some alarm? *The dog was conspiring with him.* She turned slowly and met his intense gaze. Many times, she wanted to be the focus of such a gaze. It spoke of longing, certainty, but hinted at something else. *Now that I have a man hot for me. I'm not even sure what to do with him.* The lack of birth control was a problem but mentioning it would make her sound prudish. How could she put the brakes on the situation? *Was stopping even what she wanted to do?* She had to be practical. Falling into bed together on the first day of the house sharing would not work out well.

My God, they hadn't even known each other twenty-four hours. The realization made her firm up her resolve to resist Levi. *I almost jumped into bed with him without a thought, running on pure chemistry.*

In nursing school, she often overheard other students' confessions about one-night stands, claiming overwhelming chemistry. At the time, she rather harshly labeled them sluts, because she'd never experienced such a connection until now. It was the time for a set down, which would humble his male arrogance. She came up with more than half a dozen she could choose from, but she didn't use any.

Her eyes held his. "Go ahead. Show me your worst. I'm strong, as you mentioned." The sound of her words pleased her. The words reminded her of a tough heroine from a black and white movie, back before canned laughter and airbrushing.

A gleam appeared in Levi's eyes right before he pushed her to the wall, pinning her with his body. He landed a kiss on her so hot she melted from the lips down. *Dear Lord, could the man be any sexier?*

Her arms tightened around his torso, holding him in place as he peppered kisses down her neck. *Ah, he smelled so good.* His beard stubble rubbed against her face, teasing her already heated skin. His husky whispers against her skin managed to set off explosions inside of her. Yeah, the man not only defused explosions but also set off few of his own. Her heart was beating so loudly it sounded like knocking.

"Hey, is anybody home? I brought the papers by, as I said I would. The copier was out of toner, so I copied them at home. Did you forget I was going to bring them by?"

Levi's lips stilled, except for one murmured curse. "Shit."

My feelings, exactly. Charmer's tags jingled, indicating an enthusiastic greeting, which meant at least one resident enjoyed the prospect of an unexpected visitor. The dog was a guard dog failure. Levi straightened and put his hand against the wall lifting his weight off her. Greeting the lawyer would fall to her, no doubt. Smoothing her hair, she tried to make herself look as if she hadn't been getting it on with her brand-new roomie before she greeted Oliver. Levi shook his head before putting an index finger to his lips.

Keeping silent, she listened as the lawyer gave Charmer a final pat before leaving. The screen door slammed shut followed by a car door and the purr of an expensive engine starting. Levi took a few soundless steps to see if the lawyer left. The veteran could be stealthy when he chose.

"He's gone," Levi announced the obvious. He turned with an infectious grin. "Where were we?"

Melody slammed her bedroom door and locked it. What had she been thinking? She was just a convenient female and a horny one at that. A part of her psyche she didn't know existed chose to make an appearance. *C'mon, Melody, what would it matter? It would do you both good. You could be friends with benefits. Just think. You could help Levi with his self-esteem and get him to the point where he could try dating women.*

All she needed was a bad girl persona that gave dubious advice. "I don't want him dating other women." The hard thing was she didn't know what she wanted, but she didn't wish to be a convenient bootie call. That much she did know. What did a woman do with a randy male besides the obvious? The only thing she could think of was to avoid him as much as possible, similar with how she dealt with tempting junk food. She usually didn't bring any into the house. Since Levi was already here, maybe she should leave. How could she do that? Picking up her camera, she dropped to her bed. The abrupt motion caused her laptop to bounce to the edge. A panicked lunge had her capturing the device before it hurtled to the hardwood floor.

The birds were singing in the tree outside her window. Not much had changed in their world while hers had undergone a seismic shift. If it hadn't been for the helpful lawyer, she wouldn't be thinking so much, but rather feeling how well she and Levi would fit together. A growing moisture reminded her she was still running hot. A cold shower might help, but that would mean facing Levi. Sighing, she pushed back into the pillows. "I might as well finish my dating profile."

The thought didn't tantalize her as much as it did earlier. The site even had a photo editor to make the images even more appealing. She cropped the pictures and gave herself a healthy glow before arranging them on her profile. Roy did take good pictures. A sob caught in her throat. *She missed him so. Maybe he might be able to explain his nephew to her and reasons behind making the two of them live together.*

Outside of the two of them needing to get laid, she couldn't think of anything they had in common. *Forget about him.* Her goal in joining the dating site was to meet someone. Finding available men wasn't as easy as most people thought. Her last exposure to semi-datable men was college. The majority of students in the nursing program were women, which wasn't too surprising. The handful of men in the program consisted of husbands who were attempting a career switch, guys already in relationships, and about a dozen unattached males.

She hadn't even stood a chance, even though there was one soft-spoken fellow she favored. The appearance of so few available men reminded her of a joke about an ice cream man showing up outside a dieters' meeting. There wasn't much left of the ice cream man or his supplies, and there certainly were no unattached men after the dating frenzy. Often the men went through several student nurses before settling on one.

At the time, she reassured herself that her studies were more important than a certain nursing student was, and she believed it to some extent. Of course, it didn't matter what she thought since he ended up proposing to a fresh-faced beauty. With no degree to worry about, she had the time to focus on a relationship.

After typing in her credit card number, she pushed the submit button. Would she get any potential dates? What if none of them *was* her type? What was her type? Great, now she had something else to hide in the corner of her mind, similar to cockroaches seeking out the darkest spots in the room. They were there, even when their presence wasn't apparent. The outside light diminished while she constructed her profile. The cicadas and frogs took up the evening chorus as the birds nestled down for the night.

Even though her stomach growled its displeasure at a missed meal, the image of encountering Levi kept her seated in the dark with her unhappy belly. *Seriously? Am I going to live the next year afraid I might bump into him?* She sat in the dark straining her ears for any sound of the television. Nothing. The man already demonstrated he could move around the house silently when he chose to.

The good news was that meant he was getting used to his prosthetic leg. He wasn't her patient. Why should she care? Light seeped under the door, but it could be he hadn't turned off the lights. The idea that the lights would be on all night propelled her off the bed along with hunger.

Opening the door softly, she peered out. No one. *I need to stop acting as if I am in a spy movie. I have as much right in the house as Levi. All the food in the fridge is mine, too.* Fortified by her mental pep talk, she marched into the kitchen, ready to declare her rights.

No one there, even Charmer was missing. Goodness, what type of dog owner was she? She searched the living room, bathroom, and laundry room. No dog. Even peeking into Levi's room—since the door stood ajar—produced no sign of Levi or Charmer. A glance outside the front window revealed Levi's car still in the drive. Wherever the man was, he had her dog.

Wasn't the idea of a dog to provide her with companionship? Grabbing the lunchmeat, cheese, bread, and mayonnaise, she closed the fridge with her foot. Grumbling to herself, she assembled a sandwich. "This wouldn't have happened if I'd paid more attention to my dog than my own roller coaster emotions. Good thing the shelter doesn't do home checks."

The local shelter didn't have the staff to do home visits. The team wouldn't want to anyway because a home visit might mean returning the pet to the shelter, which meant certain death.

The finished sandwich looked appetizing. All it needed was a pickle. A low-voiced conversation drifted through the screen door. It might be the couple next to her enjoying a respite from their parenting duties on their picture-perfect porch. Then again, it might be Levi. She walked into the shadowy living room. Enough lights came from the surrounding houses to silhouette both the man and the dog. Charmer pranced by Levi's side, showing much more energy than when she walked him, and Levi was using his cane more now that no one was around to observe. They came close enough for her to hear the last bit of conversation.

"I don't know what I'm going to do about your owner, boy. That woman ties me in knots. She won't even talk to me now. I did the one thing no man should ever do. I was honest. You'd think I'd know better."

Melody darted back to the kitchen, hoping he hadn't seen her standing at the door. The two of them entered, not exceptionally quiet, making her wonder how she hadn't noticed them leaving. Charmer gave a bark announcing his entrance. What to say now?

Levi walked into the kitchen with the empty leash in his hand. He acted startled to see her. "Hey. Hello. I took Charmer for a stroll." He said the words fast as he hooked the leash by the back door.

"I see." It wasn't the greatest remark, and it might indicate she wasn't pleased that he took her dog for a walk without her permission. Levi turned to stare at her, lifting one expressive eyebrow. Was he asking if she had a problem with his impromptu dog walking services? Grabbing the sandwich plate, she held it up. "I made you a sandwich for walking Charmer." His other eyebrow shot up joining the first. She placed the plate at the end of the table. "Go ahead and sit. What can I get you to drink?"

"Water is good." He slid into his seat, watching her while she poured a glass of water.

She could feel his eyes on her even with her back turned. Now that she'd offered him her sandwich, what was she going to do? Placing the glass in front of him, she noticed he hadn't taken a bite of his sandwich.

"Don't you like ham and Swiss?" It was one of her favorites, which explained why she had it in the fridge.

"Yes. I'm waiting for you to fix another sandwich before I eat yours." His lips tilted up slightly in not quite a smile, but more of an acknowledgment that she'd been found out.

"Ah, okay." Another great comeback on her part, she mentally scolded. Still, it gave her opportunity to eat and who could argue with that? She slathered on mayonnaise on the bread, slapped on the ham, and asked while her back was to him, "How did you know I didn't make the sandwich for you as, um, appreciation?"

He snorted and laughed before answering. "The slam of your door echoed through the neighborhood. I don't claim to be good with women."

You were good with me. She kept the thought behind her teeth where it belonged.

"Even I knew you were pissed. The best thing I thought I could do was take Charmer for a walk. I thought he could give me some advice."

She finished constructing her sandwich and turned to catch his shrug. He had to be unaware of it. Still, it was endearing, reminiscent of the old movie heroes making a similar gesture with respect to a woman that read, "Dames, what can you do about them?"

Charmer trotted into the kitchen and waited until Melody slid into her chair before he plopped down between her and Levi. One part of Melody considered the canine a diplomat, but another part recognized him for the scavenger he was. His best bet was to sit between them.

"Did he give you any good advice?" She bit into her sandwich, rendering herself silent as she chewed. It was just as well. Best to keep her mouth shut and prevent any other witticisms she might author. The overhead bulb threw a yellowish light over the two of them, rather like a modern painting. If titled, it would be *Late Supper,* or more appropriately, *Awkward Snack by Two Strangers Forced to Share a House.*

Levi finished his bite and chased it with a swallow of water. "Charmer didn't have any advice. I suspect his former owner was a man, which explains his lack of knowledge."

Another funny comment, the unexpected poke at men, surprised a laugh out of her, causing her to spew food across the table. *Good God, what had she done?* Using her hand, she tried to corral crumbs and rid the table of the evidence of her descent into adolescent table manners. Her eyes stayed trained on her hand, afraid to see Levi's disgusted look.

His hand covered her hand. "Leave it. I'll leave my share of crumbs before I'm finished."

He sounded normal. Not pissed, not disgusted, but rather matter of fact. A quick upward glance revealed his eyes, soft with under-standing. At least, she thought that was what it was, not a knowing smirk or superior attitude. Her lips parted to speak, but then closed when no words came to mind. Could she say, *I don't always spit food when eating, but when I do, I make sure to pick the person to whom my social gaffe would do the most damage.*

They both sat under the yellow light saying nothing. Being silent was nothing new to her. It was often her only recourse in living in unstable circumstances. Early on, she discovered defending herself with the truth never helped. Those who chose to accuse her had already made up their mind. Any defense on her part was backtalk, and that never worked out well. Silence conveyed guilt, acceptance, and even contriteness.

The hallway clock's ticks filled the space around them. Melody envisioned numbers tumbling around them as if in a cartoon. How long could they sit saying nothing? Talk about a pregnant pause. The expression took on more meaning since she was in it. All she wanted was for Levi to return to eating his sandwich. Maybe he couldn't after her stomach-turning display.

Charmer's whimper broke the stillness. The tension could have affected the canine, too. Levi lifted his hand, allowing Melody to pull her crumbs nearer to her side of the table. Her intention was to sweep them into her hand and offer them to Charmer. Her eyes stayed on her hand at the edge of the table. Levi spoke, causing her to forget to put up her other hand to catch the crumbs. Luckily, the dog was ready for such an incident.

"It wasn't anything that bad. Consider I've had soldiers blown up beside me. I saw something flash across your face just now. You were with me, and then you weren't. If you were a combat veteran, I'd say you were having flashbacks." He angled his head and stared. His expression had become contemplative before he exhaled softly. "You are a combat veteran. Not from the war, but from life."

His words resonated. She'd never thought of her past in that manner. Sure, it wasn't all sunshine and butterflies. There were very few visits from the sunshine and butterfly fairy. Somehow, the mystical entities must have misplaced her address. On nights when she couldn't sleep and lay staring up at a ceiling she couldn't see, she wondered why her life resembled an uphill battle where she was pushing a massive boulder in front of her. Other times, she felt like she was in the bottom of a well looking up.

To distract herself, she'd thought of people who had it worse than she did. Dealing with so many people who had died before their time made easy to come up with a list. To complain or wonder why she didn't have the luxury of two parents seemed wrong in comparison.

"Yeah," she readily agreed. "I guess we are all veterans in this game called life. Some of us have taken shrapnel while the rest walk around unaware there's even a battle raging." The words tumbled out of her mouth even before she fully formed the thought. They sounded right, but it made her a hardened cynic, jaded by the turns her life took.

Levi's eyes lit up in recognition as he picked up his sandwich. It hovered inches from his mouth when he asked, "Do you want to talk about it?"

His quiet voice made it hard to hear. Even still, the inquiry shot a shaft of fear so piercing her response came out as a visceral scream. "Hell, no!"

Did she want to take the dull steak knife she cut the sandwiches with, open up a vein, and bleed out in front of him? It would be the emotional equivalent. She never spoke to people about her life. Mary and Roy were the only two people she'd slightly opened up to, and mainly all she did was answer their questions. To confess to the emptiness of growing up unloved and unconnected, would make her a more pitiful character in his eyes than she already was. It might appear as if she were trying to solicit attention or sympathy when she wanted neither.

Instead of replying to her emphatic statement, Levi bit into his sandwich, consuming it in four good-sized bites. Her chair squeaked across the tile, as she jumped up to make him another one. She busied herself with placing the meat on the bread, her back to Levi, which was a good thing because he saw too much. His eyes were like some mutant superhero's, but instead of seeing her, he saw into her, the secret needy side she worked so hard to hide from everyone. As Melody Gibbons, hospice nurse, she was an unremarkable, efficient professional. Few people ever questioned the person behind the job title.

"What are you doing, woman?"

Levi's words stopped her, especially the woman part. Slowly, she bathed Levi in an icy stare. "I believe we discussed my name before. I have one. It's Melody, and I'm making you a sandwich."

A grin crossed Levi's face. "The 'woman' part got you."

Putting down the cheese, she put her hands on her hips. "You're out to bait me, are you? Is this a game you men like to play with us women?" She emphasized the last word.

He shrugged his shoulders as his eyes glittered with amusement. "I can't say about any other men. I've never tried it on anyone but you. It cracks the glass shell you wrap around yourself. Tell me, Melody, do you object to being called 'woman' because it reminds you that you're a living, breathing female?"

Her breath caught for a second as she forced herself to exhale normally. Was he implying that she was attracted to him yet again? They both knew the answer to that. Not a subject she wanted to address, so she went with a different approach. When in doubt stay as close to the truth as possible when answering. "I dislike 'woman' because it is so generic. It makes me not an individual, but just another woman or person on the planet without a face or identity. Any woman would do. Woman, go get me my coffee. That sort of thing. Growing up in foster homes, my name was usually girl, new girl, or that girl. Could be the reason behind why I resent it."

Levi took a long drink, making her wonder if he'd even heard her. It would serve her better if he hadn't. She hadn't tacked on if she even had a name since no one ever used it. When her mother left, she packed Melody's identity in her flowered suitcase before she vanished with her latest man. She couldn't refer to herself as Jill's daughter since Jill no longer existed.

Levi placed his glass on the table. "Yeah, that makes sense. I'll make an effort to use your name. By the way, Melody, I didn't ask for another sandwich."

Her hands stilled on the completed sandwich. Not one comment about her being in foster care. Did he miss that part? She went ahead and cut the sandwich. "I'm wrapping up this extra sandwich and putting it in the fridge if you get hungry later tonight."

The jingle of Charmer's tags and the protest of a chair scraping back was her only warning. A half turn had her bumping into a muscular, cloth covered chest. The scent of warmed cotton, along with the tang of sweat, and the undecipherable element that was pure male intrigued her. Taking a step back, she reached for the counter to gain her balance. Her free hand fluttered at her throat. "You startled me. It's amazing how quietly you can move."

His lips tilted up, not quite a smile—as if he considered smiling but hadn't quite made up his mind. "Yeah, amazed me, too. Being able to move silently was the one thing that kept me alive. I didn't think I'd be able to move as quietly with the fake leg, but I'm learning to. I'm just not as fast."

His proximity left her nerves a little jangled, not to mention that his nearness made other parts of her kick into automatic overdrive. Unfortunately, her body wasn't on board when she vowed to avoid romantic entanglements with her roommate. *Not a viable candidate. Might as well calm down.* She inhaled deeply. How was she going to get by the sizable man in her way? She stepped to her right intending to go around him, but his hand on her shoulder stopped her.

Children's voices drifted through the screen door as she found herself caught in Levi's intense gaze. His sharp, alert eyes missed little. His continued existence bore witness to that fact. Part of her heard a child shout, "Ready or not!" The same detached part heard the fridge make a massive shudder and then sigh, which signaled the icemaker attempting to function. The aged fridge usually produced a handful of ice at best. It wasn't a problem normally since Roy hadn't used ice.

A bead of sweat rolled down her neck and slipped under her shirt. Things were going to heat up fast. Either she was going to have to start trotting ice home or avoid home altogether to avoid overheating.

Melody found herself staring into his impenetrable gaze. Now she knew what a mouse felt when confronted by a King Cobra. Her heart pounded hard, making its presence known. Would he kiss her again? Maybe he would. Her tongue slipped out, licking her lips in anticipation. It would be a bad thing and would make things more complicated. Neither her body nor her mind listened. Instead, her mind spun a fantasy affair where the two engaged in a torrid romance all in the span it took for his words to coalesce in the air.

"I'm not Roy, some sick, old man on the edge of kicking off. Don't let the lack of a leg fool you. I don't need you taking care of me or feeling sorry for me." His hand dropped as he pivoted and headed for his room.

Her eyes followed him until his bedroom door closed softly. *Damn, girl, you screwed up again.* Grabbing a damp dishcloth, she savagely wiped the table, flinging the crumbs to the floor. Stupid, yeah, that's what she was.

She washed the two plates, two glasses, and the knife and continued her mental dressing down. Placing the dried plates in the cabinet, she decided it was what men did when they were around women. Maybe they weren't even aware they were doing it. Her nose crinkled at the thought, reminding her of something her last foster mother said. The woman lectured her numerous times to stay away from the boys. Her standard rant was that boys only wanted sex and would promise you anything to get it. Apparently, her foster father had a bit of the wandering eye.

Her lurid imagery had conjured up wild-eyed males roaming the streets, capturing any lone female with promises of moonlight walks and flowers. Melody never bothered to mention the boys stayed away from her. If that scenario didn't scare her enough, the thought of becoming a teenage mother did. Her mother was one, and she saw how well that had worked out.

Giving the counter a final wipe down, she turned out the kitchen light. Tomorrow was a workday with clients to visit. There was a new client, too, some guy in his thirties. For a moment, she forgot about the brooding man behind the door. Hospice nursing involved shepherding clients to the end of their lives. The older ones tended to accept it while the very young didn't understand. The ones close to her age were the worst. Sure, they were angry at fate playing such a vicious trick with too many dreams unfulfilled and too many things left undone. It reminded her of all the things she hadn't done in her lifetime. What if she only had a few years left?

The question wasn't an unfamiliar one in her line of work. She flicked off the hall light. Many things would remain undone. Her dreams were modest ones centering on all the things she never did as a child. Having a pet was one of them. Charmer bumped against her leg reminding her that some dreams were possible. Riding a bike was another one.

Often the families she'd lived with had their own biological children who had bikes. Foster children didn't merit bikes since their stays were often weeks, sometimes only days. An interest in a pastel bike with training wheels and a princess license plate had earned her a sudden exit from one home. A simple examination of the bike hidden in the garage, waiting to be unveiled at the daughter's birthday party was her undoing.

All she did was sit on the bike. Didn't pedal it. Didn't know how. For a brief moment, she felt special, almost like the princess the license plate declared the possessor to be. Her eyes had closed as she pretended the bike was her present. Her mother had returned with smiles, apologies, and a brand-new bike. The improbability of it happening had made her laugh aloud and shift her weight causing the bike to tumble, throwing her to the hard cement floor. Her head hit despite the bike breaking part of her fall. Indistinct yelling came from a distance. It was indistinct. For a moment, she'd pretended it was her mother asking if she were okay, before the fuzziness in her ears disappeared allowing the words to penetrate.

"Damn thief. Turn my back for one moment and you're taking what's not yours. Not only taking it, ruining it."

The words were as clear as if it had only been only yesterday, as opposed to years ago. The man had stomped off to inform his wife, no doubt. Melody had sat in the garage, dazed, looking at the bike that didn't look ruined as blood ran down her face. The social worker had arrived the same time the birthday party started. Looking back, it saved her from experiencing another thing that had been out of her reach.

Charmer nosed ahead of her to push open the bedroom door as she turned on the light. No reason she couldn't get a bike now. Of course, she had never learned how to ride one, but it couldn't be that hard. The idea cheered her as she pumped her fist into the air. "Yay, princess bike, here I come."

It wouldn't be a princess bike. She doubted they came that big. Besides, she'd attract attention mounted on such a colorful ride. Nope, a standard colored bike with no fantasy logos would work fine. It was a doable dream, not like the one she had about falling in love with a thoughtful man who valued her. The two of them would live happily ever after in a house similar to the one she was in now. In time, they would have one or two children. Then she'd be able to experience her most desired childhood dream, a family vacation.

Melody dropped to the bed, toed off her shoes, and sighed heavily. A tightness in her chest increased whenever she even considered vacations. As a foster, she remained behind when whatever family she was with decided to go on a vacation. They arranged for a dog sitter and someone for her, too. Most emergency foster parents tended to be kinder, knowing they would only have her for a few days. Even the oral reports complete with awkward tidbits about dad getting lost or mom spending too much time in the gift shop all sounded like heaven to her.

Of course, she needed the husband first. Who knows, maybe she and her husband could take in some foster children? The mythical man began to form in her mind. He'd be soft-spoken, easy to get along with, and always smiling. Too bad his face kept morphing into that of her mercurial roommate's visage.

Thinking any available male would do made her no better than him. She had enough heartache in her life. This time she'd go for the safe bet. Maybe her future date would be exactly that. A sense of dread settled over her as she considered forcing herself through the torture called dating. Walking over hot coals barefooted appealed more.

Dates were not something she did well. At best, it would be a train wreck in slow motion. She'd mishear a comment and make a wrong reply. He'd tease her, and she'd take it too seriously. Her eyes flickered shut as she attempted to stop the barrage of images from previous dates from making themselves known. Why was she trying this again?

Oh yeah, to fall in love and be part of a couple. A bike would be much easier. No matter how many times she tumbled from it, the pain would have to be less than failing to attract some strange male. "Men," she spat the word as she stood up to get ready for bed.

Chapter Seven

CHARMER CURLED UP in the blankets beside the bed. Ready for bed, she glanced at her laptop where she'd left it sitting on the floor. It had only been a few hours since she posted her profile. Could she expect any response yet?

"Don't look." She whispered the words unsure if Levi could hear her through the walls. He'd certainly heard her angry typing earlier.

Tomorrow would be here fast enough. After work, she could look. It might give the site more time to drum up an appropriate man. She wasn't sure if real people or only computers searched the profiles and sent her the matches, but even computers needed time to work. Her fingers twisted her bedside lamp off. Darkness temporarily blinded her as her eyes attuned themselves.

A sliver of light peeked under her door. Hadn't she turned off everything? The sound of the shower reassured her she hadn't left a light on. Melody punched her pillow, tweaking it into an acceptable form. *Go to sleep. Don't think about the naked man only feet away from me.*

Her mind supplied an image to go with the sound. Levi had his head thrown back, his eyes closed as the spray hit him. The water would coalesce into drops sliding down his muscular column of a neck, lingering on his wide shoulders before slipping down his muscular back. *Enough!*

She snapped on the light and grabbed her computer. A few seconds later, she had her dating profile up. A tiny envelope with a 3 on it beckoned her. She had mail. Melody Gibbons, someone, make that three, possible matches thought she was the girl for them.

Wow, a few sentences and couple of photos made her a desirable. "I better check them out first. Might not be anything worth getting excited about."

Charmer opened one eye. Possibly irritated at having his twentieth nap of the day disturbed.

Part of a chorus about it being five o'clock somewhere penetrated her door. Singing in the shower? The man did it to annoy her. Her eyes slanted in the direction of the door. Maybe she should yell that she was trying to sleep. Good chance a wet Levi, adorned only in a short towel would greet her. Her gaze went back to the tiny, glowing envelope, and then slid back to the closed door. The singing stopped, as did the water. Her window of opportunity just shut. She clicked on the envelope.

The first letter writer identified himself as Bruce the Conqueror due to Viking ancestry. Ah yes, another person convinced of his ancestry grandeur. He was very interested in the fact she was a nurse and mentioned something about his elderly father living with him. Click. Close it. She could see where that was going. Maybe instead of getting letters from old geezers who wanted a free nurse, she'd get them from geezers' sons.

With any luck, the rest wouldn't be the same. The next profile came up with a bare-chested man she considered to be on the young side of twenty. How old did a person have to be to be on a dating website? His letter started out with the words: I ADORE OLDER WOMEN. Yikes, she never thought of herself as an older woman. Close.

The third unopened letter had the subject heading *New at This.*

Should she open it? Charmer snored loudly, evidently immune to her dating dilemma. The sound of Levi closing his bedroom door reminded her why she needed a distraction. *Nothing good could come out of getting involved with her roomie.* Remembering his kiss, her body temperature spiked as her fingers touched her lips. The laptop served as an impromptu fan. *Okay, maybe it would be good, but not the forever family vacation lasting.*

Her cursor hovered over the letter icon. A picture of a well-groomed blond man with glasses filled the screen. His shy smile looked forced. The kind of half grimace people who weren't comfortable taking photos made. Something they had in common. An accountant, a stable job, similar to being a nurse, was another commonality. He collected coins, not as flashy as photography, but a decent hobby.

His profile didn't overwhelm her, but it didn't creep her out either. Might as well see what he had to say. The short message came up the same time the bedsprings squeaked next door. Melody squirmed, trying to find a more comfortable position.

Shaun admitted he wasn't good at meeting women, but he did know he wanted a wife, family, and a happily ever after. Some of his most treasured memories were the vacations his family took. He promised to work hard to be a good husband, but first, he needed to meet the right woman.

Her heartbeat picked up as she read the family vacation part. How weird was that? He had the exact same dreams. Of course, they'd have to meet, and the sooner, the better. How would she suggest that? Would it make her sound too eager?

Absentmindedly, she ran her fingers across her lips. Shaun's kisses would drive away the strange obsession she'd developed in the last twenty-four hours. A quick note about how she'd love to meet in person, but her work schedule sometimes made it difficult.

Note sent. She contemplated looking at all the matches they sent her. The company encouraged her to send premade flirty messages to men she found promising. The subject lines consisted of obvious come-ons such as "I like what I see," "Hello Handsome," and "You've got my heart beating double-time." Nope, she couldn't see herself sending anyone the cheesy remarks. Her computer pinged indicating a new message from Shaun.

Goodness, he was eager. Her eyes flitted over his message. Shaun wanted to meet immediately and even gave his phone number with instructions to call him. He wanted her to call now. Her only response was to type the word, *Now?*

Ping. The man had to be sitting at the keyboard. Her chilled skin pebbled as she read his reply. *"Yes, please."*

Wrapping her blanket around her, she contemplated calling. Not here, not in this room. She typed in his number into her cell but waited until she stepped outside before pushing send. Holding the phone up to her ear, she walked away from the illuminating lights. No reason for her neighbors to look out their windows and see her bundled up in a blanket talking on a cell phone.

The phone rang a few times before a breathless voice answered. "Hello, Melody."

The nervousness in his voice oddly pleased her. She couldn't recall anyone anxious about making a good impression on her. They talked about different things including his job and her dog. The call concluded with the two of them agreeing on a dinner date after work the next night.

The locked door foiled her plan to slip back into the house soundlessly. She wiggled the handle vigorously. It did stick on occasion. Her rattling woke Charmer, who set up a ruckus. The dog who allowed everyone to enter and go as he pleased barked at her.

"I'm coming," Levi's voice carried through the open screen windows.

Great. He'll inquire why I ended up outside. Her hands swept down her nightshirt, which stopped at mid-thigh, no pockets.

The door swung open. "What do you…?" Levi never finished his tirade. His eyes slid over her as she stood awkwardly in the porch light's gleam with the blanket wrapped around her arm hiding the phone.

"Can I come in?"

He held the door open for an answer, but his arm on the open panel narrowed the entry space she had. Turning sideways, she slipped by Levi feeling the heat emanating from his bare chest. A pair of unbuttoned jeans rode low on his hipbones. She doubted the man slept in them. Most amputees welcomed the freedom of rest that didn't require an even number of limbs.

"Thanks," she murmured as she headed to her room, keeping her phone covered.

"Hey, what were you doing outside? I double checked all the doors to be sure you were in for the night." He made her sound like a cross between a wayward teen and a misbehaving pet.

"Just went out for a walk."

"Without shoes."

Shoes, even flip-flops, would have helped. Levi had already taken her measure. As a practical, no-nonsense type, she wouldn't parade through the neighborhood in a short nightshirt. "Um, left my shoes outside."

He grunted his disbelief as he closed and locked the front door. Charmer aimed a disdainful glance in her direction. Looked like neither male believed her. As an adult, she should be able to do whatever she wanted. Melody slowly closed her bedroom door, giving herself the opportunity for another glimpse of the bare-chested Levi. No luck. He was probably hanging out in the kitchen just to frustrate her.

A date tomorrow? Talk about quick. Clothes, she'd have to wear them. The idea of wearing her cartoon character smock with matching scrub pants appealed to her. Could say she just got off from work. Why try too hard if it wouldn't work out? No, that would just be rude. Picking out a pair of dark jeans and a flowered top, she draped them across the chair.

She'd have to change at the last client's home if she didn't want Levi to question where she was going. The man had his own business to attend to and might not even be home. Still, it would feel awkward. Mrs. Fleming would be her last visit and would enjoy being part of the process. The dear would demand details on her next visit.

With her clothes laid out, she was ready for bed. The warm night invited her to open her window wider to the evening chorus of frogs, cicadas, and the occasional nightingale. Charmer's tags jangled as he circled getting ready for bed. Tomorrow, she needed to buy him a real bed. She wanted him to feel like he belonged. Maybe she could have his name embroidered on his bed. No, that would just be silly.

Half-drowsing, something startled her, as she thought of herself riding a bike and Levi shouting encouragement. Her eyes stared into the darkness wondering what woke her. A warm body near the back of her knees and a strong whiff of doggy odor indicated that Charmer had taken the issue of a proper bed into his paws. Part of her knew she should push him back to his impromptu bed, but she rather relished the fact he'd preferred to be next to her. Oh, whom was she kidding? The mattress was ten times better than a thin blanket on a hard floor.

LEVI HEADED FOR the library. His goal was to use the computer to search for possible jobs. He could have asked to borrow Melody's computer, but she carried her small laptop everywhere.

"Levi, Levi McDaniels, is that you?"

Wilsonville wasn't the biggest town around, but, on the other hand, Levi hadn't distinguished himself, either. Using his foot, he swiveled the desk chair around to face his uncle's old poker buddy, Calvin. The bearded man grinned at him and held out his hand.

Ah yes, the handshake. Using the edge of the desk, he propelled himself upward to shake the man's hand. Calvin pulled him in close and patted his back.

Confusion about what to say slowed his response since he didn't remember a great deal about the man, except he came over for Thursday night poker games. "How's business?"

The man released his hold on Levi and sat in a nearby desk chair. He walked it closer to Levi by scooting it along with his feet.

"Business is booming. All of sudden, everyone wants an old house. One that has been restored, of course. That's where my company comes in. I've got more work than I can handle and not enough people to do it, but it keeps me working twelve-hour days, sometimes seven days a week."

Levi whistled, catching the disapproving gaze of the librarian. Calvin had to be in his sixties. "Doesn't your wife mind you working such long hours?"

His companion's happy countenance dissolved, falling in on itself. Sadness, loss, and uncertainty all flashed over the man's face in seconds as he pressed his lips together. He inhaled before speaking. "My wife died. Way before you even left."

Ah yeah, he was that friend. The devastated one lost without his wife. Levi remembered his uncle talking about him. The truth was he hadn't paid a great deal of attention. All his uncle's friends, while kind to him, faded into a mass of older men, who joked, fished, and played cards.

"Ah, yeah, right. Sorry, I sometimes get names mixed up and all. Not my strong point." He nodded as if that was exactly what he did.

The whiskered man grinned at Levi. "Let's go grab some dinner. I have a business proposition you might find interesting. You don't have any pretty young thing waiting dinner on you, do you?"

Would Melody fix dinner tonight? The thought had him hesitating, but Calvin wanted to talk to him about a job, which he needed more than a sandwich. He barely exchanged a handful of words with the inscrutable redhead before she ran out of the house this morning, clutching a coffee mug, her laptop case, and clothes on hangers. Her last words were for Charmer, not him.

"Dinner sounds good. Got any place in mind?" Levi followed the man as Calvin weaved through seating areas and waved at the elderly librarian who lit up at the attention.

"Yep. There's a nice little place next door. We can walk. Thelma, the owner, makes dumplings so light they could float away. The meatloaf is great, too."

The description had his mouth watering. There was no reason to think Melody was waiting for him at home, especially since she took a change of clothing with her. *Home,* funny he thought of the house that way. The whole time he spent with Roy he viewed the house as a way station, a detour from his real life. Somehow, life had rerouted him similar to a misplaced package. It had taken an explosion and a coma before he acknowledged Roy actually had given him a home. Too late to thank him.

Calvin continued to talk, unaware of the philosophical turn Levi's thoughts took. The man held the door open as he gestured with his free hand. "Thelma's place is just two blocks that way. There's a lot of renovation going on in our little burg. Young professionals from the city are gobbling up historical homes by the dozens. I count myself lucky to get the ones I did. With the help of a good carpenter, I'll be able to turn a good profit."

Levi opened his mouth to inform him that he wasn't exactly a good carpenter. All he knew was boats and only one at that. The silver-haired gent continued talking, never giving him a chance to explain.

"You'll be working with Thomas, my master carpenter. He's been with me for the last thirty years. When it comes to wood, there isn't anything he doesn't know. A good man to show you the ropes."

A deep sigh escaped Levi's lips. Calvin didn't expect him to be the carpenter. He'd be more of an apprentice. It was a workable plan, and the only job offer he had so far. The traffic noise assaulted his ears after the quiet of the library. His companion slowed as he approached a long run of steps.

Hell, just what he didn't need. The cane was in his car since he didn't think he'd need it. Calvin stood on the stairs, staring at them as if mentally measuring them for carpet. He turned with a frown, catching Levi's attention.

"Hope you'll indulge an old man. I need to use the ramp. The knees aren't what they used to be."

The ramp? His eyes darted in the direction Calvin was moving. A large statue of twisting half-clad figures partially hid the ramp entrance. The sign beneath the sculpture called it PEACE, but it looked more like an orgy to him. The sculptor probably thought the same, too.

Levi followed Calvin realizing he should say something. "I didn't even know the place had a ramp. I came in the ground entrance."

One of Calvin's gray eyebrows shot up. "You mean you never went to the library before you went into the service?"

The idea shocked his companion. He shrugged his shoulders and fitted one hand into his pockets. "I may have come a few times with

Roy. I guess I wasn't much of a reader."

"Ah, what a shame. How about now? Are you a reader now?"

It seemed an odd question. "I guess I've got time now. I read while I was in Afghanistan. Not much to do otherwise." No need to tack on that it helped him to escape from the endless boredom of his days, his hostile environment, and the very real possibility there was nothing waiting for him at home.

Calvin moved well for a man who had knee issues. Mentioning his knee problems could have been an excuse to keep Levi from using the stairs. No way, he'd mention his lack of leg, but in a town the size of Wilsonville, secrets rarely happened. All those privacy clauses and guarantees vanished when you crossed the town boundary.

A small eatery came into view flanked by two oversized planters filled with several varieties of blooming flowers crammed into the concrete containers. An appetizing aroma drifted from the place as a couple left, leaving the door ajar for seconds.

"Ready?" Calvin asked with his hand on the door.

Why wouldn't he be ready? His stomach gave a growl announcing its state, which made his companion laugh.

"Yeah, I'd say you're ready. Let's go tuck into some excellent vittles."

The prospect of good food and a job had him smiling. His mood lightened as he entered the brightly lit diner. Waitresses bustled between filled tables, attesting to the popularity of the place. A large chalkboard announced that tonight's specials were stuffed peppers and chicken fried steak.

"They both sound good," Levi remarked to Calvin. When he heard Melody's familiar laugh, his eyes traveled over numerous couples until landing on a corner table. The woman's back was to him, but he recognized her. Hadn't he seen that same top draped across her arm as she left this morning?

A thirty-something male sat across the table from her wearing wire-rimmed glasses and sporting hair too strategically highlighted to be natural. He managed to look both artistic and intellectual. Levi's brows lowered on their own. The important thing was what Melody thought.

A server waved them to an empty booth, cutting short his scrutiny of the couple. He followed Calvin, who was on the heels of the server who led them to a booth that would make it impossible to see Melody. Realizing her direction, Levi asked, "Isn't there a table empty?" He gestured in the direction they came.

Her eyes slipped to Calvin, who answered while the woman stared at Levi. "Loretta was taking me to my usual booth, but a table would be a nice change."

The waitress gave Calvin a smile while Levi only received an annoyed look as she turned and led the way to a free table closer to the two.

Calvin headed for the chair facing Melody and the unknown man, which would leave Levi with his choice of the other three seats. He'd be constantly turning his head to stare. It wasn't something he wanted to do. He made a lunge for the chair Calvin was heading for, placing his hand on it. He dropped into the chair, thinking possession denoted ownership before he remembered Calvin was his only lead on a job. He forced himself to stand. "Did you want to sit here?"

Calvin took the seat to his right and picked up a laminated menu. "Apparently not as much as you do."

Was he that obvious? Did he offend Roy's old friend? Not knowing what to do he played the card, he'd swore he'd never play, the veteran one. "Oh, sorry, battle reflexes. Instinct, I guess."

His companion's face grew interested as he placed his menu on the table. "No reason for me to look since I know everything that's served here. I was in Vietnam. What battle reflex forces you to take a particular chair?"

That's what he got for playing the card. Harry at rehab mentioned most folks never served in combat. Any mention of it usually dumbfounded the general populace. They didn't want to respond due to a double burden of never serving and bringing up bad memories. His volunteer tutor did caution him about talking to war veterans because they could usually see through excuses or at best would want to trade war stories. *Lucky him.*

Melody's laugh distracted him from his current dilemma. Was that a real laugh or a forced one? It was hard to tell when he couldn't see her face. The man leaned closer, demonstrating he was clearly a date as opposed to a friend. Levi's back stiffened. The behavior showed the man's desire to impress her. If her laughter was any indication, he was succeeding.

Calvin half-turned in his seat to see who grabbed Levi's attention. "Know them?"

"One of them." The words came out between clenched teeth.

Calvin whistled as he turned back to face Levi. "I'm betting the woman is the reason behind your battle reflexes, too."

Even when caught in a lie, it was hard to be upset with such a convivial companion. "You're right. Sorry. What can I say?"

"No worries. Here comes Loretta back for our order. I'd recommend the chicken fried steak with mashed taters extreme. They have sour cream and chives in them."

Calvin held up most of the conversation. The man decided to hire him because of a passing remark Roy made. Being a returning veteran made it the decent thing to do, too. Sometimes Levi forgot people could be nice for no reason. It was difficult to remember when your only mission had been to not be blown up that day.

As hard as he tried not to look at Melody and her date, his eyes kept returning. After all, he was facing in that direction. Could be that blondie was a great man who would treat her well. Maybe the two of them would fall in love. She deserved someone nice. A happy conclusion to a crappy hand life had dealt her so far. His lips pulled down into a grimace as he realized he might be part of the hand. Here he was, the ungrateful nephew, ready to snatch away the only decent thing that ever happened to her.

Loretta, the gum-popping waitress, showed up saving her smiles for Calvin while turning to Levi with an abrupt, "Whadya have?"

"Chicken fried steak." He went with Calvin's recommendation since he never picked up the menu.

She penciled his choice on her tablet and gave him an approving nod. "Side?"

"Mashed tate…" he started, but Melody and her date getting up stopped him. They were leaving. What now? Maybe a movie? If they were headed out to the house to test the mattress that would be awkward. The idea made him hot and not in a good way.

Calvin finished his order for him. "The extreme ones, ya know."

"Got it. Be right back with your water." She pivoted on her sensibly shod heels and headed for the counter.

Melody passed within feet of him, turning, maybe feeling his eyes on her. Her smile slipped a little displaying her surprise. She quickly recovered, greeting him. "Oh, hi."

Her date lingered at the cash register, stocking up on the free breath mints from a bowl on the counter. Levi's eyes flickered back to Melody. "Hi, yourself. Looks like you're out for a big night, tonight." He hoped she didn't hear the jealousy in his voice because he certainly did.

"Not really." She shrugged her shoulders and turned as her date drew near. "Got to go." The man glanced at Levi and Calvin with interest.

Melody turned toward her date, who took the opportunity to

wrap his arm around her waist drawing her close. "Who's that?"

His inquiry was loud enough for Levi to hear, although he was more interested in Melody's response.

She cleared her throat before muttering, "My housemate."

That's all he was, a housemate. Not the man who plastered her against the wall and kissed her until her breath grew ragged. She made him sound more like a pet, rather like Charmer, or a stray person who needed a home. His eyes stayed on the two as they exited the crowded diner and moved out of sight.

Calvin chuckled, drawing Levi's attention. "Don't tell me Roy actually went through with his cockamamie plan? Told him it was nonsense that it wouldn't work, but by the look of your face, I may have been wrong."

Plan, Roy had a plan. Of course he did since he was one for the long game. "Tell me more."

The man opened his mouth but closed it as Loretta returned with water and utensils. Levi wished the waitress could have been a little less punctual. Good chance Calvin might rethink sharing Roy's plan. He tried not to snarl at the helpful middle-aged woman who seemed overly friendly to his companion, peppering him with questions about the weather and his children. The man must be a good tipper.

Calvin answered the woman's questions with enough elaboration to make Levi squirm in his seat. Geez, he forgot people treated each other this way. The woman's animated response indicated she liked the attention. A man seated at the counter held up a coffee cup, which Levi assumed was empty.

"Uhm," Levi interrupted. "I think the guy over there is trying to get your attention."

Loretta glanced over her shoulder at the man who now pointed to his aloft cup. "Yeah, Henry probably is. Drinks his weight in coffee."

She turned back to Calvin. "Have to go. Work calls."

"Loretta's a good sort." Calvin mused as his eyes stayed on the woman.

If you liked your women moody and contrary, Levi was tempted to add, but didn't. A thought occurred to him. The librarian had been very friendly to Calvin, also. "You're single."

"Widowed." The one-word reply brought a shadow of sadness with it. "My Helen left me in an unexpected car wreck coming home from the Ladies' Missionary Group. Her vision wasn't the best at night, even worse when it was raining. I should have driven her. Offered to, but she laughed it off, declaring she wasn't an old woman."

The guilt, so palpable, hung in the air between them. Hell, what did he say to cause so much grief? He'd only meant to joke about how the local women tended to light up whenever Calvin was around. "I'm sorry. I know what it is like to lose someone you love unexpectedly."

Calvin shuddered to shake off the fingers of regret. "I imagine you do. Bad deal with your parents dead, then Roy succumbed to cancer, and your wife left you while you were overseas."

"Ex-wife." He automatically made the correction, hoping it was true. Ah, the joy of small towns where everyone knew your business.

"Hey ya'all," Loretta bustled to their table with two side salads and with enough enthusiasm to merit her own cooking show. "Here's your starter."

The bell on the diner door jingled, causing the server to look up with a frown to deal with the new people. She drifted away in a noticeable cloud of scent that hadn't been there before.

Calvin shook his head. "Ah, that Loretta she tries too hard."

Levi raised his eyebrows. "Um, so you noticed she was flirting with you?"

"Of course." He picked up his fork and speared a tomato. He

gestured with the laden fork. "I may be old, but I'm not so blind not to notice when a woman sets her sights on me."

"From what I've seen so far, I think a lot of women have thrown their baited hooks your way." Levi picked up his fork to eat. How could he get the conversation back to Roy's plan?

His companion looked thoughtful as he chewed. He paused for a sip of water before finally answering. "At first, seven years ago when the accident happened, that might have been true. Numb from shock, I sleepwalked through those first couple of years. Sure, there were women popping by with casseroles and cakes to feed the lonely widower. Often inviting me to church socials or a production by the local theater, but I didn't go. Eventually, those invites dried up. I didn't want to go."

Levi thought of Roy going through life all alone. "Do you never want to marry again or even have female companionship?" It was an invasive question and one he wished he could withdraw. "Forget I asked."

Calvin shook his head. "It deserves an answer, maybe more for myself than you. As a young man, you're thinking about sex. When you reach my age, it isn't as important as knowing that there is someone waiting for you, loving you at the end of the day. That might be the reason I work such long hours. After all, an empty house isn't that inviting. If I wasn't lonely enough after Eleanor's death, about a month later Lily, my dog, was hit and killed."

Damn, the congenial man had it bad, but he didn't stomp around with a chip on his shoulder. He could learn something from him. "Calvin, you know you could get another dog." Another wife, too or at least a girlfriend, but he didn't bother to mention the possibility. Good possibility that dozens of people had already.

Calvin picked up his glass and brought it halfway to his mouth before speaking. "Ya know I've thought about getting a dog, maybe a rescue. Until recently it didn't seem the right time."

"Sounds good." Levi agreed, half-paying attention to the conversation, but most of his thoughts centered on Melody and her date. Wasn't he the one who encouraged her to find someone? Didn't he tell her she was attractive and to ignore her last jerky date who thought she wasn't. His lips twisted when he considered he might have pushed Melody into the arms of Mr. Well Groomed. A lingering scent cloud of cologne and hair gel at their vacated table wouldn't surprise him.

Calvin's conversation he could hear but couldn't decipher due to the image of Melody and her date leaving crowding his mind. They were laughing up at each other, not a good sign. Make that not a good sign for him. He should say something. "Melody might be able to get you a dog. She recently rescued one."

His companion's eyebrows drew down as he chewed. Did Levi say the wrong thing? That's what he got for not following the conversation. Great, did he damage the only solid job lead he had? "Um," he cleared his throat trying to think of a way not to sound stupid. "You weren't talking about the dog, were you?"

Calvin picked up his napkin and held it in front of his mouth, but it didn't hide the twinkle in his eyes. He spent several seconds tapping the tissue around his mouth to clear the non-existent food. Finally, he dropped it to the table.

"Well son, to tell you the truth I wasn't talking about the dog anymore." Calvin flashed an indulgent smile as he reached into his shirt pocket for a pen and a business card. "Don't go kicking yourself now. My Eleanor had me tied up in knots before I finally popped the question."

Levi wanted to clarify that things weren't like that between him and Melody. If they were, she wouldn't be going out with other men. Men? Did she have even more dates lined up with different ones? It was possible. Luckily, he kept his mouth shut as Calvin wrote on the back of the card.

Holding out the card, Calvin told him. "I'll see you at eight at that address tomorrow if you're still interested. Wear some old clothes, because you'll leave dirty."

His fingers grasped the thin cardboard holding the promise it represented. "I'll be there with a clearer head, too."

Calvin laughed possibly about the clearer head assertion. He motioned for the bill. Loretta rushed over, demonstrating she'd been watching for such a sign.

The older man threw a generous tip on the table before standing. Levi stood, too, wishing it were he, not Calvin, who was paying. Soon, he'd get his affairs in order. His veteran benefits should be coming soon. If he sold the house, even splitting the proceeds with Melody would leave a nice chunk of change for the lakefront property. The idea of selling the house and waving goodbye to Melody caused his heart to skip a beat similar to the moment before he stepped on the trip wire. Some animal awareness, instinct, whatever you call it, knew a split second before the bomb exploded. The jittery feeling, he blamed on too much coffee. Never one to rely on feelings, logic and action served him well, at least until the accident.

Dinner over, the two of them strolled back to the library. Calvin greeted about a dozen people on their way back. After the introduction most had no interest in speaking to Levi, especially the women. No reason for them to. He hadn't made himself likable the short time he'd lived in Wilsonville. He arrived as a troubled teen who had grown into a bitter man, sure that life had shortchanged him. No wonder Melody preferred someone who could make her laugh.

The limestone library building came into view. Calvin pointed to a conservative sedan waiting under the shade of a mature maple tree.

"There's my car. See you in the morning. Get some sleep." His hand landed on Levi's shoulder in an affectionate gesture and left just as rapidly.

Levi waved as the sedan nosed into the street. Once the car was out of sight, he slumped against the building. Damn pride caused him to bypass the cane. A moan slipped out as he adjusted his back against the warm stone wall, taking most of the weight off his prosthetic leg.

A young girl strolled past with a rhinestone lead attached to a mop-like dog. Levi assumed it was a dog since it was moving, and a flash of pink indicated a dog collar. She glanced back over one shoulder at Levi. Maybe he frightened her being a strange man and all. Evidently, her mother had warned her way from strangers.

The petite female cocked her head. "You all right, mister? Should I get help?"

Her eyes grew soft and shiny as she regarded him, making him feel a bit like a baby bird that had tumbled from the nest. There wouldn't be a shoebox big enough to contain him if the girl felt the need to nurture him.

"I'm good." He pushed himself off the wall to demonstrate this, but the toe of his shoe caught in a sidewalk crack, hurtling him to the ground. His hands broke his fall.

The girl tugged on the dog's leash while the mop-like creature sniffed at his hands. "C'mon, Molly. We need to go. That man drinks too much."

Drinks too much? Now he was a drunk. He pushed up to his feet with less trouble than he had on previous attempts. Keeping his eyes on the uneven sidewalk, he made it to his car without any more humiliating incidents.

Sanctuary, that's what he needed, someplace to lick his wounds, assume the fetal position, and sleep for nine hours. First, beer, and then a hot bath. Both sounded good. The bath would ease the pain he felt. With any luck, the beer might turn down his anxieties enough for a dreamless slumber.

He drove the familiar roads, anticipating the twin pleasures of hot water and alcohol. The anticipation kept him company along with the radio. As he slowed for the curve leading up to the house, he spotted Melody's car in the drive. A quick glance didn't reveal another car. Great. Maybe the date didn't go that well. His lips had tugged up in a broad smile before he realized how petty he was being.

"No reason Melody shouldn't have a friend. It's not as if I'm anything special. Seriously, what would she see in me? Never mind, I don't have two legs. There's the matter she thinks I'm some ungrateful jerk who abandoned Roy when he needed me. Being who she is, that would matter more. Forget the fact that Roy failed to mention he was sick. I'd have come back if I'd known."

The car wheels on the gravel grumbled as he parked beside Melody's small compact. No telling who would leave first in the morning. His monologue stilled as he realized Melody might be watching through a window. She'd end up labeling him crazy or a drunk, just like the girl at the library.

Chapter Eight

MELODY STOOD IN the kitchen, listening to the gravel crunch as Levi pulled into the driveway. No reason to run to the front room to look. No one else would be arriving. Even though he asked, she refused to give Shaun her address, despite the fact she'd agreed to a second date. The earnest accountant seemed pleased to be out with her, which was a change. Shaun made her laugh for real with his anecdotes about odd things his clients thought should be tax deductible from a yacht to a boa constrictor. Shaun explained that the snake was part of an exotic dancer's act, so it was deductible.

Everything was fine until she noticed Levi with an older man. The sight of her taciturn roommate made her realize everything Shaun wasn't. No testosterone-charged, cynical vet who always managed to rattle her. No spark went off between her and Shaun as they shook hands before they went into the diner. That wasn't fair since they just met. Enough news magazine shows demonstrated that men women experienced an immediate connection with turned into stalkers. Of course, Levi wasn't the stalker type. Even if he were, he wouldn't have to work too hard since they already lived together.

Her bedroom beckoned as a hiding place, a sanctuary. Charmer's ears went up as he heard the front door open. Her canine listened to the uneven footsteps and lurched into action, rushing to greet Levi. The canine treated him akin to the dog bakery delivery boy instead of barking insanely the way he usually did about anything. An enthusiastic greeting by her dog indicated her wakefulness. It would be churlish to hide out.

Still, she waited, not sure what to do. Maybe she could pretend she hadn't seen Levi at the diner, but they had spoken. She might not have noticed him if her date hadn't mentioned some man staring. When they turned to leave, she saw Levi. Part of her wanted to hide, but another part wanted him to see she could enjoy the attentions of another man, someone not moody. Her exaggerated laughter implied Shaun was the most entertaining man alive. It must have been believable because Shaun accepted it.

His footsteps neared but stopped, not coming into the kitchen. Where was he? Melody waited. She'd spent all this time readying herself for his reaction and now nothing. The television wasn't on. What happened? She crept forward intent on looking into the living room and spy on the aggravating man.

She made it to the doorway only to discover both Levi and Charmer waiting. "Ahh!" She jumped back in surprise. "I didn't expect you."

"I know." Levi had the temerity to grin. "I could tell by your shadow that you were cowering over by the cabinets."

The fluorescent bulb behind her did cast her long shadow on the floor. She hurried to defend herself while admitting cowering sounded accurate. "I wasn't cowering."

"Yeah? How would you describe it, then?" He hoisted an eyebrow as he casually leaned against the doorway frame.

Her mind flipped through various excuses and rejected them just as rapidly. Most sounded silly and contrived, which was what they would have been. "I was getting a drink of water when you came in."

"Sounds plausible." He nodded, accepting her reason.

His attitude irritated her. Sure, he didn't question her excuse, but he didn't believe her. Her back rigid, she stomped the two steps needed to reach the sink and grabbed the empty glass. Flourishing it, she announced, "Here's the glass. Whadya say now?"

Three long-legged strides put him right at the edge of her personal bubble. The smell of onions and country fried steak hung in the air between them. They'd had the same entrée. Odd how similar the two of them were. Her pulse kicked up, due to anger, most likely.

Putting the glass back in the sink, she whipped around and fixed him with her best glacial stare. No way she'd let Levi intimidate her. Nope, no good would come of that. "Are you satisfied now?"

Levi had blinked twice before he took a step closer, shrinking the area between them. Less than a foot separated them. She'd read somewhere that Middle Eastern people often stood very close when talking. Could be he hadn't adapted to American ways after his long absence.

His eyes held her. "No, I'm far from satisfied. How about you, Mel? Did glasses boy ring your bell?"

The unexpected question shook her. It mirrored her thoughts more than she liked. Using both hands, she shoved at his chest. "Jerk, that's what you are." Just when her opinion of him had softened a little, he went and spoiled it again, and the push didn't budge him.

Her eyes drifted down to his wide stance wondering if she should kick him to get him to move. It might work. Of course, if he fell she'd feel horrible. Part of her was curious to see what he'd do next. His large hands wrapped around her shoulders. The pads of his fingers pressed into her skin.

"Did you have fun with your date?" He pushed the words out through clenched teeth.

The idea of her date bothered him, which made no sense since he all but encouraged her, telling her there were plenty of men who'd appreciate her. "Yes, I had fun. Quite a change to go out with a guy who isn't always playing mind games with me."

"Mind games, is it?" Levi used his grip on her shoulders to pull her closer. His pupils darkened and expanded, lessening the irises.

"Mind games, you know you do it. First, you're like all prickly, and then you're—"

His lips landed on hers, stopping her words. Heat wrapped around her, reminding her of the unforgiving spandex undergarment she'd donned for her date. It squeezed areas where too much of her resided creating a high muffin top where it ended. Although the only thing squeezed out now was rational thought. Her hands linked around his neck, which was their natural destination. His coarse, short hair tickled her skin as her fingers anchored his head to hers. Sudden rubbery legs made standing difficult. Levi slid his hands down to her waist, embracing her as he walked her backward to the counter.

Her lips parted to tell him something important. The thought slipped out of her head. "Levi." His name came out as a whisper. Was it an entreaty to stop or a plea to continue? He took it as the latter, slipping his tongue into her mouth to trace the roof of her mouth, tickling her and exciting her with the same motion.

Oh yeah, the man could kiss, but he'd proven that already. It made her wonder how well he did other things. Melody rocked her hips against his, feeling his readiness, letting him know her state, too. Levi's hands stopped their downward progression, and his lips stilled on hers. His embrace loosened and then dropped. He stepped away. His inscrutable expression provided no clues as to why. He just let go of her. Had she turned into something disgusting like a decaying corpse or a woman he wasn't into?

"Does your boyfriend make you feel like that?" The words hung in the air between the two of them. He stared at her for a second before swinging away to grab Charmer's leash.

Melody's hand came up to touch her lips. How did he do that? Why did he do it would be a better question. She was all but melting in his arms, and he managed to shut off the attraction and turn away. God, she wished she could do the same. The jingle of Charmer's tags indicated Levi's attention on her dog, instead of her.

"Shaun isn't my boyfriend." She shouted the words at the departing pair, making sure he heard. No need to add she had a follow-up date with the man. The screen door slammed.

She stumbled to the table and collapsed into a chair. Breathing deeply, she tried to slow her rapid heartbeat and racing thoughts. *What an unpredictable jerk. No wonder he was alone.* Another part of her rallied to his defense. The man had issues, more than most. Sure, he was bound to act peculiar at times. She had issues, too. One of them happened to be Levi McDaniels. Cradling her head in her hands, she finally answered Levi's impertinent question when he was too far away to hear.

"No, Shaun never makes me feel the way you do. I doubt any man would. You're too much like a rollercoaster with all the hard climbs and fast falls. Shaun is a carousel compared to you. Sometimes, though," she paused to wipe an eye, "a girl might want a roller coaster, but needs to settle for a carousel."

THE TREES FLUNG out shadows as the twilight deepened. The different colored dock lights resembled psychedelic stars while porch lights served as distant moons. Charmer sniffed the perimeter of the house, snuffling through the scrubby bushes on the trail of some animal. Levi tugged the leash urging the stubborn canine toward the lake. No reason to stick around at the site of his latest disaster. Melody's shock at his behavior and her response seared itself across his memory. He'd be lucky if he could think of anything else until he reported for work tomorrow.

Acting like a Class A bastard wasn't his goal, but somehow, he managed it all the same. The endless 'talks' about thinking things through before acting—courtesy of Uncle Roy—vanished into thin air when around Melody. Instead, he acted more like a hormonal teen with a dash of jealousy thrown into the mix.

"Charmer, any insights to your owner?"

No answer came, not that he was expecting any. Verbalizing his thoughts was a technique he learned in explosive ordinance training. Often the only person he could depend on was himself and the knowledge he'd acquired. Instead of settling for a mental checklist, he spoke it, not wanting to miss a step. Yeah, a missed step could have serious consequences, like waking up in a hospital bed with a missing chunk of memory and leg. Levi had learned a lesson about vigilance.

Relaxing his guard is what caused his current dilemma. Life was easier when he considered Melody as an unscrupulous gold digger. The image of a tired bottle blonde swindling old men made him laugh. Definitely not Melody.

Charmer's ears perked up at the sound. Levi bent down to pat the hound. "Boy, you're proof enough that the woman doesn't have a selfish bone in her body. Underneath, she's soft like an eiderdown comforter."

Her life should have made her harder, but somehow a hopeful core remained, a secret belief that everything would work out in the end, maybe. "Damn, with my luck, I may have stomped that tiny spark out."

The hound investigated a child's forgotten bicycle, ignoring him. "I'm not sure why I do what I do. First, I mention how several men would find her attractive. If that wasn't enough, I hand her the camera telling her what photos men would appreciate. Of course, I was only waving a red flag in front of her as far as dating, trying to rile her."

Charmer lifted his leg over the dropped bike. Levi, realizing his intent, jerked hard on the leash. "No! I think me being the jerk is enough for the night. No reason for you to get in on the action."

The stroll reminded him of the many walks he took as a teen around the same water, though he wouldn't have labeled them walks. Usually, he stomped around in frustration at his uncle's latest idiotic edict. In hindsight, he realized Uncle Roy's decisions were sharp for a man who never had children and were what he'd needed.

"I wish I knew what to do. She thinks I'm rejecting her the way that blind date did. Far from it. I want her so badly my teeth hurt." A slight chuckle ended his statement. "Finally, I know what that expression means."

Leaves crunched under his feet as he navigated the uneven terrain, thankful he had remembered his cane as he tore out of the house. "I don't know what to do. It's me that I was rejecting. I'm no good for her. She needs someone stable, not someone with an albatross named Angelique around his neck. Tomorrow, I'll call Oliver."

The image of Calvin handing him his card jogged his memory. "Oh yeah, new job first. I'll call during lunch, then."

They walked much longer than originally intended. Levi hoped Melody would have retired to her bedroom. Of course, there would be the issue of Charmer. The dog might as well sleep with him. The way things were going, the basset mix might be the only warm body next to his.

Charmer threw him several questioning looks at his determination to circumnavigate the lake. If the dog ever looked like he couldn't make it, he'd carry him home, even if toting an unwieldy dog with his cane would prove challenging. Charmer surprised him in keeping up. By the time they completed the circle, Levi had decided what he had to do. He'd apologize to Melody in the morning.

An illogical urge to open the time capsule consumed him. Perhaps if he could pinpoint where he came from he'd have a clearer path. That's what he needed. Angelique did a number on him. What she didn't do, the war had. The time had come for him to get his bearings and decide where he was heading instead of drifting with the current like a decaying flounder.

The lights were off in the house except for one in the living room and another in the hall. Melody left her bedroom door ajar, but darkness lingered on the other side. As soon as he unhooked Charmer, the dog squeezed his body through the opening, widening it in the process.

Levi's hand rested on the doorknob as he stopped in the act of closing it. Charmer had already settled on the bed, making his nest behind Melody's knees. In the meager light from the hall, she looked so defenseless. Life had toughened her up more than many of the young soldiers he'd met in training. Of course, those he returned with weren't so naïve or trusting anymore. What soldier hadn't second-guessed his decision to enlist when faced with possible death taking the shape of an unidentified shadow appearing nearby?

He closed the door, trying not to make a sound, in case it might wake her. If the woman faked slumber, he didn't blame her. He'd rather not deal with himself at times, either.

A shower and a drink would help. A twist of the faucet started the slow process of warming up the shower. Some things hadn't changed. It would take a couple of minutes before a reasonable temperature occurred. Time enough for a bottle of beer. Twisting off the lid, he wished for something stronger. In rehab, he'd heard enough lectures about avoiding alcohol and painkillers. Too many veterans lost themselves in the oblivion of drugs and drink. It was easy to do, which was why he had to fight against it. The temptation not to work out his problems but blot them out remained powerful.

THE HUM OF the water pipes announced Levi's location and activity. Melody lay rigid, contemplating her next move. The sound of water splashing and a throaty "Ahh" reached her ears, causing her to twist uncomfortably. Talk about women running hot and cold. The stubborn man could lead a class in it. Charmer snorted his disgruntlement as her legs bumped him off the bed.

"Sorry, boy." She apologized to the dog that may have shot her a disdainful look. It was hard to tell in the dark. A year of this would just about kill her. Shaun was supposed to distract her from the difficult, sexy Levi. The soft-spoken accountant struck her as a genuinely nice person, but he didn't measure up. Like comparing lobster to fish sticks, they were both seafood, but that is where the similarity ended.

The bed groaned as Charmer landed on it. For an old dog, he sure could jump. It made her wonder how he ended up at the shelter. Obviously, he'd been a pampered pooch at some time in his life. The animals arrive with very little or no history. Many people dropped their cast-off pet and hightailed it out of there, refusing even to fill out the paperwork. Melody had held the betrayed dog in her arms as the owner left. The pet, not understanding the situation, had struggled to follow. Maybe he knew more than she thought. Maybe he'd realized his owner wasn't coming back, and it was up to him to jump into the car before it sped off. If so, the canine was sharper than she'd been. She'd always expected a return visit from her mother.

Birthdays passed then high school graduation, and eventually college with no signs of her mother. Melody hesitated to move too far away from Wilsonville, just in case her mother came looking. It would be helpful to have a mother to listen to her issues with Levi. Jill, her mother, would probably tell her to have fun until it wasn't fun anymore. The philosophy apparently served her mother well.

Mary would listen. Tomorrow she'd call and arrange a time to meet. A pang of guilt stabbed at her, but her life had turned complicated in record time leaving her less time to volunteer. Part of the reason she volunteered at the shelter was to keep busy. The other part was to take care of the creatures no one else cared for any more.

Picking up her alarm clock, she moved up her wake-up time. It would be best to be gone before Levi got up. What could she say to a man she offered herself to, and his response was to walk the dog? Damning, considering he'd confessed his sex-starved situation. Still, there was nothing cool about his kisses, much different from the chaste cheek kiss Shaun bestowed on her. If Shaun had gone for one of those plastered against the wall kisses, which seemed to be her roommate's specialty, she'd not have agreed to the second date.

Tomorrow would be a long day, especially since she had to visit her newest patient, Kevin. On her first visit, she'd met a despondent man who had barely spoken to her. His mother dragged her outside and explained that Kevin's fiancée broke their engagement when his illness became terminal. Until the final diagnosis, she was his biggest cheerleader, declaring the two of them would beat the gloomy outlook of most liver cancer patients. Something snapped. It was hard to say what, but the formerly noble woman disappeared out of Kevin's life.

Even though the mother had only scorn for the missing woman, Melody could sympathize. The younger adult patients were often the worst. They resented Melody because her arrival meant they were at the end of their life. Her being healthy irritated them, too. Still, it was her job, and not everything could be sunshine and roses. Lately, it was more like thunder and lightning. The morning would be here sooner than she was ready.

The annoying chirp sounded near her ear, as she expected, pulling her from a dream she didn't want to leave featuring a beautiful autumn day as she and Levi rowed to the island. A wicker picnic basket nestled between their feet in the bottom of the boat. A feeling of relaxed camaraderie rested over the scene.

The chirp continued, pulling her away from the dream into an uncomfortable reality. Melody turned on her side to pound the snooze button. The lighted 6:12 puzzled her for a moment. Why was she getting up so early? Hospice work didn't demand a glam up appearance. Her supervisor's advice was to downplay her hair and makeup, in particular for the female clients. Many were so sick they no longer had the energy to apply makeup or even fix their hair. The last thing they needed was an overly made-up nurse on the scene. Not to bother suited Melody. She wasn't the type to slather on the cosmetics.

The grayish pre-dawn light peeked through her blinds, illuminating the room enough to make out the outline of the furniture. Melody stared up at the ceiling. Why had she set her clock so early? Who was on her schedule today? None of her patients demanded dawn visits. Most had accepted their time was limited and took advantage of the few benefits they had left like sleeping late. Charmer moved his head onto her stomach and regarded her with his big, mournful brown eyes, the same look that had made her vow to take him home. You'd think the dog could act a little more cheerful.

A kitchen cabinet door slamming notified her that Levi was up. Levi was what she was supposed to remember. Her goal was to escape an awkward confrontation. How would she escape now? Her eyes wandered to her window. Yeah, slipping out the window with the neighbors watching would add to the talk that already existed about their odd household. It didn't help that the window only pushed up a foot, which would make it a tight squeeze at best.

Charmer jumped off the bed and padded over to the door. The kitchen sounds continued, resulting in the Charmer whimpering, eager to exit. The canine cast an imploring look at Melody. Great, he needed to go outside. Grabbing the clothes, she wore last night, she pulled them on. No way would she casually stroll past Levi in her nightie. It might look like she was offering an invitation. Well, the man passed up his invite. No more were coming his way.

It's not like it matter how she looked to Levi, but she still picked up her hairbrush and ran it through her long hair before pulling it into a side pony. No reason for the neighbors to think she'd gone all slovenly.

Slipping on her shoes, she hesitated at the door, waiting for a time window that would let her sneak past. Maybe Levi would return to his room. Cracking the door, she peeked out, feeling like a character from a melodrama. Charmer used his nose to push the door open wider and rushed out to greet Levi with a bark.

There was a reason why dogs never featured prominently in spy movies. Her eyes met Levi's. The morning scruff on his face emphasized his masculine appeal by outlining his chin line. How she could be thinking such a thing after last night's fiasco, she had no idea. The man had the nerve to smile at her. Not a mere tightening of lips, but a show all your teeth, I'm delighted to see you smile that caused his crows' feet to appear. Her traitorous body responded even though it should be on board with the *we're not talking to Levi* plan. Part of her mind mumbled something about overrated talk. Was there any part of her body unaffected by the man?

"Good morning, Melody. I know you have a busy day ahead. I fixed you breakfast." He gestured to the table where a plate laden with toast, bacon, and eggs sat.

That was unexpected. Her eyes moved from the plate to Levi, who was pouring coffee.

"Sweetener?"

"No," she answered automatically wondering if she was still asleep. "Aren't you going to eat?"

He placed the coffee cup by her plate before answering. "I already did. Sit. Eat before it gets cold. I'll take Charmer for a walk. You'll be more comfortable without me around."

Charmer pranced by his side as he walked to the peg where she kept the leash. Politeness demanded she should deny his claim about her being more comfortable with him being gone, but it would make things easier. All she had to do was gobble her breakfast, dress for work, and hit the road. Scooping the scrambled eggs into her mouth, she appreciated how fluffy they were with a hint of an unknown savory spice.

Her chewing slowed as she considered Levi's actions. No man had ever made her breakfast. She couldn't say she was ever in a long-term relationship where that might have occurred. From what she heard from fellow students, most males considered a donut and coffee breakfast. The man was trying to make up with her. That was good, especially since they had more than eleven months until the year was up. She picked up the buttered toast and bit into it. What was he trying to make up for? Acting like a jerk or not desiring her?

The lilting birdsong wafted into the room as one especially strong singer trilled a morning welcome. Most people believe that birds sang to attract a mate, but it was well past mating season. It's possible that sometimes they sang because they wanted to, which sounded like a good enough reason.

Breakfast finished, she washed the dishes and placed them in the drainer. No reason to reward the man with dirty dishes. As she dressed for work, she listened for Levi's return. The radio played in the background as she sang along with the familiar tune. A quick glance at her watch reminded her that she didn't have all day to wait on Levi. She wanted to talk to her supervisor about Kevin.

There was a good chance the man was avoiding her. Allowing food and time to work their magic. Excellent plan. A recent scientific article explained it wasn't comfort food that made a person feel better, but the time away from the disturbing incident. All the same, she'd not abandon macaroni and cheese as a cure-all just yet.

Grabbing her medical bag, she opened it. A few empty pockets illustrated a need for essential supplies. Since she was going to the office, it would give her time to stock up. Picking up a pen, she wrote down the missing items. It didn't look like Levi was coming back before she had to leave.

Exhaling deeply, she decided to go with a note. She tapped the pen on the tablet waiting for inspiration to hit her. It didn't.

Levi,

Thanks for breakfast.

It looked like something a first grader might pen. She wanted to say something more to let him know he didn't have to hide out with her dog, pretending to walk it.

I'm over my mad. No need to hide out by the lake.

Melody

A final check of her watch indicated it was time to go. The breeze pushed through the window pushing the note across the table. "Oh no, you don't. I worked too hard for it not to be read."

Snatching the note, she looked around for something to anchor it to the table. A dented popcorn tin was at the corner of the room. The design was a Christmas one with puppies wearing green and red ribbons tumbling out of a basket. She bent to pick up the can only to find it surprisingly heavy. A shake revealed something other than popcorn inside. Just as well, since it was dirty and a tad rusty. The edge of the can anchored the note to the table.

"That should do it." She washed her hands while peering out the window for any sign of a man and dog. The minivan next door reversed down the driveway to join the parade of vehicles on their way to school drop-off, and then on to work.

Taking a backward glance at the tin visible from the living room, she wondered why it sat there at all. Popcorn tins were usually an inexpensive gift option for people you didn't know well.

On the stoop, Melody used her hand to shade her eyes from the angle of the early morning sun to search the lake bank for any signs of the two. She wasn't worried about them falling in and drowning. Well, she wasn't until she thought about it. *Go to work.*

Her legs slid across the vinyl car seat, bumping into the mail from the previous day. She'd forgotten it in her rush to get to the house. Why it had been so important to be inside before Levi arrived, she couldn't say. A well-aimed throw sent the mail hurtling to the passenger seat. Despite the warm weather, she allowed the car to idle, giving the two males time to show. Nothing. "Should count myself lucky." The words sounded more like a complaint than a reassurance.

THE OFFICE RECEPTIONIST, Claire, looked up at her entrance. "Melody, good timing. Your new client's mother just called. She wants you there ASAP. Actually, she wants a doctor, but..." she hesitated, waiting.

They both spoke in unison. "What she wants and what she gets are two different things." The axiom represented so many things in the hospice industry. Most people didn't want their loved ones to die, but they did. A few wanted doctors, not nurses, answering every call at the certified nursing assistant cost. The majority just wanted the pain and suffering over.

Claire laughed at their familiar ritual. Hospice care could be soul sucking. Whenever the tiniest bit of levity presented itself, you grabbed it with both hands and held on. "Tell me about the mother, a regular tartar?"

Syringes, a roll of gauze, and latex gloves went into her bag as she pondered the term. "By tartar, if you mean a woman angry that her son is dying and there's nothing she can do about it, yeah, then she fits the description."

Claire whistled. "Damn, girl, you put me in my place. Not sure how you do what you do. I'm glad for the distance between me and the hurting ones." The phone chirped ending the conversation.

Just as well—Melody never had a real answer for why she did what she did. How could she explain that it suited her without sounding like a ghoul? No one would call her job pleasant, but it made her feel needed. The pleasure she gained from the unexpected apology breakfast dissipated as she considered what her future visit entailed. Her patients weren't disagreeable. Every one of them resented an inconvenient death, happening without their permission. A handful reacted with rage that they never got around to living the life they wanted. That was to be expected, but often it was those left behind who tied her up with endless demands and questions.

No, she didn't know why some people died, and others didn't.

She couldn't say why your second cousin, who's as mean as a snake, got the same cancer as your husband and lived.

No, she didn't think God was punishing someone for a misspent youth.

Once she made the mistake of pointing out there were plenty of ornery people living to a ripe old age to prove death wasn't a punishment. That hadn't worked out well. Better to let people vent without trying to answer their rhetorical questions. No one put that in the job description, but it was a definite, nevertheless. Most tried to tamp down their anger around the terminally ill. Spouses wrestled with the fact that their marriage only lasted years as opposed to decades. Often there were children who would be without a parent.

Inhaling deeply, she tried to control her emotions. Andi, her supervisor, would tell her not to get emotionally involved. Easy to do when a person stayed in the office, answered calls and typed out invoices. Stepping into someone's life was an entirely different thing, if only for a few hours a week.

A simple blood pressure check often had her clients verbalizing bucket lists they often considered doing but never did, only to regret the lack of time and ability to do so. Routine questions about appetite and energy level often netted her unsolicited advice about loving boldly and speaking her mind before it was too late. Occasionally, her patients leaned against her and wept as she adjusted their oxygen tubes or pain patch. She'd stored up enough anecdotes to write a dozen heart-wrenching country songs about dying. Since her patients never recovered, her songs probably wouldn't be on the hit chart.

Her fingers punched at the radio controls until she located a happy song. The fast beats and the lyrics about sun, love, and vacation romance failed to lift her mood. There was nothing for it. She'd have to handle Kevin's mother. Parents were the worst. They still expected to save their child from impending demise no matter what their age. Their anger at their helplessness somehow targeted her. Parents badgered her, calling all hours of the night. Even after doctors prescribed palliative care to keep the patient comfortable until death, they still expected her to do something miraculous.

Noting the street sign, she flipped on her blinker and slowed for the turn into the middle-class subdivision. The well-groomed yards and planters filled with live autumn flowers denoted a sense of pride and time. The development consisted of three styles of home, but everyone had the same black mailbox with gold reflective numbers attached. All the conformity made it difficult to pick out the right house. Her foot eased up on the accelerator, as she read the house numbers.

Before she fully stopped, Kevin's mother flew down the porch steps, signifying she'd been waiting. Melody's shoulders went up as she prepared herself the wave of anxiety that would engulf her as she opened the car door.

"Thank goodness you're here." Kevin's mother, Natalie, shifted her weight from foot to foot, as she wrung her hands.

Leaning back into the car, Melody snagged her bag before turning to talk. "What's wrong?" On the surface, it appeared to be a silly question. Since the problem consisted of someone Natalie birthed dying before his time.

Melody straightened to her full height and slammed the door shut. A suicide attempt wouldn't surprise her. A few of her patients had tried it but had been unsuccessful due to diligent caregivers. In the end, she figured it was a person's choice how they went, not the selection of those left. Of course, if it were someone she loved, she might change her view.

Moving closer, Natalie tiptoed stretching her petite body to be able to whisper into Melody's ear. "I think Kevin's depressed."

No shit, Sherlock. Her fingers went up to her lips, praying they weren't moving. They weren't. Good. Fifty percent of her job was medical the other part involved people skills, which wasn't always her strong suit. "What makes you think that?"

Of course, discovering in the prime of your life that you're dying might do it. Pair it with the one time you needed unconditional love and ending up being dumped could be a contributing factor, too. She'd be surprised if he weren't depressed.

"He isn't eating." Natalie confided in a low voice afraid Kevin might hear.

Loss of appetite was standard. "That's normal. Some medicines will decrease his appetite. If he's just coming off chemo, too. Some patients complain that everything tastes metallic and isn't worth eating." Most of her patients didn't possess hearty appetites. Did they not eat because they weren't hungry or because there seemed to be no purpose to it?

The two of them walked up porch steps, ducked flowering hanging baskets, and wove around wicker furniture with sunflower print cushions. Obviously, it was his mother's house. Another reason Kevin might be depressed. The whole point of going home to die is to be surrounded by the familiar and what gave you comfort. The sound of the television drifted out through the window screen. Squealing tires, sirens, and gunshots indicated a crime drama in progress.

Kevin looked up from his place on the couch. He waved, acknowledging Melody, but ignored his mother. Ah, so that's how it was. "Um, Natalie, could I have a tall glass of water, with ice." She watched her patient's eyes cut toward his mother and hurriedly added, "And lemon, too, if you have it."

Kneeling close to Kevin's head and using her body as a block, she asked. "What's going on?"

"Oh, you mean besides the dying part?" His voice was raspy.

Melody picked up the cup on the coffee table and directed the straw into his mouth. He managed a few sips and then motioned it away.

"Besides the usual." Even though everyone knew why she was there, she tried to avoid saying death and dying as much as possible.

"My mother is driving me crazy with all this hovering over me! She's sure I'm beside myself because Emily broke off our engagement."

The man acted very casually about it. "You're not upset."

"Not at all. I encouraged Emily to break it off and leave." A phone burbled in the distance, a landline. The sound of conversation indicated his mother had picked up the call.

His answer shocked her, and none of her usual platitudes fit the occasion. "That was kind of you."

"Not really. If I were kind, I would have insisted on Emily not being my beard years ago, but in a way, it worked for both of us."

Melody wondered if she heard right. If Emily were his beard that would mean Kevin was gay.

"Yep, you guessed it. Horrified?" Kevin raised his eyebrows and rounded his mouth in a surprised expression.

"No, should I be?" His sexual orientation didn't matter to her. When you were counting your future in hours as opposed to decades, it was of no consequence.

"Well, then you'd be one of the few. Now that I don't have a chance for a do-over, I realize how much of my life I've squandered doing what people expected, afraid of what someone might say, ignoring what I wanted. I'm thirty-fucking-three years old. I'll never be thirty-four and never had the courage to tell a man I love him."

"You still can." Melody didn't expect Kevin to jump up from the couch and hit the local gay bars, but he needed something, though she doubted Wilsonville even had a gay watering hole.

"Yeah." His lips twisted up as he thought. "Not sure if I can even get his number. Being engaged to a female didn't put us on the best terms."

"Give me his name and I'll look it up for you." Melody never considered herself a super sleuth, but she was determined to find the phone number, especially after watching a tear slide down Kevin's sunken cheek.

"I'd appreciate that. Robert Crane from Jackson Junction." He murmured the words as she wrapped the blood pressure cuff around his thin arm.

She wrote the blood pressure numbers down in the small note-book she used for stats. A backward glance over her shoulder revealed his mother still chatting on the phone. If she hurried, she might make it out without a prolonged conversation about the wrongness of her boy dying.

No one should die at thirty-three, but they shouldn't have to live a lie, either. Pulling out her checklist of questions, she went through them all. Scribbling down the answers in her cryptic brand of medical shorthand. The tinkling sound of ice hitting glass meant Natalie finally got around to getting her a drink. Melody's legs bent into a half squat, readying to stand up when Kevin's papery skinned hand stopped her.

"Do me another favor."

She wasn't sure she could even track down Robert Crane. "Okay." Crossing her fingers, she hoped she could deliver.

"Live your life. Be crazy. Do the thing that's not safe. The one you told yourself wasn't practical, but you wanted it just the same." He managed a slight smile. "Aha, yes, I see it in your eyes. That one."

Levi, terribly impractical, but she wanted him along with several improbable items like her mother coming back into her life. Better yet, she'd apologize for leaving in the first place. Roy McDaniels, the first person who ever treated her like family since her mother's desertion, she wanted him alive. There was a time she'd convinced herself she could will it to happen.

There was no coming back for Roy. He was dead. As for her mother, she might as well be. Ahh, but Levi, that particular image pulsated with energy and temptation. His angry edge did more to attract than repulse. Sure, she might have regrets, but she'd have more if she never acted. It was time to act, but maybe she should talk to Mary first.

Chapter Nine

THE THUD OF hammering and the scream of a power saw guided Levi to the right building. The three pickup trucks backed up to the building, and the scaffolding confirmed the location. Turning his wrist, he glanced at his watch. Yep, it was five till eight, which meant he wasn't late. All the same, he needed to get going. The newbie label would be hard enough to wear. He didn't need to add another one.

The black cane rested against the passenger seat mocking him. He should take it in case his leg gave him trouble. His hand rested on the smooth, curved handle. The first thing the other workers would think when they saw the cane was that he wouldn't pull his weight. Damn, he didn't need that. Levi's lips tightened, imagining the looks he'd receive from the other workers. Calvin could have mentioned his missing leg already, but he doubted it.

The wound site had finally knitted together, but he wasn't sure he'd ever be back to normal. There was no returning to the cocksure young man who enlisted without a second thought, anxious to leave the small burg of Wilsonville. Mistakenly, he thought with the affections of Angelique and a regular paycheck that he had it all and never had any plans of returning, especially without two legs, but here he was.

Gripping the steering wheel with his right hand, he pushed out of the car. His eyes skimmed over the workers searching for Calvin's silver head. The time it took to locate the man gave him enough time to balance his weight before walking. Maybe after a while he wouldn't need to do that, but he wasn't there yet.

Calvin reminded him of Uncle Roy. It would be up to him to prove himself. Inhaling deeply, he swung the car door closed. Technically, it would be the first time he attempted anything since he stumbled across the IED. Three months had passed since his fateful misstep. Part of the time, he'd been in a coma. The rest he spent learning to walk and healing, as the nurses liked to say. Lawrence, the physical therapist, always called his sessions work.

At the time, he called them sheer, unadulterated hell. There were times he'd wished he'd died, especially after hearing about Uncle Roy's death. It would be hard to say how happy the man would be to see him if he'd lived, considering the way he left. Fate had other plans for him. Once they decided he was ready, the Army sent him home or what used to be home.

The cracked and buckled sidewalk provided a challenge. As long as he was aware of it, he could handle it. Half a dozen steps led up to the porch, making him regret leaving the cane in the car. A rusty railing provided dubious support. Calvin turned and waved.

"You're on time. Army men always are. You can set your clock by them." His grin widened as he walked toward Levi with his hand outstretched.

Grasping the hand, he shook it hard, demonstrating he was strong enough for the job. "Glad for the opportunity." No reason to joke about the service being a constant game of hurry up and wait. Those who served would understand, but it'd still come off as whining. People tended to expect veterans to be either reticent or mentally unstable, sleeping on park benches. He wanted to be part of the first group.

Calvin's calloused hand demonstrated he wasn't one to stand

around and bark orders. Levi's respect for the man grew. They both dropped their hands at the same time when a stocky man wearing a Navy logo cap ambled up to them.

"Must be the new guy." The man smiled and stuck out his hand. "Thomas Eurton. You can call me Tom. You'll be working with me."

Levi took the proffered hand firmly, expecting a hand squeezing session. It was what his former friends did, testing to see who was the strongest. "Levi McDaniels. Call me Levi." The shake was moderate without a bone-crushing grip.

"Will do. Ready to work?"

Tom gestured to the side of the house as the rumble of a dump truck drowned out his words. Donning a hard hat over his ball cap, he passed a yellow helmet to Levi. A box of safety glasses sat on the unfinished porch. Levi reached for a pair. If he learned nothing else from his accident, it was to take precautions. His *nothing is going to happen to me* attitude disappeared with his leg. Up to that time, he'd been confident in his invincibility. Obviously, he'd just been lucky, not smart or indestructible.

Inside the house, the sunlight streaming in through windows spotlighted the sawdust dancing in the air. The safety glasses and hard hat helped some but didn't do much to prevent breathing in the dust. A spasm of coughing grabbed him as he leaned against the wall. Tom hurried to open some windows.

"Should have had the windows open. The dust gets to you. After a while, you'll get used to it."

The man looked away from Levi, knelt, and picked up a long section of wood. Catching his breath, Levi stared at the kneeling man. He hoped his tasks would be something he could do. Working on a rowboat wasn't the same as renovating old houses. More like comparing dairy farmer and a chicken farmer, while insisting they were both farmers and did the same thing.

Bringing the wood closer, Tom turned it over to reveal small red circles on the underside. "This here will be part of the banister. I need you to drill an inch and a half deep. No deeper. The wood splinters if you go too deep."

He could do this. His eyes darted around the room wondering what machine to use. A series of saws and other power tools lay around. He could ask. Tom picked up a drill and fitted it with the appropriate bit. Of course, how could he be so stupid! Had he forgotten everything Roy taught him?

Tom balanced the banister between two sawhorses. "I'll do the first one. You watch."

Levi stood on the opposite side to get a clear view. The drill bit into the wood, sending out even curls of wood. The drill whined and dust flew, as the hole grew. "Stick your finger in the hole," Tom advised, lifting the drill clear.

He stuck his index finger in, wondering if this was some joke. "Okay, what now?"

"Look at your finger. See what knuckle the hole comes up to, and that's how deep you want to drill."

Using his fingers for measurements was not exactly his uncle's way of doing things. His brows lowered. Should he ask for clarification?

Tom, sensing his dilemma, slapped him on the back. "Don't think so hard. Most of the time, you'll be moving around the house, and you won't have a tape measure." He reached for the fluorescent orange measure on his belt. "Take mine. I got plenty. Don't stress about the job too much. You're in."

Levi's fingers wrapped around the offered measure. Feeding the metal tape into the hole, he double-checked the measurement. It was exactly an inch and a half. "How did you do that?"

"A few thousand banister holes. You try it. I'll watch. You might want to sit." Tom pushed a metal folding chair in his direction.

Levi wanted to protest, stating he could stand and do the work. Did the older man think he was a cripple? Apparently, Calvin had mentioned the leg.

Tom rattled the chair. "Did you notice you're about a foot taller than me? Sitting will put you at the right height. The drill could skitter off if there is too much distance between you and the wood. Sitting allows you to hold the banister to help guide the drill."

His words made sense. Levi sat in the chair, glad for the break. Attempting to recreate the hole, he duplicated Tom's earlier action. He lifted the drill to measure the hole with his finger. Looked good, but he pulled out the tape measure to verify his guess.

Tom fingered the new cut. "You're a natural. The good news is this is a three-story home. You got plenty of banisters to do. You might say you have your work cut out for you." Tom laughed at his joke. The words soothed Levi's anxieties allowing for a relaxed work environment.

THE MORNING WENT quicker than Levi expected. The crew stopped for lunch, an eventuality he hadn't considered. The apology breakfast had gobbled up his time. In the field, lunch had more often been a meals ready to eat bag, often including candy to up the calorie content. Most were okay, although a few contained mystery meat, the reason most days he made it to the chow hall.

Tom doffed his hat and slung his arm around a younger version of himself. "Hey, Levi, if you didn't bring your lunch, Little Tommy and me are heading over to the buffet. You're welcome to join us."

The promise of food tempted him. It would also give him a chance to find out more about the job. "Sounds good. You want me to follow?"

If he followed, then he'd have a few minutes in the car to call Oliver since he inherited his deceased lawyer's cases. All he wanted to hear was the divorce was final. His Internet research revealed Angelique met the terms for abandonment. He hadn't heard much from Malachi after his initial inquiry about proceeding with the divorce. At the time, he put it down to the slowness of the legal system. That his lawyer died had never crossed his mind.

Tom slapped him on the back. "Come with us. It will give us time to talk without the whine of power tools jiggling our fillings loose."

Levi agreed but glanced back at his car when he saw Tom's over-sized truck. It would take work and ingenuity to climb into it, but he could do it. Little Tommy solved the dilemma by reaching inside the truck and grabbing a stepstool. "I'm too short to reach the seat on my own. Makes me feel like a midget."

"No problem. Think I'll use the stool, too." Using the frame of the door, he boosted himself into the back seat of the extended cab. The only problem was the stool remained on the ground. The step in question lifted and moved upward. Levi leaned forward to see why. The stool danced on the end of a thick cord as Tommy pulled it upward. "Clever," Levi added. "Got a future as an engineer."

"Yeah, that's what Dad says. I've always had to figure how to do things differently since I am so much smaller than other guys my age."

The boy was a little on the skinny side, but not too typical for a pre-teen. "How old are you?"

"Eighteen."

The answer stunned Levi. He'd thought the boy was barely out of middle school. He knew he was as big as he was now when he was eighteen and twice as foolish. People all over had issues, but he never recognized that fact until recently.

Tommy's words ran together as he explained his service project for his Eagle Scout badge, something about refitting a scout camp to allow disabled children to attend. The noble effort made Levi feel about two inches tall. When he was Tommy's age, when he wasn't arguing with his uncle or getting into trouble at school, he'd put the majority of his energy into chasing girls. Apparently, it took him much longer to grow up.

THE BUZZ OF the phone gave way to voice mail. Melody depressed the end key without leaving a message. What could she really say? *I'm thinking about jumping my roommate. I need you to tell me all the reasons I shouldn't.* Mary could give her plenty. Most people would, but the truth was she didn't want to hear rational reasons. She hardly ever did anything spontaneous. Her mother's free-spirited ways never took root in her. Order was her religion. A glance at her file carrier sitting next to her zippered laptop case proved her point. One of Linda's dates informed Melody he could get her a good trade in on her car since she kept hers in showroom shape. Of course, the man was a car salesperson, which made her discount his evaluation. A new car wasn't in her budget. Her present compact was reliable.

Safety was the second rung in her ladder. Never do anything that could end badly. Organization allowed her to gain control over a life as a foster child that often went off the tracks, many times through no fault of her own. Other times, she may have caused it to derail. At last, she had some stability, but no real joy. Keeping to the speed limit, she proceeded to her next appointment, Lilah. Even though Lilah was only forty, she'd surpassed many other Cystic Fibrosis patients as far as life expectancy, proving her doctors wrong.

Melody pulled into the modest neighborhood where her client lived. The splashes of color against the still green lawns caught her eyes. Little things told a lot about the person who lived there. The bright pots of geraniums denoted a gardener. Fussy wicker lawn furniture belonged to someone who spent time outdoors. Various toys strewn around the yard indicated a growing family. A fairy flag flapping in the wind reminded her that magic happens. It was a fitting flag for Lilah.

Jim, the husband, opened the door to her knock. His lips stretched into what most would call a friendly smile, but Melody saw the strain in his eyes.

"Lilah's in the bedroom. In fact, she was just talking about you." He gestured to the back of the house.

Melody weaved her way around furniture and boxes piled haphazardly on one another. The neon marker penned labels announced the contents accompanied by a name. Without meaning to stare, she read *romance novels for Darlena*. "You aren't moving, are you?"

Jim's eyes grew glassy as he gestured to the boxes. "Lilah wants to move out everything of hers while she's here. Get it to the person who could use it. She doesn't wish to wait until she's…" Jim turned away to try to control a sob.

"No worries. No need to explain. I'm sorry I asked." She continued to the bedroom, giving the man needed privacy.

Lilah sat up in bed in a lacy lavender bed jacket, labeling a cardboard box resting on the mattress. "You're here. I'm so glad."

Her patient's eyes danced with excitement, even though her words were faint. Death crowded into the room along with the two oxygen canisters hovering nearby like silent vultures waiting to swoop in.

"What are all the boxes for?" Melody tried to be as upbeat and matter-of-fact with her patients as possible. They had too many friends and relatives hanging over them, wringing their hands, and talking about the unfairness of life. No one wants to dwell on dying, especially when death is imminent.

Lilah pushed the current box, attempting to move it off her bed without success. Melody gently removed it and sat it beside the bed. "Thanks," she acknowledged while pointing to the area near the window. "Go find the box with your name on it."

Melody complied, lifting and moving around boxes until she located a surprisingly light medium-sized box. Her name was in bright purple block letters. Underneath her name was *romantic dresses*. Apparently, she'd picked up the wrong box. Could be Lilah labeled the box wrong, too. It would be easy to do being on so many painkillers.

Lilah's breathy voice stopped her from replacing the box on the floor. "That's it. You got it."

"This one? You're sure?" Hugging the box close to her body, she carried it to back to the bed. If her slight patient thought anything she owned would fit Melody, then she was sadly mistaken. Her game plan was to take the box with her as she left. Eventually, the box would find its way to the local thrift shop.

A twinge of pain shot across Lilah's face as she shifted, but it didn't stop her excited burble of chatter. "I had an idea, a great one. Instead, of just waiting to die, why not share my life with others while I'm still here?"

"Sounds good to me. You already do that simply being you." The remark seemed like something from Saturday morning kids' shows. Lilah's eye roll concurred. Taking a seat in the chair near the bed, Melody balanced the box on her knees.

"Seriously. Back to my plan. I'd rid the house of all my personal items so Jim wouldn't have to go through that after I'm gone." Her words were casual as if she were checking off items from a list. Pack up things. Check. Second item, die.

"Makes sense, but don't you think he might want something to keep?" Grief often overwhelmed those left behind. Some managed by wearing the deceased's clothes or playing their favorite music. Some therapists thought it best to haul everything away and make a clean break. Melody didn't agree with get rid of anything that remained from the deceased, and then go on to live your life. On some levels, she understood. Still, as a person who had so little mementos of her past life, it seemed brutal and abrupt. Grief couldn't be compart-mentalized.

Lilah's lips pursed as she considered the suggestion. "He'll have the wedding photos, the furniture we bought together, the dishes, and my jewelry. I imagine he'll remarry in time, and the new wife will insist he gets rid of everything. I might as well do some cleaning while I'm here. This way the items go to the person I believe needs it the most."

Melody choked back a cough at the way Lilah considered a new wife chucking everything. Guilt twisted around her when she realized she'd be doing exactly what the new wife would do if she got rid of the dresses. What else could she do?

"Open it." Lilah leaned forward, her arm tangling in the oxygen line as she tapped the box.

Pulling off the tape, Melody pulled the flaps apart, expecting to see miniscule dresses. Instead, colorful fabric popped out. Gauzy floral prints, along with rich purples and yellows, even a red and white polka dot pattern tucked under the others. Her fingers rubbed the fabric. She'd never even looked at dresses like these. Too impractical, no place to wear them, and no one to wear them for, either.

"Pull out the purple one."

Melody complied, pulling yard after yard of fabric. Did the dress go on forever? It wasn't as tiny as she thought it would be. Manners stopped her from looking at the size, but she wanted to. "It's beautiful."

"Yes, it is." Lilah sighed, reaching out to stroke the dress. "I wore it the night Jim proposed. I knew he was going to do the deed because he had felt me out beforehand."

"Surely you'd want to keep this."

Lilah shook her head slowly. "You suck at taking gifts. If you forgot, I'm dying here. That's why you're visiting. Humor the sick woman, try it on."

Oh great, it had come to this. Didn't the woman have eyes? "I'm not sure it would fit." How could you graciously get out of trying the dress on? It would be nice if it fit, especially since she planned to have her way with Mr. Handsome and Embittered. A dress like this would make her feel beautiful.

"Is it too out of style? I wanted to share what I considered my lucky dress. Might do the same for you." Her eyebrows went up and down in a comical fashion as she mock leered.

"Yeah, right. I'll give it a go, but I'm not promising I'll be able to get the zipper up." She placed the box of dresses on the floor and kept the purple one. "Be right back."

In the attached bathroom, she wiggled out of her scrubs. Should she even bother trying the dress on? It could only lead to disappointment. Still, Melody prided herself on honesty. She should at least try it on. Part of her was secretly hoping it would fit. Well, maybe not so secretly. If it did, it would be another sign to go for it.

Guiding her arms through the big-skirted dress, she wiggled into the elasticized bodice. There were no zippers. Smoothing out the underdress, she stood and shook her shoulders. It fit. Did it? That couldn't be right. Turning to the full-length mirror, she gazed fascinated by the stranger in the low-cut party dress. The white anklets were the only thing she recognized from this morning. Even her face appeared different, somehow more attractive.

Pulling out her hair tie, she shook out her long, thick hair. Waves of auburn tresses danced around her shoulder, making her look like a shampoo commercial. It was a miracle. A tiny tap sounded on the door. Melody opened the door a sliver and peeked out. Lilah stood by the door, holding onto the frame, her oxygen line trailing behind her.

"What are you doing up?" The door banged against the wall as she shepherded her patient back to her bed.

"You were taking too long, so I had to check." She fluttered her hand in the direction of the living room while her eyes cut to the door. "Don't tell, Jim."

Melody tucked her patient into bed, fluffed up the pillows, and fisted her hands on her hips. "Well, since I got you back in bed without a whimper, I won't mention it."

The woman rolled her eyes again, stating, if only by her actions, that she never truly feared revelation. "You look hot in the dress."

"You think so? I was surprised it fit, me being as big as I am and you being you." Her hands wrapped around the skirt, pulling it out at the sides, demonstrating the width. "I could go dancing in this dress."

"Why not? I did. As for the size, I think you and I aren't that different. True, I lost weight these last few months. When I wore that dress, Jim thought I looked fantastic, too."

The mention of her husband resurrected the doubts Melody had managed to put to rest. "Are you sure Jim won't mind?"

Lilah managed to heave a heavy sigh, which wasn't that comfortable with her compromised lungs. "Jim will not be wearing my dresses, nor will he convince any female in future relationships to don my clothes. It's up to you to guarantee my clothes a real life."

"Well, if you put that way, I guess I should." Swishing her skirts, she pivoted and then spun allowing the skirts to bell out. "I feel like a princess."

Clapping her hands together in delight, Lilah announced, "You look like one, too. Got any glass slippers to wear?"

The mention of shoes stopped her impromptu dance. "No. I only have practical nurse's oxfords, athletic shoes, and sensible pumps for job interviews." Since it wasn't a date, she could go barefoot.

"Hmm, what size do you wear?" Lilah knuckled the spot between her eyes while grimacing.

"You're in pain." Melody reached for her bag. "Let me get you another pain patch. I was going to apply one anyhow. Instead, I'm fussing about shoes."

Lilah held up her hand. "Go change your clothes. Then we'll do the patch. Think about the shoes. I want to figure this out before you leave."

The dress came off with a twinge of regret. The return of the smock and uniform pants meant the end of Princess Melody, at least for a couple of hours. Grabbing a handful of hair, she twisted it into a knot and secured it with a tie. The mirror reflected back her unpolished self.

Her ill-begotten date with Mr. Gripey cost her more than wounded feelings. She'd spent good money on a new outfit and shoes. The strappy sandals would be a good compliment for the new dress. Carrying the dress, she caught Lilah unaware. Her closed eyes gave no indication if she were asleep or just resting.

Tiptoeing closer, she heard the ragged, forced breathing. The woman needed a ventilator. No use bringing it up since she'd refuse. Lilah wasn't a proponent of extending life using mechanical measures. Creeping up to the bed, Melody hung over it, staring at her client. What would it be like knowing you were on a death watch?

Lilah's eyes popped open. "Did you think I was dead?"

"No, you were snoring." It was always hard to know how to answer questions like that.

Often her clients would joke about death. Might as well get the vitals done and the patch on. The blood pressure cuff and stethoscope rested on the covers as she proceeded to do the routine procedure. Tucking her pen behind her ear, she turned to her patient who looked considerably paler after her exertions.

"I'm not sure why you bother with all that. It's certain I'm going to die soon. Why the fuss?" Her eyelids fluttered shut. The impromptu trip out of bed drained her.

Wrapping the cuff around her arm, Melody debated how to answer. The tracking of temperatures, heart rate, blood pressure, even weight gain and loss was something she did. Not that it made any difference. Pain control served as her primary purpose. Reassuring the loved ones without inspiring unfounded hope had to be the trickiest part of her job. Lilah's dropping blood pressure was not a good sign, but not unexpected, especially since Lilah already announced her time was short. In her experience, patients predicted their deaths within hours.

Realizing she hadn't answered the question, she mumbled, "It's what I was trained to do."

Lilah's eyelids opened, revealing her vivid blue eyes. Her thin hand wrapped around Melody with an intensity that seemed impossible for such a fragile creature. "Do... you...always...follow...rules?"

Each word tumbled out on a raspy exhale pushed out from her soul, sounding more like a statement than a question, but Melody answered because it apparently meant a great deal to Lilah. It didn't take much thought. "Yes, I do."

The fact she never considered bending the rules showed what a real dull dog she was. Why did she follow the rules? Where had it gotten her?

"I always follow the rules in an old-fashioned belief that someday a reward might come my way. Sounds silly, right?"

Her attentive questioner managed a strained smile. "No. I didn't," her hand released Melody's and fluttered to her chest as she attempted to catch her breath with an ominous rasp, "follow the rules."

Her practical nurse side wanted to tell her to rest, not talk, but both recognized there wasn't much time left for talking. The bright posters consisting of rainbows, flowers, and unicorns epitomized Lilah. "What did you do then? Ride a cow down Main Street buck naked?"

A snorty, gasping giggle, and a headshake was her answer. "No, never thought of it." She paused as if getting her thoughts together or sucking in oxygen to continue. "I lived. Doctors told me I'd never see twenty."

How hard that must have been expecting every day to be her last. Melody was familiar with the daily maintenance Cystic Fibrosis patients endured, reminding them every day they weren't normal and one step closer to death. The woman could give her some pointers.

"What did you do to live?"

She tore open the wrapper on the patch. Lifting Melody's shirt, she carefully peeled off the old patch. An alcohol pad cleaned away the remaining adhesive residue, scenting the air with an antiseptic bite. Centering the new patch below the diaphragm, she gently pressed it into place.

"Everything and anything. My parents were indulgent. They drove me to Florida every spring break. I went to college like a real kid and even had the nerve to fall in love. I never lied to Jim. He always knew. He believed whatever time we did have would be precious."

A dreamy look signaled she was still very much in love with her husband. The besotted expression caused a tiny ping of envy Melody immediately shook off. What type of person was she to want what a dying woman had? Schooling her features into what she liked to refer to as her listening face, she told her, "You're lucky. You've had a full life."

Lilah's chin came up and the look vanished as she directed an intense stare Melody's way. "Luck had nothing to do with it. If I were lucky, I wouldn't have been born with CF. Lucky is winning the lottery. All I have, I grabbed with both hands and held onto tightly. Do me a favor."

Oh no, not another deathbed favor. She sucked in her lips, knowing she'd be helpless to refuse, but often couldn't carry out the convoluted and sometimes bizarre requests. The pain medications clouded thought processes. One man asked her to make sure his son didn't turn into a llama. That was one promise she delivered on. Another matriarch asked Melody to stop her adult children from fighting. That was a failed promise since not even the United Nations peacekeeping forces could placate the warring siblings. Crossing her fingers, she asked, "What?"

"Start grabbing." Her eyes drifted closed as a contented expression crossed her face. The slight hiss of the oxygen machine continued, but her raspy breathing stopped.

Melody reached for the woman's hand determined to check her pulse, but already knowing the result. Lilah's mouth dropped open making a light exhale. Some people might mistake it for breathing, but it was the death rattle, the soul leaving the body. Realizing what she needed to do, she arranged Lilah on the bed. Plumping up the pillows, she arranged her body and pushed Lilah's mouth closed. This would be the last image her husband would have. It might as well be a good one. She sensed Lilah hovering over her shoulder, whispering in her ear. *Put my left hand on top to display my wedding ring. Tell him how much I loved him.*

Melody could hear Jim's running footsteps. The man burst into the room, looking wild-eyed and distraught. She wished there was some way she could comfort him, but there wasn't. "Her last words were about how you were the best thing in her life and how much she loved you."

The man knelt beside the bed, resting his head on the covers. His shoulders shook with his sobs. Not wanting to witness such heart-wrenching grief, she stepped out of the room. Her hand was on the cellphone to call it in when she felt Lilah's presence again. *Well done. Thank you. Now, it's your turn to go grab some life.*

The barely whispered words froze her in place. Then they faded away, similar to breaths visible on the frozen air for only seconds. Did she imagine it? Never before had any of her deceased clients chosen to speak to her after their death. It could be they didn't know how. Leave it to Lilah to find a way. Rules, guidelines, and predicted outcomes had little meaning to the woman.

The words lingered in her mind as she called her office, filled in the death certificate info, and consoled Jim. She chose to wait for the ambulance to pick up the body before leaving for her next appointment. Death not only stole your breath, but it tended to humiliate you, too, by emptying your bladder and bowels.

Those who were on death wagon pickup were used to the indignities associated with dying. Her job was to shield the loved ones from seeing the recently departed in such a manner. Of course, she always thought of it as a duty to her patient more as an unspoken promise that she would do her best to make their death not such a huge embarrassment. That was the least she could do since she could never make them better.

The two uniformed workers passed by with the cloth covered

gurney between them. The doorway proved problematic as they attempted to wiggle it through with some difficulty. One of them caught her eye, signaling her. A dazed Jim stood about a foot away from her, looking breakable.

Putting a hand on his arm, she steered him away from the gurney and its passenger. "Can you show me the box that Lilah wanted me to have?"

He blinked a few times having trouble processing the words or even hearing her voice. "Oh yeah." He turned back to Lilah's room while Melody made a shooing gesture to the attendants. It wasn't the best thing to go back into Lilah's room with the grief so recent. No reason for Jim to see gurney legs flipped under and his wife turned sideways to fit through the door. Theirs must not be a standard size entry door.

Jim handed her the box with the purple dress trailing out. His face crumpled as his fingers brushed against the cloth. Her heart spasmed to see so much pain. Melody had called Jim's sister who promised to rush over. Not knowing how far away she lived, it was hard to know what that meant.

"Do you want me to stay until your sister gets here?"

A peek out the window revealed the ambulance's brake lights as it readied itself to leave. Truthfully, she didn't want to stay. Her desire to leave made her feel a bit like a rat fleeing a sinking ship. Jim's fingers dropped from the material as he turned away.

His hands covering his face muting his voice. "Go on."

Melody tucked the box under her arm and bent to retrieve her medical bag.

Jim's tear-soaked voice sounded behind her. "I'm grateful for the time we had together. Lilah taught me how to love. If we'd only had a day together, I'd be grateful for that."

The agony in his voice rattled Melody's composure. Hands full, she turned to look back at the hurting husband. "I know. She knows, too." Eyes already glassy, she walked out of the bedroom before she broke down.

Minutes later, she drove trance-like to her next appointment, never bothering to turn on the radio. Death always shook her. A quick glance at her smock revealed there were no tell-tale blood spots or even signs she'd been at the side of a dying person. All the same, she didn't want to walk into her next client's home with the smell of mortality clinging to her.

A quick stop at a gas station allowed her to scrub down with antiseptic soap and change into a different cartoon animal smock and clean pants. Her blanched face looked about the same, a bit fresher, at least. The blank stare reminded her of the one time she'd tried fishing with Roy. The bass she'd hooked flipped about on the line, its gills fluttering. Finally, it stilled as Roy lifted the lid of the cooler. It knew its end was coming and froze in the face of it. Good God, she needed to snap out of it.

She wadded up her old uniform and threw it in the trash. Whenever she'd been with a patient who died, she discarded the smock and pants. Another reason she never wore street clothes to work. Her patients would never know the history of her uniforms, but she did. Whenever she'd put on the uniform, she'd think this was the uniform I was wearing when Lilah died. It would be like experiencing her passing again every time she wore it. Luckily, she picked up her work clothes second hand or at discount shops and always kept a replacement in her car. Dressed in a fresh uniform, she stepped out of the bathroom after a trio of hard knock signaling need and impatience for the facilities.

Her lips tried for an apologetic smile as an irritated woman rushed past her, slamming the door, almost catching the end of Melody's bag. A quick sidestep saved her that ignominy and brought her into the mini mart area. The combination of survivor guilt and wanting to live life to its fullest caused her to load up on junk food. She cuddled a frozen drink, a bag of chips, and a sleeve of cookies to her chest. As she turned toward the register, she passed the condom display. Without too much thought, she snagged the box that promised extra sensation. Why not? It was about time she grabbed life with both hands.

Chapter Ten

MELODY'S CLIENTS LIKED to talk if they were able. Sometimes, because of the advanced state of their illness, they didn't have the energy. Taciturn men who had never been in the habit of speaking, wouldn't start. While dear old ladies like Mrs. Fleming must have stored up conversation for years because it bubbled up like a fountain whenever Melody visited.

"Did I tell you about my nephew, Marcus?"

Melody looked up from her notepad. Usually, it was enough for Mrs. Fleming to talk. She seldom expected interaction. "Uhm, no." Maybe she had mentioned him, and she hadn't been paying close attention.

"He's a good one. Single. Never married. Good boy. Takes care of his mother. You two would suit, I think. Maybe I could match the two of you up, heh?"

Melody checked her watch. It was already half past five. If she wanted to start Operation Seduction, she needed to get home and shower first.

"Oh, checking your watch, that must mean you already have a young man."

Melody smiled at the woman, well aware she'd missed a portion of the promotional ad for the nephew. Instead of explaining the intricacy of modern relationships, she quietly answered, "Yes, I do. I need to be going."

"Hot date? Where are you going?" Mrs. Fleming leaned forward in her wheelchair with an avid expression.

To bed might not be the most appropriate answer even if that is what she hoped. "It's a surprise. I'll tell you on my next visit."

"I can't wait. Something to look forward to besides those dreadful reality shows." The woman rubbed her hands together, anticipating the future news.

Melody kept her face downcast as she stored her supplies to keep from laughing. Mrs. Fleming's health care aide, Lola, rolled her eyes when the woman started protesting how she hated the reality shows. It was no secret the woman loved them. She even called 911 once, when the cable went out.

Lola walked her to the door. "Make sure you have a great time. We'll both be expecting an exciting story."

"Will do," She agreed while thinking *no way*. C'mon now, some things should remain private. Usually, she'd sit in the car and input the data from her visits, but not today. Guilt rode on her shoulder as she shot through yellow lights rushing home. "No one is in the office to even know if I put the data in immediately or not."

Her declaration eased her guilt a little. Casting caution to the wind wasn't exactly how she did things. She'd never seduced a man. Her foot eased up on the gas. What was she thinking? Not exactly femme fatale, any action she'd seen had been by capitulation. It was mutual consent, but it was more along the lines of she wanted to see what all the fuss was about. Unfortunately, she still didn't totally get it.

The cuddling, the kissing, and necking on the couch she'd been a fan of, but apparently it was only part of the three-step plan to make it to the bedroom. Those lukewarm encounters never developed into a relationship as she hoped. Instead of shooting through the next yellow light, she slowed and came to a stop before it even turned red, much to the irritation of the honking driver behind her.

The grand plan she had fizzled before she could put it into play. No reason to rush home now. No three-step seduction plan to fall back on, a shower, her best lingerie, perfume at the pulse points, and then she'd don the dress. A bottle of sparkling wine was still in the fridge, a thank you from a client's family. It was a bit odd, but the family was also a liquor distributor.

If she'd arrived home earlier, she could have whipped up a romantic meal. Although, all she could remember seeing from her brief peek in the fridge this morning were cold cuts, eggs, and condiments. There was a good chance Levi used the majority of the eggs for breakfast this morning. He could already be home, too.

Her shoulders drooped as her impromptu plans spiraled downward, losing steam. Her right hand blindly reached into the passenger seat. Where were the cookies? Her fingers brushed over the laptop case and her medical bag before finally snagging the sack from the quickie mart. Clutching the cylindrical sleeve of cookies, she held it up to her mouth to bite through the cellophane.

A passing driver did a double take as she shoved the sandwich cookies into her mouth, two at a time. Her mouth was so full she could barely chew. Good thing she hadn't picked up a six-pack. Twisting the sleeve closed, she shoved it back into the bag as she painfully swallowed the dry cookies. Too bad her slushie was gone. Of course, if she hadn't eaten like a bear coming out of hibernation, then she wouldn't need a drink.

The familiar streets reminded her that she was close to home. What were her plans if she wasn't going to ravish her roommate? They were at least on talking terms, especially after breakfast. A sandwich and a little television would be nice if he didn't draw some parallel that she did the same thing with his uncle. She had.

No sedan, no Levi, which meant Charmer hadn't been out. Melody swung open the car door and made a grab for her laptop, box, and snack sack. She'd quit carrying a purse a while back since she could put whatever she needed in her laptop case or pockets. A purse was just another thing she could leave in a client's home. Leaving it once had left her considerably lighter in funds. It could have been anyone from the home health care aides to the live-in grandson. Her money was on the grandson since she'd caught him removing granny's pain patches and sucking on them for a contact high.

Charmer welcomed her arrival with a flurry of barks as she pushed open the front door. Dropping everything on the kitchen table, she turned to pat her dancing canine, and this was possibly his version of the potty dance. Yeah, she'd better hurry. Clipping on his lead, they both lunged toward the door. Outside, Charmer headed for the few plants she'd planted around the house. She pulled him away before he could initiate them.

Dogs and flowers, who suspected they were natural enemies? Melody looked back at the house, which was growing smaller in the distance. She needed to get back and get a shower before Levi got back. Technically, she may not have smelled, but psychologically she needed to scrub the stench of death away.

LEVI WHISTLED AS he drove, glad he'd had the chance to work with his hands. His shirt stuck to him. Where it didn't stick to him, sawdust did. His day had moved fast, not leaving him time to call Oliver and discover anything new on the Angelique front. His old lawyer should have put ads in the surrounding papers after he filed for divorce on the grounds of desertion. His avaricious wife most likely didn't even remember his name. She was probably working her way through the ranks of naïve GIs.

The car wheels on the gravel road sang to him. Home and the possibility of another encounter with Melody made him grin. Would she be fiery or friendly? Either way had merits. His hands tighten on the steering wheel. Fiery might have an explosive outcome.

Her economical compact sat in the driveway, indicating she'd beaten him home. Pushing the car gear into park, he wondered what approach to take. He reached for his cane before opening the door. Even though he sat most of the day, his leg still ached. All the uneven surfaces and steps took their toll. Tomorrow he'd not be such a victim of his pride. His lunch with Tommy revealed that Calvin took on the hard luck cases, the ones most people wrote off as damaged. What he received in return was a dedicated workforce.

Using his cane, he walked slowly up the path considering how he was now the turtle in the race between the tortoise and the hare. Before he left, he was more like the hare, taking off fast but becoming distracted along the way.

Calvin got a lot more done with his tortoise staff than most did with a crew chock full of rabbits, anxious to dart off to the next new adventure or hung over from their latest. He'd learned his lesson on what distraction got you. The front door stood open, which surprised him. Melody struck him as a practical, safety first type of gal.

The lack of canine nails skittering across the hard floors indicated Charmer's absence. The two of them must be out on a walk, which made sense. It would also give him time to grab a shower. The small pile of items on the table attracted his attention. Naturally, she dropped everything to cater to the dog. He'd have done the same thing.

A half-eaten sleeve of cookies rested near the corner of the table. Levi bent to retrieve them before Charmer discovered them. He wouldn't consider himself an expert on dogs but knew enough to know that chocolate was dangerous to them. It did something to their hearts. He figured the cookies must have rolled out from the sack on the table. If he shoved them back in the bag, Melody would never know how close she came to sickening her dog. The woman wore guilt the way some women donned makeup, daily and thick. Lord knew she didn't need anymore.

When he pushed the sleeve in, he couldn't help noticing a famil-iar-looking box. Without thinking, his fingers brushed over it, then wrapped around it. He pulled it out, confirming it was what he thought. He read the words aloud the same time the screen door slammed. "Ribbed for her pleasure."

Charmer barked his greeting. Melody's was less friendly. "What are you doing?" She charged forward to grab the box from his hands.

He allowed her to take the box from him with misgivings. If he held onto the box, it would somehow slow down things, though most men had at least a condom or two in their wallet. The rare exception was a guy who wasn't expecting to get lucky, like himself. "The better question is what are you doing? You go out with a guy once and go buy condoms. It may have been a while for you, but if that's your M.O. It's no wonder no man stays. They get what they want and move on."

Melody's skin flushed as he talked. Redheads had little ability to hide their emotions, and she was no exception. Box in her hand, she still managed to put her hands on her hips and gave him a glare that should have knocked him to his knees. "So, you're the expert on relationships now!"

Ouch, that hurt. Sure, his record wasn't great. It was hard to say how much his uncle chose to divulge. "No, but I know men. Anything that comes too quickly comes without value. Don't sell yourself cheap. You're the real deal, a treasure." His leg ached, and a headache was building behind his eyes. Arguing with Melody over her sex life was the last thing he wanted. It wasn't any of his business. The thought only made him grind his teeth.

The flush faded from Melody's cheeks as her eyes became soft, wondering. "You sound like my last foster mother. Of course, she never called me a treasure or the real deal. Go ahead. Explain yourself. I'm willing to listen." Latching onto a kitchen chair, she dropped into it, throwing her head back and closing her eyes for a brief second. Good. That meant he could sit, which he did with a sigh.

"Why didn't you sit if your leg was hurting you?" Her brows knitted together.

Why didn't he sit? Of course, he couldn't sit. It would put him at a disadvantage when arguing. Besides, it would make him look weak. He opened his mouth to speak, but she waved away his reply before he could even form one. "Never mind. I know it's that stiff-necked male pride thing. Tell me about the other."

Ah yes, that. "You're an extraordinary woman." Melody raised her eyebrows as if doubtful, but he chose to plow on. "You have a lot going for you."

"I do hope you're not going to tell me what a sweet personality I have." She grimaced.

Sweet, not hardly. "Fiery, determined, stubborn, loyal—those would all fit, but not sweet. The Melody Gibbons I know is smart, hard-working, honest, and kind."

"You make me sound like a cross between a boy scout and a mule. I guess I'd be lucky if any man wants to have sex with me."

She uttered the words with a weariness that did not suit her. Really? His eyebrows drew together as he considered her lack of expertise. "You don't know much about men, do you?"

"I'm not an expert, like you," she sniped back, drooping in the chair like a helium balloon on its second week of existence.

"As an expert," he brought his hand up to his chest, "I'll tell you this. You are a gorgeous woman. Those curves of yours would give any man wet dreams. It would be surprising to find a man who didn't want to have sex with you."

"I've never found them."

The muttered words were still audible. Damn, the woman wasn't making it easy. The awkward conversation made him uncomfortable in many ways. Right now, the shower sounded incredible, although he'd better make it a cold one. "You ran across a variety of men. Some saw your strength and considered it as a threat."

A slight chuckle emerged from her side of the table as she rolled her eyes. "Now I'm no longer the loyal scout, but I'm some muscle-bound monster roaming the streets, terrifying men."

God. The woman tied him in knots. He ran his hands over his face. How could he explain things to her? "You twist my words. You're so used to thinking of yourself as not valuable that you won't hear anything good about yourself."

Melody shot to her feet, proving that his singular lack of smooth-ness with women hadn't changed.

"You," she pointed her index finger at him, "think you know so much about me. You don't know anything." She stomped her foot for emphasis.

He expected her to whirl away, slamming doors behind her, but she stood, glaring at him. His urge was to stand, but he didn't. It would be an intimidation tactic using his superior height. The last thing he wanted to do was cause her to withdraw. He started uncertainly, gentling his voice to tempt the untamed creature in front of him to trust him.

"This I do know. You're more desirable than you ever give your-self credit for. You think you have to earn love."

Her face blanched as she sat abruptly. A tear tracked slowly down her face. "How do you know that?"

Instinct, but that was hardly an answer. He leaned forward and wiped her tear away with his thumb. "Most of it was my story, too, except for the part where I tried to earn people's love by being nice."

"Yeah, I can believe that. What changed your outlook?"

That was a hard one. It certainly didn't come all at once. He hadn't even realized it had changed until now. "It was when I didn't die. At first, I couldn't figure out why I lived. I screwed up. I deserved to die. Plenty of soldiers died for lesser things."

Melody reached to entangle her fingers with his. Her eyes conveyed concern while she nodded for him to continue.

"In the hospital, there was this nurse. He was certain I had a destiny, saying I lived because I had a purpose. No big surprise that when I lost my leg, I also lost my sense of identity. When I arrived as a kid to live with Roy, I was a regular badass. The truth was, I wasn't all that bad, but I acted the part until I started believing it."

"What changed?"

She tightened her fingers, afraid he might draw away. No chance of that. He loved the way her hand felt in his. "It's hard being a one-legged badass."

"Pirates manage."

"Yep, maybe. We have our stories. In the end, I'd be fighting all the time. I was tired of the war, tired of fighting altogether."

"You could have fooled me." A slight smile brightened her face. "I mean you're always arguing with me."

It did seem that way. "The two of us do fight. At first, I think we didn't trust each other, so sure the other didn't properly respect Roy. I thought you'd be some middle-aged gold digger."

"Well!" She gave a snort and tried to act affronted but didn't withdraw her hand from his. "I thought you were the thoughtless nephew who allowed his uncle to die alone."

He shook his head slowly knowing her words hit closer than he'd like. "I was the thoughtless nephew. I allowed pride to come between me and the man who treated me like a son, an unexpected son, but a son nonetheless. I would have come home if he'd told me he was sick."

"He wouldn't have said. The two of you are more alike than you know. He wrote you a letter. I'd see him working on it for days. He wouldn't let me read it, but he did tell me it was for you, and it would explain everything." "A letter? Where is it?"

Melody bit her bottom lip as she considered the possibilities. "I figured Oliver gave it to you."

"No." It would make sense if he had. "Maybe he forgot. I'll ask him tomorrow." Oliver Douglas did not strike him as the type who'd forget such a matter, but he'd ask just the same.

"So why do you think we fight now?" Melody's question tabled the issue of the mysterious letter.

He knew why they fought. "Why do you think we fight?" It would be interesting to hear her perspective. Emotions flittered across her face.

A slight flush indicated her thoughts were similar to his, but then the blush faded. "I think we're both very much alike."

Her answer surprised him, not the one he'd have picked. Still, it had merit. "I guess you are right, although we approach things differently."

"What was your answer?"

Her eyes peered into his, making him catch his breath. She had no clue how beautiful she was.

"Okay, you're not going to like it." He inhaled deeply, ready for her to turn into a spitfire. "We fight because we are fighting our attraction to each other. The harsh words keep us apart, preventing what we both want, but we keep telling ourselves it would be unwise."

"Really?" Melody arched her brows but kept her hand in his. "Is that all? I knew that."

"You knew that!" Here he was twisting in the wind, wondering if being a horny male made him a jerk. Melody stirred up a maelstrom of emotions inside of him, some he never experienced until he met her.

"Of course I did. Did you forget I kissed you back? I think I was more disappointed when Oliver showed up than you were. You kiss me or entice me, then stomp off. You accuse me of treating you like an old man when that is the last thing on my mind. Why do you think I bought the condoms?" She tugged her hand free to cover her mouth. Her shocked expression revealed she let the last part slip accidentally.

This changed everything. Part of him screamed caution, but it was hard to hear over the rest of him revving his engines. He was past ready when it came to Melody. Still, she deserved to be treated like a princess. Apparently, no man had ever made the effort. He changed the subject to spare her some humiliation.

"I thought the two of us might go out and celebrate tonight. How about the Clam Digger restaurant?" It was as close to fine dining as Wilsonville had. There were even tiny votive candle lamps on the tables.

"All right," Melody agreed with slight hesitation. "Would we be celebrating me buying condoms?"

In some ways, yes, but he decided that was not the best answer. "Actually, me landing a job. Today was a trial period for me. It's something I can do."

"That's great." Melody stood and circled the table to hug him. "I'm so glad."

He sat unresisting in her embrace. To stand would expose what all the talk about mutual attraction and condoms did to him. "It can be our official bury the hatchet dinner. I'll even let you have the first shower."

She released him, giggling a little. "I'm going to use all the hot water." Her feet did a little shuffling dance step as she turned to the bathroom. At the last minute, she grabbed the large dress box on the table and took it with her. The smaller condom box sat on the table, taunting him. He needed a beer. Good thing he bought some.

Chapter Eleven

THE COOL SHOWER caused Melody to hurry while shaving her legs. "Ouch." Not too surprisingly, she nicked her knee. The dress would cover her self-inflicted wound. Sure, she could have used warmer water, but she wanted to leave some hot water for Levi, despite her taunt. The excitement caused her to break into an impromptu song.

Twisting off the water, she toweled herself dry. A date at a nice restaurant, she couldn't wait. Didn't she go on a date last night? Yeah but, that didn't really count. It was one of those trial dates to see if people might be able to tolerate one another for a follow-up date. Shaun was a nice, stable man, not hard on the eyes, and he displayed good manners. Still, he didn't charge her battery the way Levi did. Maybe she should cancel their second date. It wouldn't be fair to the man.

Melody peered at the woman in the mirror. She should be familiar, but she didn't recognize the woman who had two dates in forty-eight hours. Cocking her head, she narrowed her eyes and attempted to see herself as others might see her. Straightening her shoulders, she dropped the towel.

The hair she clipped onto the top of her head cascaded down in fiery tendrils around her face. Her green eyes looked overlarge in her face and reminded her more of a cartoon character. Big eyes were fashionable. Why else use so much makeup to make them appear larger? Her skin was paler than she'd like, but she'd have to put that on ancestry. It made an excellent contrast with her hair.

Standing sideways, the curves Levi seemed so appreciative of were there. Stick-thin models didn't have to worry about her stealing their runaway jobs. Healthy, that's how Mrs. Fleming defined her look. A sigh escaped at the thought. Healthy did not equate to sexy. Turning her back to the mirror, she cast a sultry glance over one shoulder. Wow, she looked hot. Instead of bemoaning what she wasn't, she was able to accept what she was, even celebrate it thanks to Levi. A knock stopped her self-evaluation. "Clam Digger closes at nine on week-days."

Oh my goodness, what time was it? She shimmied into her underwear, then her dress in record time, deciding to apply her makeup in the bedroom. Rushing to get out of the bathroom, she swung the door open to find Levi leisurely leaning against the wall. Seeing her, he let out a whistle.

"You look good! Delicious. I think I might need a wardrobe change. He brandished the dark jeans and polo shirt he held.

"No, those are good. This is only a sundress. A frou-frou one, but still a sundress. Kind of like an alternative to jeans." She wasn't even sure if Levi had anything better to wear. No reason for him to change.

"Whatever it is, you look breathtaking." He shook his head as if he couldn't get over the change. "Like a princess. I like your hair like that, too."

"Okay, if I'm a princess, you must be Prince Charming. Hurry up, Charming, I'm hungry." Pivoting on her heel, she flounced to her bedroom, his masculine laughter filling the hallway.

Melody wanted to insist it was just a dress, but it wasn't. The bathroom became her personal transformation chamber. He liked her hair. A jumbo tortoiseshell clip held it in place, but she could duplicate the effect with enough bobby pins. A light dusting of blush and mascara was the base of her makeup routine. Shimmery lip gloss and a spritz of perfume finished her toilette. Now for her jewelry. She'd never invested in more than a few cheap pairs of earrings and a wristwatch. None of them would be unique enough.

Might as well get her shoes. Standing on her tiptoes, she stretched to reach the back of the closet shelf. Her expensive ill-fated sandals were behind everything else because she couldn't imagine ever wearing them again. After the date, she was tempted to trash her entire outfit, but her frugal side wouldn't let her. Tonight would be exorcism of sorts. Exceptional memories would replace the bad ones.

A slim, jeweler's box tumbled into her face. Quick reflexes had caught it before it hit the floor. The pearls Mary gave her. At the time, she wondered why Mary would give her such a valuable gift. Her animal-loving friend explained none of the dogs would look good in them. Besides, a woman always needs pearls. She couldn't imagine wearing pearls until now. The box housed a cultured pearl choker and a pair of matching pearl studs.

Her outfit came together without the help of a fairy godmother. Well, maybe she did have some non-magical ones. A tear trickled down her face. How did a woman who wasn't any good at relationships forge ones without knowing it? Levi had been dropping hints ever since he showed up about how attractive she was. At the time, she wasn't willing to accept them as true. At first, she considered he might be teasing her. Lilah's generous gift along with her sudden willingness to see herself as appealing made the difference. Levi planted the seed. It took a while to bloom.

Shoes. A green shoebox at the very edge of her reach taunted her. A quick glance surveyed her room, looking for something she could stand on to reach. A wastebasket would serve. The small base made it hard to balance herself, but she only needed it for a second. On her tiptoes, she snagged the shoebox, pulling it toward her as her impromptu stepstool crumbled. Her fingers clutched at the box even as she fell. A loud thump marked her landing, but the yards of material in the dress skirt softened her landing a little.

Rushing footsteps were the only warning she had before the door swung open. "Are you okay?"

Melody looked up into Levi's concerned face. Taking in the sight of him in uniform, she was unwilling to admit her butt was a trifle sore. A downward glance revealed her legs splayed out, but her full skirt kept her from looking like some provocative perfume ad. "I'm good. The wastebasket I used as a stool might be beyond repair." Her head angled in the direction of the remains.

Levi glanced that way, giving her the opportunity to scramble to her feet. "I'm just about ready." She pulled on both sandals and opened the pearl box. Holding the pearls up, she asked, "Could you help me with the necklace? I don't wear jewelry much."

He cautiously avoided the crumpled wastebasket, discarded clothing, and other items she'd scattered around the room while dressing. It could be a minefield for a man who was unsure of his footing. "Here, let me pick up some things."

"Don't bother." Two large steps took him directly behind her. He held out his hand for the necklace.

Melody dropped it into his open palm and turned to the mirror reflecting the two of them, where her eyes could feast on him without being too noticeable. His uniform jacket emphasized his broad shoulders, and she had a fixation for a man in uniform. "Nice outfit. Army's blue now?"

"Class A's are. They changed it for some reason."

He draped the necklace around her neck, allowing his warm hands to linger on her bare shoulders, teasing her skin, starting a chain reaction of electricity that arced through her body. How it affected him, she couldn't tell. His bowed head hid his expression. As for her, they needed to get going before she lost control. "How do you keep the Air Force and the Army uniforms separate?"

His hands dropped as he grinned at her in the mirror. "The Army uniforms look better."

The pearl studs went in without any trouble, a sign of quality. "I think you're biased."

"Could be but consider the Air Force has had the same uniform for a donkey's age. The Army's uniform is new and has some of the dash that makes the Marines look so good. Air Force members are often mistaken for mailmen."

Her nose crinkled, realizing he must be joking. "I'm ready. Whose car do you want to take?"

His hand covered his heart and stumbled backward feigning horror. "I asked you out. Of course, I'll drive. I'll be paying the bill before you bring that up. Lady, you got yourself a high-class date here."

Levi held out his bent arm for her to hold. Charmer escorted the two of them to the door, dancing wildly under the mistaken assumption that a walk was in the offing. "Look, your son thinks he's going. We'll sneak you something home, boy."

"Be a good dog while we're gone." Too bad Charmer couldn't take a photo of the two of them. "Wait, let me get my camera." She darted back to the bedroom.

"Why do you want a photo?" His question followed her.

Was she silly? This was as nice a date as she'd ever been on so far. Would it be wrong to want to save the memory with a snapshot? Plenty of people took selfies of themselves doing nothing. Why not? The urge to drop the camera battled with her need to obtain a keepsake.

Levi called from the hall. "I'd like a picture, too, of us both gussied up."

That settled it. The camera was going. The thin, silver device slid into her purse taking up residence beside her cell phone. The phone's picture resolution sucked, which was the reasoning behind the camera.

Levi donned his beret while she'd gone in search of the camera. Her footsteps slowed as she realized the man somehow notched up the hotness factor the few seconds she'd been gone. His arm swept out, swinging open the door. Outside, he bent his arm again, allowing her to rest her hand in the crook. Instead of parting ways at the trunk as she expected, he escorted her to the passenger side and opened the door.

No one ever opened the car door for her, if you excluded the car sales representative. A woman could get a man to open the car door if she were willing to spend several thousand dollars over a six-year span. *Be still my heart, a gentleman.* She slid into her seat, holding her lips firm to prevent herself from gushing about the gesture. "Thank you."

"I should be thanking you for agreeing to go out with me, especially since I've been all kinds of crazy."

Melody disagreed, although at times, the man didn't make sense. Before she could formulate a denial, he shut her door and walked to his side. Just as well, she was never a convincing liar. The first part of the drive to the restaurant went relatively well with none of the misunderstandings or flare-ups that marked their usual conversations. They conversed more like friends as opposed to warring factions. Halfway there, she got Levi to open up about his Uncle Roy.

"Do you know I have no clue how old my uncle was? I figured he was around my father's age since they were brothers. Still, when you're a teenager, everyone seems ancient." He turned his head slightly away from the road to grin at her.

"Yeah, I know what you mean. He was sixty-eight." She heaved an inner sigh when his attention returned to the narrow road the same time a fast-moving semi-truck drew close. Melody was a nervous driver and a worse passenger. Life taught her to be cautious since you never knew when it could veer out of control without warning.

Was she out of control? Of course not. She was having dinner with an attractive and congenial man. That's all. Part of her wanted to grab all the gusto she could with both hands per Lilah's instructions. Then there was her usual self, who always took the paved road instead of the unknown path.

A handful of cars filled the restaurant parking lot. Levi scooted into the closest parking space. Melody almost reminded him he could get a handicapped tag but bit her lip. He wanted no reminders of his difference. He'd even left his cane at home. Though understandable, he was pushing himself too fast for a man just out of rehab. She'd be his cane. Instead of hanging onto his arm, maybe she could wrap her arm around his waist and use her body to alleviate the stress on his leg. *Just helping him out, yeah. It has nothing to do with wanting to touch him or be close to him.* No reason a person couldn't achieve two goals at once, especially since they coincided.

"We're here." Levi announced while parking the sedan. The restaurant, perched on a jutting cliff, glowed above them in the diminishing light. The only way to reach it was a steep set of stairs. "I didn't remember the stairs being so long or steep."

She was ready to suggest they go elsewhere to avoid putting Levi through the ordeal of climbing the stairs when she'd remembered building guidelines. Any restaurant, store, even churches built after 1993 had to be wheelchair accessible. Even though the Clam Digger opened in 1983, they had to update to meet code, which meant there had to be an elevator or ramp somewhere. She knew their opening date, not that she ever visited before, but the foster family she stayed with had. She spent the time with a respite family to allow the natural family to go out and have fun without the burden of foster children. It sure wasn't like the commercials they ran for foster care.

As soon as Levi opened the car door, Melody scanned the area for any signs depicting the familiar wheelchair logo. Levi cupped her elbow and steered her in the direction of the stairs. A sign below eye level, but not if she were in a wheelchair, pointed the direction to the elevator. "Oh look, they have an elevator."

Levi looked to where she pointed and back at her. "I know what you're doing. We can take the stairs. It will be good therapy for me."

The man had to go all brave and stoic on her. Melody hooked her arm through his. "Please, let's use the elevator. I'm tired. It's been a rough day."

His eyes drifted from the stairs to the elevator entrance. A metal shaft tacked onto the side of the cliff. He looked undecided, so she pushed a little. "Not sure I could make it up the stairs tonight. One of my patients died today. It was tough. She was only forty." A tear trembled at the edge of her eyelash from thinking about Lilah. She chose not to mention the dress was Lilah's, afraid it would steal the romance from the night the same as an arduous step climbing session would.

"Okay, if…" he emphasized the last word, before continuing, "…it would make you feel better."

A vigorous nod bobbed the tendrils beside her face. The ride up took mere seconds. The two of them inside the small box, standing close to one another, felt amazingly intimate, especially with his arm wrapped around her waist. They'd been closer when they locked lips, at least physically. Their nearness came more from knowing Levi better than from touching. Each peek into his past allowed her to understand the guarded man who stood beside her.

The elevator doors opened. Levi dropped a brief kiss on the top of her head before cupping her elbow to propel her forward. "Thank you. I know what you did back there, and I appreciate it."

Stepping out with him, she placed a hand on her chest right above her low-cut neckline drawing his eyes. "Me, do something?"

"Give it up. You're as subtle as a sledgehammer." He winked at her, which caused her heartbeat to skip.

An alert host swung the door open at their approach. "Good evening. Are we celebrating anything special?"

A denial formulated in her mind, but Levi answered before she could reply.

"Of course we are. We're alive. It's a gorgeous Indian Summer evening, and I have the most beautiful girl in town on my arm. Sounds worthy of a celebration to me."

The most beautiful girl in town. She'd never heard those words in connection with her. A huge, silly smile bloomed on her face. The man had charm. Who knew? Manners and charm. What else would the night bring?

The host led them to a window table with a remarkable view. Wilsonville might be small potatoes, but Lauren across the river wasn't. The skyline glittered like a handful of stars thrown out on the dark backdrop of the approaching evening. The small votive lamp cast flickering shadows onto Levi. Typically, shadows made people look threatening, but on Levi, they only made him more mysterious. What would it take to peel back those layers, similar to the skin of an onion?

A waiter showed, flourished menus, and proceeded to relay the special of the day. She only half-listened, too caught up in the experience. The waiter suggested the crab bisque to start and Mahi Mahi with roasted vegetables, which sounded good. Levi chose the

Salmon New Orleans and a salad.

A dark-suited man appeared with a towel draped over one arm and a bottle of champagne. "A patron has gifted you with this champagne in honor of your service. Will you accept?"

Levi's eyebrows shot up as an elderly man stood and saluted him. He stood up, faced the man, and snapped out a crisp salute back. "We'll accept."

The wine steward opened the bottle and poured two flutes provided by an alert waiter. The same waiter returned with a wine cooler for the bottle. The wine steward and waiter left without a word, hurrying off to serve the other patrons. Levi lifted his glass. "To appreciating what we have, to life."

The crystal tinkling of the glasses as they gently tapped together made something well up inside. She took a sip to quell the need to burst into tears. Today had been an emotional roller coaster, but she certainly didn't expect it to end like this. If she were someone else watching, she'd see a romantic love story unfolding, hero boyfriend returns from war to a devoted girlfriend.

Her eyes met his over the rim of the glass. What was not to like about the man—besides his tendency to jump to conclusions and assume the wrong thing? She'd done the same. What was he thinking? Did he feel the magic of the evening?

He put down his glass and glanced back in the direction of his beneficiary. "Never has anyone given me anything."

"What?" That made no sense. "What about your parents and Uncle Roy?" Sure, her life had been rough as a foster kid, but she didn't expect anything else. Images of her previous residences crowded her mind. Calling them homes would give them qualities they never possessed. Occasionally she got a gift for her birthday or Christmas though never anything big, flashy, or something she wanted. Usually, it was practical cotton underwear and socks. One family gave her a manual on how to be a good foster child. The awkward phrasing and photos that didn't go along with the text made her think it was self-published even before she found the box full of copies hidden in the garage.

"My parents and Uncle Roy got me stuff. I'm talking about people not related to me." He picked up the champagne bottle and refilled their flutes. "How about you?"

Her first instinct was to say no, but then she reconsidered. "My foster parents gave me a present occasionally on my birthday or Christmas, not always. Often, they forgot. I lived with one family who didn't celebrate Christmas, birthdays, or even holidays."

"Wow. That must have been lame." Levi shook his head in disbelief.

A waiter arrived with their first courses, keeping Melody from answering. The steam wafting up from the bowl smelled delicious. The waiter held a large pepper grinder over her soup. "Pepper?"

She nodded, wondering where the grinder came from. A second waiter arrived with a basket of hot bread. Both the dark-shirted employees left as quickly as they came. Melody glanced around before wrapping a roll in a tissue to take home. "For Charmer." Levi merely nodded reaching for a roll of his own.

No need to explain how lame foster homes had been. It was a depressing place to live. The usual joy most kids experienced with school holidays was missing because there were no holidays for foster children. Just a long stretch of days without the interruption of school to break up the routine of earning her keep. She also had to make sure never to mention the holidays that others regularly celebrated. It was better to concentrate on the good in her life.

"Mary gave me the pearls I'm wearing." Her hand reached up to touch the necklace given in love.

Levi picked up his fork and speared a tomato from his salad.

"Never heard you mention Mary before."

Ah, he made it sound like they had regular conversations about everyday things instead their daily head-butting sessions. "Mary volunteers at the shelter with me. She's a sweetheart, a retired bank employee, who helps out at all the surrounding shelters."

"Really? Calvin, my new boss, is looking for a pet. Maybe you can get Mary to talk to him."

Her lips pursed as she blew on the soup, before tasting the creamy broth. The flavors danced on her tongue, the cream and butter she could identify, along with pepper. The sweetness must come from the crab. "This is delicious."

Fine dining was a novelty for her. Dinner out at the local diner was as fancy as she ever got. The memory of her last date surfaced, but she ruthlessly pushed it down. Now wasn't the time. She'd deal with Shaun later. She dipped her spoon back into her bowl.

"You never answered me. Could you get Mary to call Calvin? Recommend a pooch or two?"

Goodness, she'd forgotten the question. "Your boss can go to the shelter on his own. It's on Pleasant Street."

Levi shook his head, apparently confused why she wasn't following him. "He could. Maybe he should have. He's been a widower for a while. He talks about being lonely but seems to be unwilling to do anything about it. Maybe he needs a push. You got your dog from the shelter."

An idea began to form in her head. Mary was lonely, too. "Mary could do that. How old is your boss?"

Levi cut his eyes at her as he chewed. He swallowed before answering. "Why does that matter? I guess he's around Uncle Roy's age."

"No reason." Melody was unwilling to elaborate or even expose her friend to this man if he was a jerk. "What's your opinion of him?"

"Calvin's a good guy. He hired me." His eyebrows lifted with the pronouncement. "Seriously though, everyone loves him. He's always willing to help those who need it. He has that old-world charm that has the white-haired ladies all aflutter."

Melody put down her spoon since her bowl was empty. She'd even tipped it to scrape up the last bit of deliciousness. "He's a player then, the senior version?" No way did she want her friend making the acquaintance of a lady-killer.

Levi buttered another warm roll as he talked. "I don't think the man has ever dated after his wife died. It certainly isn't because there aren't available women. On our outing to the diner, the silver set practically threw themselves at him. He was polite, but not interested and told me he wasn't interested because he buried his heart with his wife."

"That's so romantic." She sighed a little, causing Levi to give her a skeptical look.

"Yeah, the idea of living your life alone is so romantic. I think Calvin may be looking to dig up his heart again. The willingness to have a pet is the first step. It helps to have someone glad to see you when you get home every day."

Yes, it did, but she wasn't thinking about Charmer. Two glasses of champagne created a desire to confess her secret feelings. The only thing that held her tongue was that she wasn't entirely sure what they were. Physically, he drew her rather like chocolate, encouraging an insatiable appetite. Other times, he was helpful and easy to talk to, and then he went and acted like a jerk, sometimes a jealous idiot. The thought made her smile.

"I hope that smile is for me." Levi rested his hand on top of hers, warming them, and strengthening the invisible connection between them.

"It is. This has been an incredible experience. I never went to my school prom. I like to pretend if I had it would have been something like this with a handsome escort, beautiful dress, and an extravagant dinner."

He half-stood, leaned across the table to place a tender kiss on her lips, and sank back down. Her fingers touched her lips. That kiss meant more the others. She wasn't just a woman. He saw her for who she was.

"I didn't say that so you'd feel sorry for me and kiss me. Not sorry for the kiss, though." Feeling audacious, she winked. "Bet you had a blowout prom date."

Her words caused him to laugh. "You'd be wrong. I was suspended. Truthfully, I can't remember what I did to earn it. Sure, I'd fought with all the boys at the school who wanted to pick a fight. By the time, prom rolled around, I'd calmed down. Most guys were no longer foolish enough to pick on me. I think the suspension served as a preventative measure on some bogus charge. Uncle Roy wanted to challenge it. I didn't care too much since I didn't have a girlfriend."

The waiter showed up with a dessert cart, displaying several wedges of mouthwatering cakes, along with a few pies, and a fluted dish of crème brûlée. Levi managed to talk her into splitting a wedge of peanut butter pie with him. Talk about a hardship.

THE NIGHT WOUND down even though she never wanted it to end. The last thing she remembered was Levi making sure all of her dress was in the car before closing the door. Her eyes opened as the car tires rumbled over the driveway gravel. The fact she dozed on the way home flushed her cheeks. Some date she was. Generally, a date kept her so on edge worrying about what to say, how to act, that there'd be no chance of relaxing, let alone sleeping.

Dashboard lights silhouetted Levi's chiseled profile. The man could be a model for a recruiting poster. A love song played on the radio, something about unrequited love, something she'd experienced numerous times. In retrospect, they were only infatuations. A boy or a man caught her eye, but apparently, the opposite was never true. What was so different about Levi?

The fact that he was handsome wasn't it. Plenty of attractive men were around, although most were in relationships. Most of the time he was abrupt, stubborn, and unflinchingly honest. He made her see things she'd never seen before, truths about herself that her spotty upbringing had distorted. After all, when people housed and fed someone else's child, they seldom cared about their self-esteem. Their charity ended with the inconvenience of an unrelated child in their home.

Trust, that's what made Levi different. She held up one hand in the dim light, counting whom she trusted. There was Roy. She folded down the index finger. Could be he didn't count since he was dead. There was Mary. The middle finger went down. Dr. Caldwell from nursing school ended up being the ring finger. Her pinkie wiggled as she contemplated counting Levi.

"Are you counting all the times I made a social blunder tonight?" He steered the car into the driveway to park behind her car. The porch light cast a welcoming pool of light onto the stoop. A mixture of barks and bays announced Charmer was on guard duty. "I'm not any good at fancy restaurant stuff."

Did he actually imagine she'd ever been in a place that upscale? Balling her fingers into a fist, she dropped it into her lap. "No, I wasn't. It would be hard for me to know since that was my first fancy restaurant. Could be that I did something wrong."

A twist of the key shut off the engine, although the radio played a few bars before going silent. Home, should she get out of the car on her own? It was hard to know as Levi stared at her in the dark. Without the glow of the dashboard lights, it was impossible to distinguish his expression. His stillness, similar to hearing what sounded like a footstep in the dark, unnerved her. She'd strain her ears waiting to hear that next ominous footfall. Usually, she fell asleep listening for a step that never came.

"Why are you staring at me?"

Levi managed a husky chuckle that would rate an eight on the seductive scale. "That would require me having better eyesight than I do. No, I was more in shock, puzzled as to why none of your dates took you out to a fancy restaurant."

All of her dates? That was rich. "Trust me, there weren't that many. Going to a mid-chain restaurant was as elaborate as it got. I considered myself lucky if I got a meal before the man vanished." Unfortunately, talk of her dating history undermined her newfound confidence.

His shadowy form moved closer, reaching across the expanse to cup her face. "Their loss. You deserve beautiful things. You looked so elegant sitting across from me. You made me the envy of every man there tonight."

His caress and his words melted her like butter left out on the counter. Her eyelids fluttered shut as she leaned into his embrace. His scent surrounded her with notes of crisp starch, citrusy cologne, and underlying muskiness that reminded her of a walk through the forest after the rain.

His lips landed on hers, not surprising her, but fulfilling her wish. Her hand rose to cradle his head, urging on the kiss and taking no chances that he might pull away. His tongue traced her lips, reverentially. The longing between the two of them grew in the dark car, filling it, heating it up, and creating a world of sensation of muttered sweet nothings. Melody could live in the place they created forever until a long baying pierced the night.

Charmer. Who knew a dog could seriously complicate a love life? She'd never considered that when adopting since she never expected to have a love life. "I better take care of him before he annoys the neighbors."

Levi loosened his embrace, retreating to his side of the car. "Right, I'll help you. A moonlit walk along the lake sounds promising."

Interesting. She expected him to be upset at the interruption, but the man took the situation and made it work. "Sounds great." She placed her hand on the door handle when Levi captured her hand with this own.

"Remember, when you're out with me, I'll be the one opening and closing doors. Got a problem with that?" He growled the question playfully.

His fingers curled around hers, holding her in place. "Do I have a problem with being treated as if I'm special? No, can't say I do. I do need to get to my over-reactive dog before he annoys anyone besides us."

"Order received." His hand dropped hers and gave her a mock salute before opening his door. His actions made her giggle. His shadowy form moved around the car to her side. What would happen once they were inside? Would they go to separate bedrooms after Charmer's walk? It might be up to her to make the first move. What should she do? Turn on some slow jazz and light a few candles. Invite him to her bedroom and place the box of condoms on her bedside table. No, she could never be that bold.

The car door opened, stopping her impromptu seduction plans. Melody took his proffered hand as she stood. Her heels wobbled a little on the gravel, not the best shoes for walking. "I might need to change shoes and clothes before our walk. It will save the gauzy dress from branches and briars snagging it."

"Mm sounds like a good idea." He tucked her hand into the crook of his arm. "If you give me a minute, I'll change too since this my only set of the new class A uniform. Hate to ruin them."

It would give her time to shed her dress for something appropriate. The idea of discarding the dress made her wonder if her evening of romance was over. Sure, she knew people flirted in jeans and T-shirts all the time, but that was other people, not her. Beautiful dress, elegant restaurant, and handsome escort gave the night a fairy tale quality she wasn't quite ready to relinquish. Charmer would be either the pumpkin or the rat coachman.

Chapter Twelve

T HE CANINE IN question welcomed them with a series of sniffles and licks. Melody offered the smuggled bread as Levi went to change. "Give me a minute, boy. I need to change out of my party clothes."

In her bedroom, she stripped off her dress, laying it on the bed. Attired only in a strapless bra and panties she stared at the dress. The extravagant concoction of whisper thin multiple skirts and a fitted bodice embroidered with tiny flowers and butterflies made her fairylike, allowing her to dance in the dew and lift off with the breeze. Now that it was off, she'd settle for a pair of shorts and a T-shirt for the evening walk.

The sulfur smell of a spent match rode the air. Odd, the scent propelled her to her dresser where she dabbed perfume on her neck, her wrists, and in between her breasts. Never hurt to be prepared. Exotic guitar music stirring up images of moonlit beaches on foreign shores slid from under Levi's door. Was he coming, or had he changed his mind? Could be she read the whole evening wrong, but if that were true, then she read everything else wrong since the first time they met. She doubted it. Sure, she never won any awards for flirting, dating, or driving the opposite sex crazy, but she knew chemistry even if she only went by textbook examples of physical attraction, although none used arguing as a courting behavior.

His bedroom door held her attention as it opened, allowing a brief glimpse into Levi's shadowy room. Her slightly tousled roommate stood briefly in the doorway, looking uncertain. "Let's get this walk done."

Charmer shadowed his steps as he moved toward the leash hook. Melody stood, perplexed with her mind shooting off in a hundred directions. One part immediately noticed he looked buff in his brown T-shirt and a pair of fatigues. Still another section obsessed on his words that made it sound like he didn't want to go. Still he snapped the leash on Charmer's collar.

His cane leaned against the table, attracting her eye. It was right next to everything she'd dumped onto the table, including the sack containing condoms. She'd need to get the box to her room without being obvious. Her fingers wrapped around the cane. No doubt the man would deny he needed it, but the ground outside was uneven and difficult to negotiate in the dark.

The two of them met at the door with Charmer in tow. Levi eyed the cane treating it akin to a coiled snake. "Humor me," she asked as she held up the cane. He took the proffered aid with reluctance. Melody reached for Charmer's lead while explaining her need to walk the dog. "I like to remind him that he's my dog even though he prefers you."

"I doubt that." Levi swung the door open for Charmer and Melody. He followed, snapping on the flashlight snagged from his room. The yellow beam illuminated the area four feet in front of them. A couple of beetles scurried through the light.

"Good thinking. I never thought of using a flashlight." Melody felt like hitting her forehead and murmuring 'duh'. She'd have stumbled around in the dark, her hound pulling her whatever direction he wanted to go. She hadn't taken Charmer out too much at night. Levi usually offered to do the deed. She accepted without too much protest. No wonder her dog had developed such a bond with her roommate.

"Army training, rather like the scouts' always be prepared motto." He allowed the cane to touch the ground. The loose soil shifted under his feet causing him to plant his cane like a pole-vaulter. "You could have been a drill sergeant. Forcing me to take the hateful reminder of my infirmity, knowing I might need it. Thank you."

Melody's lips lifted in a smile. She should say something, realizing how hard it must have been for Levi to concede she was right about needing the cane. "You know a man with a cane has an air of sophistication about him."

"Please." He stretched the word out. "Who is humoring whom here?" His gait matched hers as they strolled down the path worn down by hundreds of feet over the years.

"You think I'm humoring you? I'm not. A lot has to do with your attitude. If you're okay with your cane, then everyone else will be." There were times she wanted to dope slap the man. How could he not see what he had going for him? His loss was so recent it might be unreasonable for him to accept it. Most people would assume the fetal position as they battled acute depression.

Tree branches threw out deeper shadows, challenging the small beam of light. The three of them existed in the tight circle of light, their own private world. Levi stood close enough for Melody to feel his body heat. His body drew hers. It wouldn't be too surprising if she were leaning at an angle. Levi held the flashlight at waist level making it difficult to see his face. How would she know if he wanted her as much as she wanted him? His voice startled her.

"Are you okay with my cane? Would you find a man with only one leg attractive?" The flashlight dropped to his side, leaving only their feet in the circle of light.

That was it. He was afraid. Melody's heart raced as she began to piece together his previous behavior. "If you're asking if I could crush on any one-legged man, then the answer is no."

He took a step back. Good heavens, she gave him the wrong impression. "No, wait." She threw her arms around him, stumbling and taking him to the ground. Fallen leaves crumpled under them. The flashlight rolled away, shining off in another direction. Her body sprawled over his with her head next to his. His labored breathing ruffled her hair.

"Oh, I'm hurting you." She tried to scramble up, but Levi's arms went around her pulling closer. His mouth was close to her ear as he asked.

"What were you going to say before you knocked me to the ground?"

The feel of his muscular body made it hard to remember. His mint-scented breath touched her face, making her realize he'd brushed his teeth before they left or at least chewed a breath mint. Something a man might do if he hoped to get lucky. Half the time, she thought it might happen, but he'd backed away. Ah yes, she knew why now. "You're the only guy I care about, one leg, two legs, or three legs. It doesn't matter to me."

His chest rumbled as he pushed out a raspy laugh. "Three legs, huh? Sometimes, the players like to call it that."

He sighed deeply, causing her body to move with the action, rather how she imagined it would be riding a wave on a human shaped surfboard. His embrace tightened holding onto her, possibly afraid she'd somehow slip away. Never mind the fact her hands were behind his head and pinned to the ground.

"Melody, you have no clue how you torment me every minute of the day."

"Wait a minute, I may be difficult, occasionally argumentative, but I'm not that bad." If she was so horrible, why was he holding onto her as if his life depended on it? Something was digging into her thigh. She wiggled a little trying to remember if she'd put anything in that pocket before she left. "Damn woman, is it your goal to kill me off?" His husky complaint stopped her movement.

Okay, she should have considered that. "Sorry," she whispered the word but remained secretly exultant. The evidence he found her arousing pleased her. It was far from the first sign, but he always managed to throw cold water on both of them. Okay, sometimes she did. Another time it was Oliver. Maybe tonight no one would interrupt. Ignoring his grumbling, she shimmied up a couple of inches and peppered small kisses across his face, starting at his forehead. The first kiss she initiated, and the man had to talk.

"God, I want you so bad, but there are things I need to work out first."

If he was talking still, she must not be doing it right. She kissed his eyebrows, his nose, his cheeks, and had to scooch down to reach his mouth.

"Melody, I think you should know…"

She placed her lips on his cutting off his words. His lips moved under hers, but he was no longer speaking. The firm pressure signaled his ardor as their tongues tangled with one another. Life was good. The sensation of being important, needed, and beautiful wrapped around her as tightly as Levi's arms. Talk about a heady feeling. No wonder people did stupid, often disastrous things in pursuit of it. Levi rocked underneath her. Was he trying to get up? Maybe it wasn't the same warm feeling for him. His final rock rolled them both over, putting him on the top.

The leaves crunched, sending up an earthy aroma. Through the tree branches, a few twinkling stars could be seen as Levi lifted his head to whisper. "I thought I was never going to get you underneath me. I told myself all the reasons I shouldn't."

Her hand moved down over his hair, lightly tracing his ear. "What reasons?"

"You deserve better than me." He was ready to say more, but Melody put her fingers to his lips.

"Hush. You're an amazing person. I get to decide what's right for me. Right now, I can't think of anyone better than you."

His beard stubble brushed her cheek as he rested his cheek against hers. "I like the sound of that."

Enough talk, it was time for action. Using both hands, she guided his lips to hers. He didn't need any more encouragement in bestowing toe-curling kisses that made her long for more. Her sensitized skin felt everything from his firm body to the crumbling leaves and soft moss underneath her. Even the breeze, hot and fetid smelling, bathed her face. That didn't seem right. Not part of the romantic memory she wanted to preserve. A loud bark right in her ear burst through the lovely romantic cocoon. Charmer.

Somehow, she'd forgotten about her dog. The canine shoved his cold nose between their two startled faces, giving them both a long swipe with his wet tongue. Talk about a mood buster. Apparently, the dog wanted to get in on the love fest between two of his favorite people. It was enough to cause them both to scramble to sitting positions to avoid another dose of canine saliva. Melody used her shirt to wipe off the dog spit.

Levi scrubbed his hands over his face. "I thought you were supposed to be man's best friend."

Charmer didn't realize it was rhetorical and answered with a hearty bark. Hand over her mouth, she smothered laughter as she bent to grab the flashlight. It allowed her to find the cane, which was tricky since it was black. Levi was already standing when she returned and handed him the cane.

"I should have done that." His lips moved down in a frown.

She wrapped an arm around his waist and gave him a tight squeeze. "Sorry. No one informed me of the protocol. Next time, we get carried away under the evening stars, you're in charge of finding the flashlight."

"Damn right." His arm draped over her shoulder with his hand cupping her upper arm. They climbed the hill together in companionable silence. It felt familiar as if they'd done it before in another lifetime. A slight scuffling noise sounded to her right, froze Melody in her tracks and pulled Levi to an involuntary stop.

"Do you hear that?" Sure, she'd witnessed chipmunks, rabbits, and squirrels playing among the trees, but nothing bigger. "What do you think it is?" She hissed the words afraid the creature might hear them.

Levi whistled, causing the beast to break out of the undergrowth and jog straight at them, floppy ears bouncing. "It's your dog."

She shrank in relief against Levi, unwilling to admit she'd forgotten her dog again. Some dog owner she was. Grabbing the leash, she held onto it and passed the flashlight to Levi. With his cane in his right hand and the flashlight in his left, there was no free hand for her. With the inclusion of Charmer, they were two separate people as opposed to a couple.

Levi switched off the flashlight and stuck it in his pants pocket. "There's enough light from the moon and the porch lights to make our way back. Come back here." He held out his arm, allowing her to nestle back into his side.

The terrain flattened as they approached the long gravel driveway with a full moon hanging low in the sky. "When I was in Afghanistan, I'd look up at the moon and experience such a cold, deep feeling of loneliness. It felt as if I was the last person alive. Sounds silly, doesn't it?"

"No, not at all. I know how you feel, not that I've been in a foreign country or anything. I've spent most of my life alone even though people were around me. There just wasn't any connection there. I remember feeling that way after my first hospice patient died, a relatively young man, he was forty-two."

"That's young," Levi remarked but gave her a nudge to continue.

"I called the ambulance. Anton was one of the unlucky ones who didn't have anyone beside his bed when he died."

Levi interrupted, "He had you."

"Yeah, but I was paid to be there. Not quite the same."

"Better than no one."

"I'll give you that. It wasn't my point, though. I went outside to wait for the ambulance. It was my first time being there when someone died. I think I saw his soul leave. I knew when he wasn't there anymore. I didn't have to take vitals—I just knew, but I did it anyhow because it was the procedure.

After I had called, I went outside. The moon was big. If it wasn't full, it was close to it. The air was still like tonight, the same, except for the katydids singing in the tall weeds. I stood there looking for some evidence that the world had a clue that Anton had passed. Nothing. It made me think that when you matter to no one, it's as if you don't exist. You never even lived. I realized I was one of those unremembered people standing out under the moon."

The cane hit the gravel and Levi's hands gripped both of Melody's shoulders. "Don't ever think that. You're very important. To me, to your friends, your patients, even Charmer. You've made the world a better place by being here. I'm so grateful you were able to take care of Uncle Roy when I wasn't here. Those people who don't see your worth are idiots. Plain and simple." He dropped a tender kiss on her head as his grip on her shoulders relaxed. "Believe me?"

Her life hadn't been aimless. There was a purpose, even when she didn't know it. Her brow furrowed as she mulled over the thought. "I think I do." A gentle wave of euphoria stirred deep within her. Despite the countless self-help books, she'd read explaining how she was good enough as she was, nothing ever stuck until now—until she believed. Standing on her tiptoes, she landed a kiss on his lips. Dropping back to her heels, she murmured, "Thank you."

Levi bent to grab his cane. As he stood, he held out his hand to her. The three of them walked the rest of the way without speaking. Sometimes words weren't necessary when you knew what was in each other's hearts. Often words served as a disguise.

A SOUND WOKE Levi. He wasn't exactly sure what it was. A thin, pinkish light streamed into the room. A raspy snore indicated Charmer was somewhere in the room. Melody, snuggled against his bare chest, made soft, little noises that turned his heart over. His hand played with the fiery tendrils hanging over her face. Never did he expect someone like her, especially someone who understood him the way she did.

He expected it to be a huge ordeal making love to a woman after he lost his leg, but she made it easy and natural. No embarrassment, not even blinking when he took his leg off to sleep. He could have searched the world over and never found a woman as perfect for him. Uncle Roy set him up from the grave. He originally suspected his dead relative of possible machinations, but he thought it was to punish him. Who knew Roy was still looking out for his nephew? He certainly hadn't.

A car door slammed very close, awakening the sleeping dog. Charmer lumbered to his feet and trotted out the open doorway, barking as he went. Levi winced as Melody stirred against his chest.

"It's just Charmer being his usual self. Go back to sleep."

Her eyes blinked twice, looking up at him, but still a little unfocused. Her lips tipped up in a sleepy smile. "Okay, honey." She snuggled back into her original position. He could get used to this. He was someone's honey. Had he ever been anyone's honey? A southern belle nurse at rehab had called everyone honey. The term flattered the wounded soldiers until they realized it had no more meaning than Buster did.

Charmer's animated barking continued, which was both puzzling and irritating. Melody wouldn't be able to sleep through the noise. He considered yelling at the dog, which would be no help. It would be the same as his drill sergeant screaming in his ear, startling him into a panicked wakefulness. A hard knock on the front door sent the canine into a bigger frenzy.

Great. Who would show up at dawn? Who would show up period? Melody stirred pushing her hair back. "I'll get it," she half-mumbled the words as she slid out of bed.

Levi knew he should argue, but he was enjoying the view of her naked body as she picked through the clothes on the floor. Not finding her shirt, she pulled on his that hung down to her thighs. Still, he had to admit she filled it out better than he did.

"It's probably Courtney, one of the kids next door. She sometimes wants me to look at her homework or even comment on her outfit. Can't figure out why she even comes over here." She stepped into her shorts.

With the scenery this pleasant, he had no incentive to move, although he would have to eventually. Crossing his arms behind his head, he grinned proudly, thinking Melody looked well loved. He doubted a grade school kid would notice, though. "You're sweet is the reason she stops by. Anyone else would ignore her."

One hand on the doorframe, she gave him a sultry backward

look. "Hold the position. I've got plans for you, soldier."

It just kept getting better. His ears followed the slap of Melody's bare feet. Charmer ceased barking. Maybe now would be a good time to strap on the leg. Later might kill the moment.

Leg in place, he slipped on a pair of shorts, although he didn't expect Melody to let the child in, but you never knew. He heard voices. Melody's he recognized, but the other was an adult woman. Possibly it was Courtney's mother asking a favor?

The voices grew intense. A disagreement was brewing, but about what he couldn't imagine. He pulled on a shirt but hesitated to leave the room only in shorts. Pants were his disguise for his prosthetic. If people didn't see it, they wouldn't know. The sharp edge of the other woman's voice sounded vaguely familiar. His heart dropped into his stomach. It couldn't be.

Both thighs ached from his unusual exertion the day before causing his gait to be more awkward as he lurched down the hallway to see the woman he hoped never to see again standing in the living room. Angelique had more makeup on than most drugstores stocked. Her teased hair surrounded her face reminding him of a dark cloud.

Melody stood there looking natural and beautiful in comparison to Angelique's plastic veneer. It was hard to believe he ever thought the artificial bitch was beautiful or even lovable. Both women turned at his entrance. Angelique gave him a cold, disdainful stare. Melody's glare should have incinerated him.

Melody spoke through gritted teeth. "This woman claims she's your wife."

Before he could answer, Angelique marched up to him only a foot away. Placing both hands on her hips, she announced. "I am his wife. I want what's mine. I figured this house would do for me. I'm not interested in you, especially since you're not a real man anymore. I got me one of those. I'll sign the divorce papers as soon as you sign over the house."

Wasn't this why he hired a lawyer? It didn't help that the first one died on him. Worse yet was the shock and hurt on Melody's face. She thought he'd played her, made her into a booty call. Nothing could be further from the truth. The one woman who mattered in his life would end up disappearing. He expected her to dissolve in tears, stomp out of the room, or at least cuss him out. Instead, she placed her hand on Angelique's shoulder and squeezed.

"You're not wanted here. This is half my house. Nothing gets signed over to you. Levi is a better man than most walking around on two legs. You're more the fool because you never realized that."

Angelique wiggled her shoulders, trying to shake Melody's hand off her without luck. "Would you call off your giant guard girl?"

Before Levi could even think of an answer, Melody pulled back on Angelique, causing her to stumble back in her Lucite high heels, and shout, "What are you doing?"

He wondered, too, realizing he should be doing something, but Melody took control when his past decided to bite him. Keeping her grip on the smaller woman, she escorted her to the door. Charmer kept pace, emitting a menacing growl that made Angelique move a bit faster. His soon to be ex grabbed onto the door frame before Melody pushed her out.

"I am going to press charges against your he-man girlfriend for assault," she declared.

Levi knew how vindictive Angelique could be. "It wouldn't stand up. Your word against the two of us. You have no credibility in this town. I imagine I could press charges for criminal trespass, terroristic threatening, larceny, and extortion." Before he continued naming the various crimes, she might be guilty of, Melody kicked open the screen door with one foot and pushed the still protesting woman out. Charmer escaped with Angelique and followed her out to her car.

Levi stood beside Melody as the two of them watched the brittle woman climb into her car. She gave a one-fingered salute before tearing off in a cloud of gravel dust.

"Nice car," Melody commented before turning away.

"Bought with my enlistment bonus." He growled the words, thinking how about how much she stole, and her shameless attempt to take his present and future, too. "Glad she's gone."

He turned back to an empty room. With Charmer on the wrong side of the door, he might as well put on his shoes and walk the dog. While he was out by the lake walking her dog, Melody stormed out of the house and drove away. It was easy to interpret her mood. Tornadoes showed less aggression. Her car grew smaller and smaller as it drove down the road taking with it his last hope of any future.

MELODY'S FOOT PUSHED the gas pedal down to the floor, shooting past the posted speed limit. It would be just her luck to get a ticket today. What else could go wrong? Her foot eased off the pedal as she considered the children in the area. Most of them played at their bus stops and often darted into the street. None of them feared angry drivers because nothing bad had happened to them yet. If it had, they'd stay on the sidewalk.

A complete jerk would not have walked her dog. There was no reason to walk her dog since he'd gotten what he wanted, but still he did. She slowed and stopped to allow an older couple to cross the street. The two turned and waved at her. Melody didn't know their names, but the two of them always took a morning and evening stroll. The fact that they held hands always touched something deep inside of her. What must it be like to be able to rely on someone? Know that he would be there for her. It must be amazing. Apparently, it wasn't anything she was destined to have in her life.

She smiled at the couple and waved back while her heart did a somersault. The genial couple she saw daily morphed into an older version of Levi and herself. Her gray-streaked chignon rested at the base her neck while Levi's hair was noticeably thinner. Her creations turned and looked at her. The pair seemed so peaceful and content.

A sharp beep alerted her that she'd been sitting for too long. Goodness, what was happening to her? She couldn't even drive down the street correctly. Her stomach gave a decisive growl, alerting her to the fact she'd skipped breakfast. Maybe that was her problem. A detour to a fast food restaurant netted her breakfast, which she ate in the shelter parking lot. Animals never judged you, but they did recognize those who actually cared about them. It was even early for shelter employees. There were three cars in the parking lot, but a few of them may have been overnighters, people who met for a date and left their car in what they considered a safe place. Since the shelter never towed, afraid they might lose a possible forever home for one of their residents, their assumption proved correct.

The breakfast biscuit crumbled as she bit into it, dropping crumbs into her lap. Sighing, she licked her finger and tried to pick up the various pieces. It was her breakfast, and she was going to eat it all. A knock on her driver side window startled her. At least she wasn't drinking her coffee. Mary peered through the glass with her eyebrows raised.

A slight punch to the power lever moved the window down enough to talk. "Melody, what are you doing here? It's not even eight o'clock, and you're not scheduled to volunteer."

She hadn't expected to meet anyone. It was an impulse decision to eat in the shelter parking lot. People always looked pathetic eating in fast food parking lots as if they had some disease and couldn't be around others. Usually, their only issue was that they were alone.

Often that seemed like a curse. Most would jump through hoops to prove they weren't alone, even to chatting on cell phones as they shopped to show someone was listening to them. Although at times, she often wondered if there was someone at the other end.

Mary's kind eyes compelled her to confess all. "It's a long story."

"I've got time." She looked at her watch. "I'm early anyhow. What are they going to do, fire me if I'm late?" They both laughed at the familiar joke since you didn't fire volunteers. Sometimes if they were no help, you might tell them their services weren't necessary. Of course, Mary had no fear since the various shelters depended on her free labor and community connections.

"Get in the car, then. I choose not to share my humiliation." She unlocked the door and rolled up the window, pushing a series of levers. It would be good to receive some affirmation, although she hadn't decided what to do.

Mary carefully sat down and swung her legs into the car reminiscent of old Hollywood actresses. The woman had class and beauty. Even though Melody knew her story of lost love, it still puzzled her that no man ever fell for the vivacious woman.

"Men are idiots." The words summed up her life up to now.

"That may be, but I had the feeling you're talking about one in particular." Mary reached over and patted Melody's knee. "Tell me the whole story."

The whole story would sound stupid. "Well, I wish I'd talked to you yesterday. As you know, I had my patients to see. My new client urged me to be bold and live my life with gusto since he never did, and now he's dying."

"Not such bad advice. I wish someone would have given me similar advice when I was your age." Her hand circled for her to go on.

The car seemed to be getting hotter, but not too surprising since she had the windows rolled up, and they were baking in a terrarium. A twist of the ignition switch started the engine, enabling her to turn on the air conditioning. "Then I went to Lilah's. I knew she didn't have long, but I didn't expect her to die while I was there."

"Oh, sweetie, it must be so hard for you being a hospice nurse."

Melody accepted the concern and the reassuring pat before continuing. "It wasn't that, although I guess a part of it was. Lilah told me to push the envelope, to do things that scared me, and then she gave me all these gorgeous dresses before she died."

"Okay." Mary's brows pinched together. "I thought I was listening well, and you mentioned it wasn't the death that unsettled you. I guess I'm missing something."

The tears started to fill her eyes as much as she fought against it. Looking up at the car ceiling, she tried to hold them off. "It's Levi, the guy I inherited the house with."

"Ah, that explains it some."

"Last night was the most magical night of my life." The memory of how handsome he looked in his uniform caused her to sigh.

"Hmm, I may be old, but magical nights usually do not equal tears. Forgive me, but I still don't understand." She shook her head slowly.

The aroma of coffee had her reaching for her cup. The bitter brew didn't taste as she expected, but it did delay her reply. Putting down her cup, she turned to face her friend. "Last night incredible. Levi looked hot in his dress uniform. I had on a wispy dress that made me feel like a princess. We went to the Clam Digger."

Mary whistled. "That's a fancy place. Must have cost a bundle. I'd say a man must be smitten to take a girl there."

"That's what I thought, too. A veteran there sent us a bottle of champagne. We talked, ate, laughed, and it all went so well. On the way home, I fell asleep. Maybe too much champagne."

"I assume the rest of the night was fantastic, too."

Melody put a hand over her face to cover her blush. "Ahh, yes."

"Be generous, you're all I got as far as getting a little vicarious thrill." Her eyes twinkled as she teased.

"Ya know you could still meet someone. You're not too old."

Mary waved off her suggestion. "Pshaw. I've forgotten even what to do on a date. I imagine much has changed. Besides, let's concentrate on you. So far, the night was magical, did you wake up next to a toad?"

Her top teeth worried her bottom lip as she tried to think of a delicate way to put it. There wasn't any. "I woke up with his wife banging on the door insisting she wanted the house signed over. I should point out his wife is a size zero tart. I wouldn't be surprised if he met her at a strip club."

"Wouldn't be the first to do so, but there's a lot missing in your story. Did he ever say he had a wife?"

The question made her stop and consider. "Yes, he did admit some woman hooked into him after he got a sizable enlistment bonus and convinced him to marry her just before he shipped out. Roy didn't much care for the girl. She was the reason Roy and Levi quit speaking, I think. A woman came between the McDaniels.

"It is difficult to remember exactly what Roy said about Angelique. Toward the end, the painkillers often had him mumbling to himself, but he often thought he was talking to other people. When I surprised him in a room, I'd make no mention of it. I heard him more than once cursing Angelique. Other times, he'd curse himself because he chose to write the letter revealing the woman's perfidy." Her friend looked straight ahead, her lips moving, but no sound. Did she have this effect on everyone? "I can't remember all the conversations we had. I do remember Levi saying something about making sure the divorce had gone through before he could think about dating."

"He did tell you that much."

"Yes." Maybe Levi wasn't as big as a creep as she thought. The thought cheered her a little, but it wouldn't do to get too hopeful and have things come crashing down around her. "Angelique came in screaming something about a letter, after all those notices were put in the paper."

"Notices." Mary's lips pursed as she held her fingers up counting. "Often people put up notices to find people for an inheritance or to demonstrate desertion. He could have been pushing a divorce through on desertion or abandonment. What letter?"

"She kept saying she wrote a letter. Levi walked in about that time. She got in his face and demanded he sign over the house to her, and she'd give him the divorce. Then got even nastier, calling him half a man because he lost a leg, telling him she didn't want him, and she called me the giant girlfriend." Her fists clenched in remembrance.

"I'm sure you agreed with her and offered to sign over your share of the house." Her friend reached toward the floorboard picking up the mail Melody had thrown there a couple of days ago.

"I did no such thing. I threw her out, and then Charmer followed her to the car, growling the entire time. It was hard not to laugh at the woman trying to balance herself on the gravel driveway in her Lucite stripper heels."

An envelope appeared in Mary's hand. She tapped it on the dashboard. "This might be the letter in question." She held out a purple envelope with flowery handwriting. There was even a heart over the 'I' in Levi.

Good heavens. She was part of major screw-up this morning. If she'd taken the mail in then, it might have circumvented the surprise visit. "I forgot to take the mail in. I think that was when I met my new patient, Kevin. His mother was over the top. One of those please make my son not die, despite the fact that me being there means he's terminal."

Melody reached for the envelope, but Mary pulled it away. "No doubt, being the honorable type, you'd present this to Levi unopened."

"Yes, I would. I should have already done it a couple of days ago." She wasn't sure what Mary was getting at, but her friend's eyes took on a sly knowingly look.

"Come in for tea and we'll discuss what we'll do." Mary opened the car door, taking the letter with her, not even waiting for her response.

What'll we do? Where did the *we* come from? This was a new side of Mary. Her problem energized the woman. If she had a solution, then Melody wanted to hear it. First, she needed to get the letter back. The receptionist greeted them both with a wave as she listened to the messages left on the machine. The woman had the thankless job of listening to a slew of messages, most coming from inebriated men who were unaware an uninterested woman had passed them the animal shelter number as opposed to her own. A few thought the shelter offered pickup service for unwanted pets. Very few messages were inquiries about adoption.

She slipped into the kitchenette where Mary already had a teapot on the compact stove. "I'm not steaming that letter open."

"Of course not. You're too honorable. I'm old. I've learned that scruples often leave you lonely. I'll be the bad guy. Besides I think I owe it to Roy McDaniels." The pot began to steam. Mary held it by the edge as she positioned it, so the flap was over the steam.

"Why are you determined to help Roy McDaniels, a man you never even knew?" Her friend's emphatic need to help seemed peculiar.

Placing the envelope on the counter, Mary used the edge of the butter knife to lift the flap without tearing it. "We can read it and reseal it while the adhesive is still damp."

The handwriting she could see bleeding across the page. Apparently, Angelique used a marker instead of a pen. "It's running."

"Oh, Mercy!" Mary began flapping the page trying to dry it.

"Wait, I think that is making it worse." She took the paper from Mary's hand and placed it on the table. "This is what comes from being sneaky."

"Hush, child. I've opened many a letter with this method with success. This is what comes from using a child's washable marker to write with instead of a proper writing utensil." They both hovered over the paper squinting trying to make out letters. "Are you sure this is English?"

"Reasonably. It's written in cheerleader bubble writing. I'm proficient in it," she explained as she deciphered the first line. "My Dear Sweet Husband Levi." She covered her mouth and made a gagging noise.

"If it's that bad, maybe I should read it." Mary nudged Melody aside. She blinked a couple of times and turned the paper upside down. "I don't think this is English. Wait. I think I see the words, love, hot, house."

"Mm let me see." She bumped into Mary as she straightened the letter. "I'm not sure how you saw anything with it upside down. Let's see. 'My heart beat with joy when I heard you were alive.' Why would she think he was dead?"

Mary snorted. "The woman has to have some explanation why she wasn't around during her husband's recovery. What else does it say? Why are you so good at reading this stuff anyhow?"

"I used to do one of the cheerleader's homework and had to

mimic her handwriting. Kept me from getting beat up and allowed her to graduate, barely. I couldn't take her tests for her." She traced her fingers under the words as she read. "I am hot with love for you. I am rushing to your side to make our house into a home."

"Phew." Mary held her nose. "Laying it on a little thick, isn't she?"

"Trust me—this wasn't her song and dance when she showed up this morning. She was all ultimatums and threats as if she were the wronged party. Thank goodness I didn't do anything that might have gotten me in trouble with the law. I didn't even invite her in. The woman already had the screen door open when I went to the door and stepped in like it was her house, which she apparently thought it would be."

"Wish I had been a fly on the wall. Miss Sneaky Pants comes prancing up the walk hoping to ensnare Levi with her wiles, and then you answer the door, a beautiful, tousled woman who has obviously been well-loved." Mary cocked her head in an arrogant fashion and began a mincing walk similar to Angelique's. Once she drew close to Melody, she acted surprised, and then scratched her head.

Her act did cause Melody to smile when only earlier she was sure that expression would never cross her face again. "By the way, I didn't mention any of that well-loved stuff."

"I know. You wouldn't be half as upset if you'd slept alone in your bed last night. Think about it."

The woman was right. Even Levi told her she didn't have a poker face, but she was no closer knowing what to do than she had been when she'd left the house in a huff. "What can I do? I'll see Levi tonight. We have to share the house for an entire year."

"Invite me over. I'll take his measure and tell you his real intentions." She rubbed her hands together at the prospect. "I'll even bring dinner."

"Okay. Will six work?" She wasn't sure if this would only the stir the pot more, but she'd welcome a buffer between her and Levi. All she could imagine was him with his dark-haired, negative sized bimbo. The woman brought out all her insecurities big time.

Mary grinned as she folded up the letter. "I'm keeping it. No reason for the goods to be found on you. See you at six."

The friend she'd worked with for the last three years was suddenly talking in a gangster fashion. Her fingers crossed, warding off the possibility of her day getting any stranger.

Chapter Thirteen

L EVI PACED OLIVER'S small office waiting for the lawyer to finish reading legal briefs. His inner turmoil was so apparent Calvin had ordered him from the work site to take care of his personal business. The man didn't ask for details, for which Levi was grateful. Not a great way to start a job, bailing on his second day.

The memory of how Melody defended him was glorious. Tossing the mercenary Angelique out on her ass, complete with a growling canine escort lifted his mood some. The humor of the situation ended when she turned her eyes on him. So much pain resided there. He caused it. If he hadn't pursued her, she wouldn't feel so betrayed.

Oliver rocked back in his chair with a squeak. "Son, don't get your shorts in a bunch. Your request for a divorce went on record over a year ago. True, it didn't get pushed through due to a vanishing wife and ailing barrister, but it was recorded just the same. Once started, the assets are frozen. If Angelique hadn't pulled that missing person act, the divorce would have been final long ago. Notices went out at that time, but obviously she had no need to return."

Levi placed both hands in his pockets as he tried to reason out Angelique's sudden reappearance in Wilsonville. "News travels fast through small towns. A cousin in the next town could have told her about Uncle Roy's passing and the inheritance. I imagine she thinks the man hid away a fortune. I wonder if she'd even bother coming back if she knew she was duking it out for a modest house and a rowboat. The car she blew my enlistment bonus on retails for more than the house." He pounded his fist into his hand, wishing he could hit something hard. Despite Oliver being an easygoing man, he'd object to him damaging his office.

"Sports car, huh. She bought it while you were married." He stroked his chin as he thought. "It is an asset. She'll have to sell at a fair market price and split the proceeds with you. None of this selling it to a friend for a dollar and buying it back later."

"She won't go for that." Levi rubbed the bridge of his nose. Uncle Roy did everything in his power to keep him from Angelique. His warnings were the ramblings of an old, bitter man, or so he thought at the time. "The woman is about appearances. I'm surprised she'd even be interested in the house."

"Could be she's between men and a home would be a soft place to land. Then again, she'd sell it if she got her hands on it. Roy did worry about her coming back on the scene. One of the reasons he wrote the will the way he did was to protect the house from falling into the wrong hands if the worst happened and you didn't make it back. He wanted to make sure Angelique could not lay claim to the house. If you couldn't claim the house, none of your heirs could. It would be the sole property of Ms. Gibbons. At the time, I thought Roy was being reactive, but hearing what happened at the house, I guess I owe my friend an apology when I meet him at the pearly gates."

"You and me both." Levi straddled the straight chair resting his forearm across the back. His head drooped until it met his arm. Exhaustion weighed down his eyelids. Maybe he could close his eyes for a few seconds.

"Levi," Oliver's deep, resonant voice caused him to open one eye.

"This seems like a major upset right now, but it isn't. Losing a leg and an uncle were both a big deal. What you got is a spoiled little diva who bats her eyelashes or flashes cleavage to get what she wants. The law doesn't work that way. Since she's in town, I figured we might as well push the paperwork through. Judge Clement will be presiding." The lawyer steepled his fingers and smirked. The man appeared to be amused.

"What's the punchline I'm missing?"

"Judge Clement is a mother with a son in Afghanistan. I can shoot the paperwork over to her by the end of the day. Typically, divorces go through uncontested, being a no-fault state and all. If Angelique were to contest it, she'd need a lawyer and about a twelve-hundred-dollar retainer. Normally, I don't do divorce, but I inherited your case. All the same, most of the lawyers I know will refuse to take her."

"Because you're that good?" The plainspoken lawyer did not strike him as pit bull adversary.

The lawyer brushed his nails on his shirt. "There is that. I also heard a rumor the woman doesn't have a dime to her name. No lawyer will take her case until her credit card clears. Then there's the stigma going up against a wounded warrior. Bad business. Few people want that attached to their name. Roy was popular in these parts. The general respect and affection Roy had is yours by default. Honestly, I feel sorry for the woman. Go home. Relax. I've got it taken care of."

Levi opened both eyes and held up his head as he considered the man's words. He sounded confident. It would be good to let someone take care of the dirty work for a change. The lakeside house exerted a pull on him, except that Melody would be there and would look at him with those hurt puppy eyes.

Her transparent face might as well flash BETRAYED or USED. The effect would be the same. He would have no clue what to do when they came to face-to-face.

An apology wasn't enough. What else did he have? He spent a bundle on dinner last night, a little more than he expected. Fine dining didn't come cheap, but he'd do that a hundred times just to see the sparkle in her eyes again.

"Yeah, I believe you do." He stood slowly, using the chair to balance him as he swung his leg back. It was harder than swinging the leg over. Gravity handled that. Maybe he wouldn't sit like that anymore. His perverse desire to do everything the same way he'd had before the accident was wearing on him. Some things just wouldn't be the same.

Once up and balanced, he stretched. "I think I will go home and take a nap." His eyes scanned the austere office. "I didn't bring my cane in, did I?"

"Don't remember seeing it. Not too many places to hide it, either." He swept his arm wide to indicate the entire office.

"Yeah. Point taken. Must be in the car. What were my uncle's other reasons for writing the will the way he did?" His hand was on the doorknob, but he hesitated to wait for the answer to his question.

"You're a smart man. I bet you can figure it out." The phone rang, setting the lawyer into motion as he pulled a yellow legal tablet close with one hand and picked up the phone with the other.

Levi pulled the door softly closed behind him. The drive home took longer than usual because he drove slower, unsure of his reception. Some women would even change the locks just to be spiteful. "I am so clueless. Give me a bomb and I know what to do. An upset woman and I'm close to useless." *Did you open the capsule?*

The thought popped into this head as clearly as if spoken. He hadn't thought about the capsule. First, he was so anxious to get it, and then things got complicated. Today, he'd open it. He didn't expect more than a handful of photos and predictions of what he'd be doing ten years from then. He was willing to bet going through a messy divorce wasn't on the list.

A glimpse of the lake between houses as he turned onto the last road relaxed him. The water soothed and comforted better than any other element. It would be a great day to take the rowboat out after he opened the capsule.

No sign of Melody's car as he pulled into the driveway. It might be a nice gesture if he made dinner, but he hadn't done anything wrong, had he? Charmer met him at the door, insisting on an immediate walk by trying to push past him.

"C'mon boy, wait until I get the leash."

The dog sat and waited as if he understood. If he did or not was questionable. Snapping on the leash, they stepped outside into the fall afternoon. Summer had hung on for an absurdly long time, but he could smell autumn. Some cosmic switch changed the season. Not too much longer before frost would be on the ground, and vegetation would start the slow die off. Some trees had already dropped their leaves. Another reason for him to get out in the boat. Not a lot of joy rowing in winter. It could be done, but why unless you were intent on rescuing someone?

"Charmer, you may not have heard, but your owner is not speaking to me. If you could help me, I'd appreciate it. Consider I walk you more than anyone and allow you to linger longer at your favorite trees, enjoying the odor stories left by your four-footed friends."

The dog didn't answer but sniffed at the trees that most of the neighborhood dogs tended to favor. They were usually the bigger trees. They made better bulletin boards, more space to leave a message written in urine.

"I think I mentioned starting the divorce while I was overseas." A heavy sigh escaped him as his eyes flickered to Charmer, who was investigating a calling card left by a previous dog. He wasn't exactly a great listener.

Not having solved his conundrum with Melody, he tugged on the leash, anxious to get back to the house where he could retreat to his room. His only shelter from what was sure to be an emotional storm. Still, if she weren't upset, it would mean last night meant nothing to her. He meant nothing. It was better to have the storm.

"Charmer, I think you were not a counselor in a previous life. Tell the truth, we both got carried away last night. It's natural when two people are attracted to one another. Maybe it was a little too soon."

The dog, oblivious to the conversation, rolled in some stinky, dark blot on the leaves. A hard yank brought the dog upright, but the dark spot on his back glistened. Whatever it was, it stank to high heavens.

Kneeling he grabbed handfuls of fallen leaves and rubbed Charmer's coat down. A little came off, but the rubbing action intensified the smell. A bath was the only solution. Seriously, the dog had to roll in crap today. Charmer had the nerve to wag his tail as if he'd done something noteworthy. Dogs. Who knew what went on in their minds? He was no closer understanding dogs than he was women.

A mockingbird on a branch cawed, sounding similar to a crow. The feathered creature laughed at him. If he hurried, he could get the dog bathed before Melody arrived. The only problem was Charmer wasn't ready to go. The canine pulled in the opposite direction, anxious to renew his acquaintance with the odiferous mess.

"Charmer!"

The dog looked up at him inquisitively questioning his tone of voice. He lowered the volume and tried to inject a wheedling aspect to it.

"C'mon, boy. I need your help. It's been a long, rough day for me, full of surprises after I considered it the best morning of my life when I woke up next to your mistress. She's not going to be happy with the way you smell. She might even make you sleep outside." The dog's ears went up demonstrating his ability to comprehend.

"Yep, you don't want that. It's a bath for you. Doesn't matter how much either one of us doesn't want it." A tug on the leash tested Charmer's willingness to follow. This time he followed without a protest.

The bathwater ran as he searched for something to remove the smell. An industrial cleaner might do the job but would irritate the dog's skin. He finally settled on a bottle of peach bubble bath while making a mental note to buy more. The fruity scent filled the room, invoking an image of naked Melody surrounded by bubbles, not an image conducive to dog washing. He shook his head trying to dispel it, knowing it would only return to tantalize him.

Charmer cowered in the corner, wedging his tail and back leg behind the toilet. Since he was a good-sized dog, it wouldn't be a gentle dunking. The dog would struggle as if his life were at stake. Levi shrugged off his shirt. Surely his hand-to-hand combat training should pay off in dealing with a dog. He noted Charmer's location as he pushed the door half-closed, cutting off any avenue of escape. Not making eye contact to signal his intention, he approached cautiously.

He expected a dash for safety, but the canine shook, looking so forlorn that guilt attacked Levi as he snagged his collar and pulled him out. Charmer's refusal ended up with him picking up the dog and placing him in the tub.

The action allowed him an extra strong whiff. "Phew. You smell awful. Melody should be extremely grateful to me."

MELODY WANDERED INTO the house with some trepidation. Sure, she'd left in a huff, but a full day of rethinking the morning had her wondering if she'd given the man a fair chance. After all, she knew about the divorce issue. It hadn't mattered too much last night. Whom was she kidding? She'd been lusting after Levi since they met on the dock.

Fate kept throwing roadblocks in her way, showing why the man wouldn't be a good fit. Was it fate or her mistrust of men, love, and life in general? Whatever it was she'd have to confront Levi sooner rather than later, especially with Mary coming over.

The first thing she noticed was the absence of Charmer. Dogs always made you glad to be home, except when they were missing. The sound of running water and Levi talking took her to the partially closed bathroom door.

The light scent of her peach bubble bath floated out, making her anxious. There must be someone in there with him or why would he be talking? Tiptoeing to the doors, she heard. "Melody should be very grateful to me."

Grateful, grateful for what? What was going on in her bathroom? Technically, half her bathroom. Her hand was on the door before she even considered the appropriateness of her actions. If she found that woman in her tub, she'd have no trouble tossing them both out without giving them time to dress. Her heartbeat sped up as she slowly pushed the door open, afraid of what she'd find.

A bare-chested Levi knelt beside the tub lathering up Charmer who appeared reconciled to the situation. "I know you think it's a hardship now, but you'll be glad later. Women prefer sweet smelling males."

Her heart rhythm slowed. Thank God, no showdown. Her shoulders, which had been practically up to her ears, relaxed. For a few seconds, she admired the way the light played across Levi's wet skin highlighting his rippling muscles. The man was handsome, but there were plenty of handsome men out there. The fact he was washing her dog after she ran out on him said so much more.

Charmer noticed her first and barked his welcome. Levi rocked back on his heels, one hand gripping the tub to turn and look. His eyebrows shot up as his mouth dropped open.

It was enough to make her laugh, but she didn't. Her goal was to recapture what they had yesterday, not alienate the man. "I see the two of you are making use of my bubble bath."

"Caught." An easy grin spread across his face, hinting at his willingness to be back on good footing.

Her mood lightened as she observed the two. The homecoming was supposed to be hard. After all, she'd been dreading the encounter all day. How could she be upset at a man shampooing her dog? "Should I ask what brought on this impromptu bath?"

Levi wrinkled his nose before replying. "Your child decided to roll in something disgusting. A bath was in order."

His words made perfect sense. Anyone else would tie the dog outside. At best, hose him down with frigid water and a high-powered nozzle. The man was a bigger softie than he was willing to let on. "Could you use help?"

His eyes traveled over her work smock down her pants to her sensible oxfords before returning to her face. "You might get wet."

"Not a surprise." She dropped her laptop and medical case outside the door and toed off her shoes before stepping onto the slippery floor.

The passive dog lunged and jumped acting as if the water was electrified. Levi kept a good grip on the wet canine. "Before you arrived he was fine. Maybe downcast at the prospect of a bath, but no real issues. Not sure why he has to put a show on when you arrive."

Dropping to her knees beside him, she wet her hands before

working the lather into her pet's coat. "No idea really?"

She kept her eyes on the dog as she spoke. "Could be he's trying to attract my attention, especially when I only have eyes for you."

"What?" Levi's hands slid off the dog as he turned to stare at Melody. "I didn't think you were even going to talk to me again."

Ah, she was afraid of this. Biting her bottom lip, she looked into his understanding brown eyes. "Well, I was mad this morning—very mad—because of the moron you married. She brought back all the bad memories of feeling ugly, unlovable, and worthless."

His wet hand grasped her shoulders as his face drew closer. "Melody, you are far from worthless and so breathtakingly beautiful, it's hard for me not to think about you. As for lovable, I find myself falling hard."

Her hands slipped off Charmer's soapy coat to embrace Levi as he lowered his lips to hers. The kiss, so full of promise and forgiveness, sent waves of energy pulsating through her entire body. This must be what others took for granted. She wrapped her arms around his back, returning his kiss with equal fervor.

A jingle of dog tags and a huge splash announced Charmer's escape. They jumped apart in time to see the canine's soapy tail disappearing out the door. A cluster of bubbles clung to her man's face. She wiped the bubbles away realizing she never thought of anyone as hers after her mother left.

A feeling of wonder built and expanded in her chest, reminding her of a tiny sun, growing with each second, filling her with warmth and joy, spreading out to her fingers even to her toes.

Levi stood and offered her a hand up. "Are you okay?"

"I'm marvelous." She took his proffered hand and stood. "I guess we need to grab Charmer for the rinse cycle."

Half an hour later, Charmer sulked behind a chair. Levi and Melody sat at the kitchen table with the time capsule between them.

A butter knife served as a pry bar as he worked the lid off. "I've had a feeling for a while there's something inside the can I need. It makes no sense since I put everything inside."

Melody watched while he worked the can open. The clock on the wall reminded her that Mary would arrive soon. She'd confessed to the reason for Mary's visit when Levi suggested making dinner. Maybe she should have called and told her there was no reason for her to come. Still, it would be nice if two of the most important people in her life met.

The lid popped off and hit the floor with a metallic clank, startling Charmer, who threw them both a baleful look. Apparently, they were both to blame for the bath.

An array of old photos, rocks, a couple of paperback books and envelopes littered the table as Levi lifted the objects out. A rock shaped like a heart caught Melody's eye. The smooth rock must have been a creek stone formed by running water.

Holding the small stone aloft, she asked, "What's this?"

"My stone heart. When my parents died, and I came to live with Uncle Roy, I thought my heart had turned to stone. I carried the stone with me for a while. When I decided to make a time capsule, I put it inside wondering if I would feel the same years from now."

Melody put the stone heart in his palm. "Do you still feel the same?" Instead of answering, he leaned forward, kissing her tenderly. "What do you think?"

Her breath caught. Why could he always do that to her? Knock her for a loop with a kiss, a wink, or even a word. "I'll go out on a limb here and say no."

"A perceptive woman, a rarity." He grinned before returning to shuffle through the can contents.

The bundled photographs called to her. Faded dates and locations written a decade or so ago graced each photo. She cradled one in her hand, imagining the woman who penned, *my darling Reuben and me by Lake Calico*. The dark underlines under 'darling' emphasized the newness of the relationship. The instant photos had faded with time, but it was still easy to tell that the couple was very much in love. "You look like your father."

There was no reply. Levi sat there with a letter in his hand and tears rolling down his face. "What's wrong?" Something he wrote when he was a teen moved him.

His hand shook as he held out the letter. "It's both forgiveness and explanation from the other side. Read it."

Dear Levi,

I know you think I'm a crotchety old man who doesn't know anything about life or love, but you'd be wrong. I was young like you once, full of energy, dreams, and an endless hunger for living. I had an eye for the pretty girls, too. One named Mary caught my eye. We fell in love as deep and hard as anyone can. I wanted to marry her before I went off to Vietnam. Her mother convinced her it would be a bad thing since her father never returned from war.

Her mother thought she was saving her daughter from a life of heartache. Her acceptance of her mother's edict bruised my pride and wounded my heart. When I returned unhurt, I heard Mary never married, but my pride kept me away.

In a town as small as ours, I heard rumors about Mary. I wondered if she heard any about me. Stiff-neck pride and fear of rejection kept me from going to her house and begging for another chance.

What I'm trying to say is I had a shot at real love. I know the shape and feel of it. Love is often sacrificial. Even though Mary loved me at the time, she thought her mother needed her more.

Could be she did. Hard to say. Often, we do things with the best intentions that blow up in our faces.

I did that when you took up with Angelique. From my time in the service, I was familiar with her type, a woman who knew the GIs' pay grade better than the paymaster did. A man's worth wasn't based on intrinsic values and beliefs. Instead, what he could do for her was all that mattered. I tried to warn you off, but all I did was alienate you. The last thing I wanted to do. You were all I had left, and I drove you away.

Maybe your father told you that the two of us parted ways over a girl. She preferred your father to me. He was the better-looking McDaniels brother. He dropped her a couple of months later when he met your mother, but I kept the hurt close. Meeting Mary was my second chance at love, but I allowed her to slip away, too.

When you came to live with me, I was a lonely man whose only joy was making things with wood. In some ways, I felt sorry for you having me as your last living relative. I tried to do right by you. I only hope I didn't leave any lasting scars.

If you're reading this, then you know I died. I wanted to make up for the way we parted. I left the house and boat to share between you and Melody. At first, I know this might seem like another disastrous trick, but it isn't. I wrote the will to accomplish two things. First, to keep the greedy Angelique away from my home and to give you a chance to get to know Melody. She reminds me so much of my beloved Mary. Try not to be a fool like me. Love is rare and is worth the price.

Don't let pride or hurt feelings cheat you out your opportunity to love and be loved. It may be hard for you to believe, but I loved you as if you were my own son.

You may have suspected me of the anonymous letter inform-

ing you of your wife's infidelity. I was trying to fix what I thought I caused. If I had sat back and waited, you would have seen past Angelique's brittle charm. My fear of you being stuck in a soul-draining union caused me to blunder in when I should have kept my mouth shut.

I hope you can forgive me. Work hard to hold onto love since it's the only thing that matters. Trust me, I know. Years have gone by, and nothing has ever measured up to Mary's love.

If you decide to share this letter with Melody, I want her to know I loved her, too. Her sweet personality and gentle concern were a salve for this battered soul.

A teardrop fell onto the paper. Melody placed it on the table to prevent any more tears from hitting it. She glanced up at Levi, catching his eye. They rose spontaneously and hugged, crying a little, both celebrating and grieving the passing of a good man. They stood quietly, Melody resting her head on Levi's shoulders. *Hold onto love.* The words came back. Roy didn't hold onto love and had always regretted it.

A knock on the door interrupted their contemplation of a man who had a profound impact on both their lives. Melody straightened, brushing away the tears on her face. "It's Mary."

She turned away to answer the door. Could her friend be Roy's Mary? Wouldn't it be too weird? Charmer came out of hiding to greet their guest with a yip and a hand lick. Opening the door, she beckoned the woman in who was loaded down with restaurant carry out sacks.

"Come in. Let me take your bags." Melody moved the food to the kitchen while Mary pulled a dog treat from her pocket.

Melody sorted the food on the counter while Levi introduced himself with a smile and a handshake. Mary held onto his hand without speaking.

Melody left the food to stand by her friend who looked unsteady. "Are you okay?"

"Not really. Can I sit down?"

Melody pulled out a chair while Levi escorted the woman to it. She settled into the chair with a sigh. "Forgive me, both of you. I tried to prepare myself. I realized Levi might look like my Roy, but I never expected him to look so much like him. Your age, your hair cut, remind me of the last time I saw Roy, kissed him goodbye, told him I couldn't marry him." Her voice caught, and she rested her face in her open hands.

Both Melody and Levi busied themselves giving Mary a chance to gather her emotions. Grabbing the time capsule can, Melody helped Levi stuff everything back into it. Her fingers touched a crisp envelope. Roy's familiar handwriting stood out against the white background. Her eyes drifted back to her friend who was wiping away a few stray tears.

"I'm okay. I'm just an emotional, old woman." She directed a shaky smile at Melody. "I bet I ruined my chance for a return invitation."

"No," Melody disagreed, glancing back down to the envelope. Levi gestured to the envelope. She turned it allowing him to see the name of it. His eyebrows arched as his eyes cut to their guest.

She shrugged her shoulders, not very sure what to do. In the end, Roy wrote the letter with the expectation it would be delivered. Strange, he put it into the can.

"Uh, Mary, I have something here that I believe is for you."

"Really?" The pale woman was not the same woman who steamed open Angelique's letter. She held out her hand.

Melody had given it to her with apprehension before she turned to Levi. "Let's set the table for dinner."

They set the table without speaking, sneaking occasional glances at the reading woman. No waterworks yet.

Melody stuck a spoon in the sides and placed them on the table. She arranged the chicken on a platter. "What does everyone want to drink? We have water, coke, tea, wine, and beer."

"It feels like a wine night to me," Levi suggested while angling his head at the still reading Mary.

"Wine, it is."

The cork came out with a small pop, releasing a crisp, fruity aroma. Levi took the bottle from her and placed it on the table. Mary was still reading. It might be a two-bottle night. Opening the produce drawer, she grabbed a white wine. Grapes were produce. It made sense to her as a storage bin.

A deep sigh drew her attention back to Mary. Her face was dry, and she was smiling. She had no clue what was in the letter, but she had to hand it to Roy. Whatever he wrote made Mary significantly lighter and happier.

They gathered around the table to eat when a knock sounded at the door. What was this, Grand Central Station? Melody froze thinking it could be Angelique. Levi rose, skirting the table to answer the door. The masculine timber of a man, conversing with Levi reassured her the vindictive woman hadn't returned.

Thank goodness. She didn't know who it was but was glad it wasn't plastic girl. Levi entered the kitchen, escorting a handsome older man.

"Hey, I want you to meet my boss, Calvin. He brought my cane by since I forgot it at work. I was wondering if he could join us."

The invitation surprised Calvin, who looked abashed. Melody did a mental calculation of the food, not seeing any reason not to invite him. Mary sat up a mite straighter, patting her hair. Ah yes, the widower who needed a pet.

"Pull up a seat," she invited. "I'll just get another plate."

Calvin took a seat by Mary, leaving Melody to sit by Levi. The night went well. At one point, Calvin and Mary were deep into reminiscing when Levi winked at her. It was more than just a wink to her. It was their secret language. Of course, he was telling her he was right about getting the two friends together. No way she'd mention it was her idea.

The best part of the night is when they stood at the door and waved goodbye. It was the best part because they both knew love was worth the trouble in the end.

Epilogue

A YEAR LATER, another beautiful Indian Summer day, a perfect day for a wedding, Melody couldn't have ordered a better day. Glass fairy balls bedecked the surrounding trees glistening in the afternoon sun. There were several guests with dogs on leashes. Each animal wore a T-shirt emblazoned with ADOPT ME across its back. Mary suggested an outdoor wedding would be the perfect opportunity to reveal several lovable pooches to the public. Melody quickly agreed.

The guests mingled around the colorful tubs of zinnias Melody planted earlier in the season. Kevin arrived with Robert looking healthier than she'd ever seen him. Love could work miracles. It brought a man with only a few months to live back to life. It turned Levi's stone heart into a real one.

From the living room, she peered out the window, hoping for a glimpse of the groom. He stood next to the bridal arch dressed in white shirt and slacks. At the time, she thought the choice impractical but went along after he explained. Their love and marriage would be his only real one. Nothing else had mattered before they met. Ironically, all the side streets led to now.

She chose to wear her purple dress that Lilah gave her. In this dress, she finally allowed herself to fall headlong in love with Levi and life.

Mary hurried up the path to the front door. Opening the door, she called. "C'mon, honey. It's time."

Melody stepped away from the window ready for her wedding. Mary reached for her hand drawing her into a tight hug. "I'm so excited. It's like you are my own daughter."

Their embrace tightened as Melody hugged her close. "Thank you. You've been more than a mother to me." Their heads touched as she wondered about her biological mother who chose to walk away from her own child. Surprisingly, it didn't hurt anymore. She picked up her bouquet of yellow roses. "I'll throw the bouquet your way."

Mary laughed as she wiped away a tear. "No need, sweetie. Calvin already proposed."

"What?"

Courtney, the neighbor girl, burst into the room. "They're already playing the music, and Levi looks worried."

"Oh!" Melody slipped her shoes on. She didn't want to keep her groom waiting. She gave Mary a quick kiss.

She tapped Courtney as she walked by. "Remember, you are in charge of the ring bearer."

The sunlight made her blink as she stepped out of the house. Her future was bright. It wouldn't hurt to invest in sunglasses. A lilting flute solo wafted through the air as light and lovely as a butterfly.

Taking a deep breath, her eyes skimmed over the large crowd, surprising for a woman who didn't think she had friends. Mary scurried around the edge of the crowd to return to her place as maid of honor. Calvin looked dignified standing beside Levi. Her soon to be husband turned and smiled at her. Her heart soared. Roy was right. Some things are worth holding onto forever. She started the slow, measured steps she'd practiced the night before.

"No, stop, not yet."

The words alerted her something unexpected was about to happen. Charmer ran down the aisle with a ring pillow tied to his back.

The dog darted passed her to reach his true love, Levi.

The few guests tittered as the hound sat beside the groom looking as poised as a dog food model. Fortunately, all the shelter volunteers had good control of the canine guests. A few yipped their desire to follow.

Being a Justice of the Peace, as well as a lawyer, Oliver Douglas stood under the arch ready to officiate. Truly, there was no one better to do it since he inadvertently brought them together.

When she reached the arch, she handed her flowers to Mary and took Levi's outstretched hands.

In his eyes, she saw their future. There would be fights, apologies, and makeup sex. There would be long walks, boat rides across the lake, companionable silences, and love.

Oliver addressed the crowd with his trademark humor. "Some you may know Melody and Levi were required to share the house for a year to inherit. Those of you who knew Roy realized what a canny man he was. Like all good Scots, he was a thrifty one, too. I guess it's not too surprising he insisted the two of them live together in hopes of his two favorite people falling in love. A year and a day later, I am happy to be uniting these two fine, young people."

The crowd laughed as Oliver intended them to. It was time for their vows. When they started planning the wedding, she thought writing their vows would be a good thing. The idea of reciting them in front of everyone caused her to have doubts. Levi chose to go first.

He dropped one of her hands to reach into his pocket. He placed the familiar stone heart into her hand.

"There was a time in my life I never expected to love again or be loved. I thought of my heart as being a dead, lifeless stone. It took a very special woman to teach me to love, to challenge me to live. Thanks to my uncle and his interfering from the great beyond, I met the woman of my dreams. The stone heart I give her is a symbol of my love. It is all yours, forever."

Her eyes were getting glassy, making it hard to see. She couldn't cry it would cause her mascara to run, and she'd end up looking like some 70's rock star.

Mary handed her a tissue she used to dab away her tears. Inhaling deeply, she tried to remove the tears from her voice, but it still shook a little.

"I was never a believer in love, happy endings, or even heroes. When I met Levi, I thought he was a sarcastic jerk."

The uniformed soldiers crowded together in the second row hooted and chuckled. One shouted, "Oh yeah, she's got that right."

"As I got to know him I discovered he could be a kind, considerate, gentleman. He didn't woo me with romantic poems and empty flattery. Instead, he impressed me by walking my difficult dog, Charmer, making me an apology breakfast and making my secret romantic dreams come true."

There was a rippling of 'ahs'. Someone clapped. Another woman said loudly enough to carry, "Take notes," which caused additional giggles.

"Levi made me believe in love. He is my happy ending, but most of all, he's my hero."

The guests broke into applause as Levi leaned forward to kiss her. Melody kissed him back, caught in the moment, realizing she never dared to dream dreams this magnificent, too afraid to believe.

Oliver cleared his throat and blustered. "I think I'm the one to tell you when you can kiss the bride."

Levi pulled back to regard Oliver. "I'll let you pronounce us husband and wife."

"That'll do, but first the rings. Levi reached down to untie the pillow from Charmer. He actually put their rings on the pillow. He trusted her dog more than she did. Well, their dog. He always was.

The End

The Soul Mate Search

By
Morgan K Wyatt

Chapter One

NINA LOOKED AT the placard promising Tarot readings taped on the window of what appeared to be a junk store. The display crammed with decorative vases, statues of Greek Gods and Goddesses even had a few tribal masks that leered out at the passing crowd. It was the first time she'd noticed the small shop jammed between the carpet remnants store and yoga studio. Every other time she'd driven to the spice shop. Today she had walked since it was a gorgeous, sunny day. Besides, she could use the exercise. Tucking one finger into the waistband of her skirt, she tugged it outward to ease the bite. Her impulsive decision to go with a size smaller to encourage weight loss felt stupid and painful now.

Nonsense. That's what all card readings were. They were no more accurate than reading a fortune cookie and certainly no reason to waste good money to hear she had a handsome stranger in her future or that she couldn't decide between two men. Any real fortuneteller would know there were no men in her life. The lack was beginning to worry her, which was probably the reason she attacked every diet that came out. If only she'd dropped ten pounds, she'd be a knockout according to the trainer at the gym. He dropped the conversational grenade while trying to interest her in individual sessions. The man expected an expensive financial outlay for planting his seed. Nina dropped over a thousand, not on sessions, but on a treadmill. It allowed her to exercise at home without seeing his smug face.

Still, the doubt lingered even though she cut Mr. Obnoxious

Trainer out of her life. Her best friend Ellie swore by the ginger regimen. The ginger water she tried at her friend's house didn't gag her too much, which was the reason she was off to buy an industrial size container of the stuff.

Two large steps took her past the lure of Tarot reading when an elderly woman appeared space between the buildings. She wore her hair in a chignon while an elegant black dress skimmed her slender frame. A few colorful necklaces hung from her neck while some sizable jewels glittered on her fingers. Her dark gaze met Nina's surprised one.

"You are leaving without even knowing the answer to your question."

Biting her lips, Nina debated what to say. At first, she wanted to deny having a question, but she did have one. If the woman knew she had a question, did that make her legitimate? It could be the fact she had hesitated in front of the store that had the woman hurrying out to drum up business. "Um…" What did one call a fortune teller?

The woman's eyes sparkled as if holding back laughter. "It's Helen, just Helen. I did not come out to drum up business." Her lips turned up into a smile at the phrase. "No, I came because I care about you."

Nina understood the retail business and *pretending to care* sold merchandise, but even knowing that the woman intrigued her. "Why do you care?"

Helen raised one delicately plucked eyebrow. "You are running out of time."

Nina automatically looked at her watch, wondering how late it was. What excuse could she use to get away from the woman? Weren't those who told your fortune for money supposed to say good things? How else would they get any repeat business? "I am in a bit of a rush."

"Perhaps that's your problem." Helen held up an admonishing finger and then added two more. "Three times you've passed your soul mate without giving him a glance. It is rare to have a soul mate, even rarer to have so many chances." Helen dropped her hand and contemplated her cuticles.

Soul mate, what soul mate? Somehow, she had passed the man. Trying to think of how many people she encountered every day working in at one of the biggest malls in the tristate region boggled her math ability. All the same, she had missed him three times. Three times? "How old was I when I missed him?"

Helen gestured to the shop door. "Perhaps you would like to keep your private life private."

Of course, she would. The idea of her missing *the one* had her demanding answers on a busy sidewalk. Who knows how many people overheard her? As the regional manager of men's suit and formal wear outlet, she did have a business reputation to keep. When she took the management job ten years ago, constantly surrounded by men, Ellie had predicted wedding bells. In a way, she had the same thought, the reason she left managing a trio of candle shops.

She and Ellie failed to consider one thing. Most of the men who came to her shop for tuxedos or suits were usually getting married or very close to it. Often the fiancée showed up too, which really killed any chance of flirting if the men considered it. Still, she got a few dates from sales representatives who were trying to get her to pick up their line. Unfortunately, most of the dates were little more than sales pitches with wine and food.

Might as well listen to what the women had to say. It could be no worse than the ginger diet.

Leading the way, Helen skirted tables laden with curios and dust. After a long, twisted path, they reached a small room with a cloth-covered round table and two chairs, surprising her after the clutter of the outer room.

"Have a seat." Helen gestured to the chairs, turning to remove something from a cabinet built into the wall.

Nina sat in the seat, perching on the edge, wondering if it was too late to leave. Helen turned and placed a white candle on the table along with a round glass sphere. It was an honest to goodness crystal ball. Leaning closer, Nina examined the object. Only a little bigger than a softball, instead of being clear, it had a whitish, frosted aspect to it. She wondered how anyone could see anything in it. A cynic would reason that was the idea. Helen walked around the table, making Nina wonder what she was doing. Every time she passed behind her, Nina twisted in her chair to keep her in view. She didn't expect the woman to mug her, but crazier things happen. A little old lady with a butcher knife in the hospital parking lot assaulted one of her employees. It went to show you never could tell.

"Rest easy, Nina. This is a safe place. You are safe." Helen made her third turn around the table and slipped into her chair. Pulling out a box of matches, she lit one and held it to the wick of the white candle until it caught.

No cards on the table. How would she do a reading? Nina was about to point this out when Helen spoke.

"Pick up the sphere and hold it. Consider your questions. Close your eyes."

She reached for the ball, vowing not to close her eyes. She rolled the ball between her fingers feeling the smooth glass. The frosted inside began to look cloudier. Indistinct shapes moved inside the glass ball. The outline of her old elementary school solidified as she held the globe closer with the image of her mother walking her to school.

She twisted and danced at the end of her mother's hand, convinced she did not need parental supervision to walk the two blocks to school. Her mother determinedly held on, believing otherwise. The school buses roared up to the school, ejecting their load of noisy children.

One dark haired boy with a superhero backpack ran up the school stairs, turned, stopped, and looked back at her. Their eyes met for the briefest second.

His red polo and jeans could belong to any other male student, but she knew in an instant that it was he, her soul mate. She held the globe at eye level to get a closer look. No doubt, the man had changed in thirty years, but something might remain to help her find him. A name on a folder or some identifying mark on his clothing, there had to be something.

The crystal, instead of cooperating, grew foggy again. A sudden urge to pitch the faulty ball swept over her, but her hands remained locked in position. Her gaze went to Helen's, curious if she had something to do with the ball remaining stationary as opposed to airborne.

"Crystal balls are expensive." She winked, confirming her mental hold over Nina's throwing arm. "Look quickly or you will miss your second meeting."

The ball fogged and shifted once more when another image formed.

Her small car was loaded down with all she thought essential for college life. It included twenty pairs of shoes, her laptop, no less than 200 romantic comedies DVDs, and enough toiletries and makeup to do one floor of her dorm. She struggled with a large box she had over-packed. A masculine voice broke into her struggles.

"Could you use some help?"

She gave up her box with a sigh of relief and recited her room number. She watched the box walk away with the assistance of two jean clad legs and athletic shoes. She didn't even see his face. He left the carton in front of her door, never giving her the chance to thank him. She never

knew who carried her box. Her intentions were to make him cupcakes,
which were difficult with the dorm's limited kitchen facilities, but even
harder since she didn't know his name.

She watched him walk away in the globe, admiring how well he
filled out his jeans. One of her girlfriends bragged how she could
identify any man by looking at his backside. She could recognize him
walking away, but it would make her no better than the men who
always looked at her breasts and never ever made it up to her face.
She wanted to whine but felt the psychic's grip over her hands. "I
wasn't going to throw it this time."

"I can feel your frustration." Helen nodded as if agreeing with
herself.

Exhaling deeply, Nina rolled her shoulders while keeping a firm
grip on the ball. "How would you feel if you discovered you went to
the same grade school as your soul mate, even the same college? Yet,
you both managed to pass each other."

Helen smiled wistfully as if contemplating a memory Nina
couldn't see. "I would feel very, very blessed. You aren't always
reunited with your soul mate in each lifetime. It is such a grand
experience. The euphoria lingers into the next life." The rapturous
look on her face faded, confirming the suspicion that Helen's soul
mate had not appeared in the current time.

"Oh." Nina grasped for something better but came up with nothing. The ball started to heat under her hands as if responding to her
emotional state. The McMillan and Sons building materialized in the
glass.

Her first job after college, but already she'd given her notice, anxious
for a chance to prove her worth at Candle World. However, before she
could start her new adventure, Mr. McMillan gave her the odd job of

hiring her own replacement. She shuffled through the resumes putting them in the order the interviews would be.

Antonius Dunn was last out of five candidates. The first name sounded foreign, but she noticed they graduated from the same college, which caused her to discount his first name. By interview number three, Mr. McMillan informed her that Joseph, who was nephew of the owner, had the job. Joseph wasn't well qualified, but Mr. McMillan made it known he wanted Joseph. The interviews and the ad in the paper were all a smokescreen to hide a clear case of nepotism. It didn't seem fair to interview the other candidates, leading them on with the possibility of being hired. She walked into the company lobby where the last two candidates waited, a well-groomed blonde woman with an air of superiority and a gorgeous, be still my heart, man.

Ah yes, she remembered now. She could hardly bring herself to look at the two of them since she was the bearer of bad tidings. The woman didn't matter too much because she had the look. Daddy could pull a few strings and get her a much better job than this. The man she remembered. Just one look at him and her heart stumbled. If she ever designed her ideal man, it'd be him. His dark curly hair skimmed his shoulders with the emphasis on artist as opposed to MBA. He had a pair of trendy wireless glasses and deep brown eyes. How she noticed so much in the time, it took her to say, "The position has been filled. Thanks for coming," amazed her.

The woman left in a huff, while he stood, towering over her a few inches. He held out his hand, and she touched it hesitantly, knowing touching it would be electrical. It was. He thanked her for her time, repeated his name and left. She stood there with her hand out as if turned into a statue. Peggy, the receptionist, broke into her stupor. "That one was a looker. I would rather have him around than dumpy old Joseph."

Nina stared into the crystal ball at her younger self, transfixed by the closed door. She didn't need to remember what she was thinking then. Any woman would wish for a return visit. Helen cleared her throat, catching her attention.

"Helen, that gorgeous guy is my soul mate? I don't get it. Men who look like him don't go for me. I'm average, a sparrow while he's a hawk. If I remember correctly, hawks eat sparrows." Her hands still clutched the ball as if she could bring back the image.

The woman's laughter tinkled and shimmered like wind chimes. "My girl, you have to see past the outside trappings to the man within. You two are destined to be together."

This sounded great in theory. "How do I meet my soul mate? Will he know I am his soul mate? I know his name, and he's probably in the area. All I have to do is look him up, right?"

The woman's forehead beetled as she chewed her bottom lip, not a good sign. Holding her hand out for the crystal ball, Helen took it and returned it to the cabinet. With her back turned, she started talking, making it hard to hear her clearly.

"It won't be easy. Your last meeting was almost thirteen years ago. Things change. People change. Antonius could have married."

"What?" Nina shot to her feet. "First, you tell me I have a soul mate and I need to find him because time is running out, then you inform me that he might be married. Why?" Her fingers gripped the table.

Putting her hands together in front of her chest, Helen waited, probably for Nina to appear less hostile. Realizing the elderly woman might view her as threatening. She sat and loosened her grip on the table. Her hand went up to her neck, which felt a little heated. Turning forty stalked her the way a cat did a bird. She'd given up any hope of children and a husband too. Now she discovered her soul mate existed mere miles, possibly blocks from her. Instead of watching endless romantic movies, she could have been starring in her own.

Wait, she could have gone to her prom with Antonius, instead of Ellie's cousin. The name was a mouthful. She could call him Anton. No, it didn't sound right. Tony felt better, a regular name, not pretentious.

Helena held out her hand as if pleading for her understanding. "Some things I know. Others I don't. You walk pass the store and your thoughts shout '*Where's my soul mate?*'"

Nina's eyes narrowed. She didn't like the image of her thoughts shouting. It made her sound pathetic. "My thoughts don't yell."

"They did." Helen disagreed. "That's why I had to come out of the shop to quiet them down. I had no clue how long you and your screaming thoughts would be in the area."

"Now, they're screaming thoughts." This was not helping in the least. "Tell me about my soul mate and how I am running out of time."

Helen sat down, spreading her long fingers out on the table, showing off her rings. Nina noticed none was a wedding ring.

"That's right, no soul mate for me in this lifetime. My gift allowed me to see this so I did not hope for one. You have had more chances than most. Chances come in magical denominations. Three is one magical grouping, but lucky for you, three isn't it. You have four more chances."

Four more chances sounded as if a multitude. Surely, with four chances she could make it work. She'd always managed to get what she set her mind to, including her MBA, her home, and her current job. Why not Tony? "Is Tony looking for his soul mate?"

"I can't tell you. He may think he's already found his soul mate. He may be married." She shrugged her thin shoulders.

Not what she wanted to hear. "Please stop. Such possibilities are no help to me at all. What am I supposed to do with a man who is married?" She didn't consider herself a femme fatale who would cause a man to abandon his wife and family. Her Nona would be appalled at such behavior. It turned her stomach too. Who knew finding a soul mate would be so frigging hard.

Helen stretched across the table to pat Nina's hand. "Don't fret too much. Even if he's married, I doubt it will last long. Marriages seldom do these days. Besides, you can't force the meetings. They just happen when everything falls into place."

Her plan to search the Internet using the services she used for employee background checks skidded to an abrupt halt. "I can't do what?" Her other plans, where she'd get the works, complete with eyebrows and other areas waxed, ended up on temporary hold also.

"No, you cannot mess with fate. She can be a cruel bitch. Consider you know more than most people do in your position. You've seen your other half. You even know his name. All you have to do is be aware, ready, for the next chance." Helen gave her a hand a squeeze before letting go and standing.

It didn't take a rocket scientist to recognize the signal for the reading was over. Standing, she grabbed her purse and rifled through the wallet, thinking she should give the woman something. "How much do you usually charge for a reading?"

Her fingers rested on a twenty as Helen said, "Sixty-five."

The twenty would make a decent tip. You'd think if she charged so much the place would look better.

Helen laughed again, motioning her through the store. "It wouldn't do me any good to look too prosperous in this neighborhood. An update on how your soul mate search concludes will be my payment."

The door closed behind her. Standing on the sidewalk, Nina stared at the people walking around her. She needed to be on full alert. She would never know when Antonius might show up. With that in mind, she headed for the spice shop. No time like the present to drop the ten pounds settled stubbornly on her torso.

By the time, she returned to her office the sales rep from the Allegro line had dropped off a pound of free trade, Sumatran coffee. The bag rattled when she shook it, indicating beans. No good. Her grinder broke a couple of weeks ago, probably due to overwork. A good cup of coffee sounded like heaven. Sighing, she pushed the bag aside and paged through the suit catalog that accompanied the beans.

Most people believe when you advertised custom suits that each man gets one designed just for him, which wasn't the case. They had to start somewhere. Usually, her tailors had a series of suits they fitted to each client. They did an excellent job, often making the customer better dressed than most millionaires. The Allegro line catalog featured glossy page after glossy page of lean, sexy models, wearing light colored suits. Sometimes the suits were even unconstructed. Her clients preferred padding. The more padding in the shoulders, the better the waist looked.

Allegro. She considered the word, rolling it around in her mouth. It reminded her of allergy medicine. It was hard to sell a suit with a similar name to allergy medicine. Too bad, she pushed the catalog away. Some of the suits had potential, especially if she wanted to appeal to a younger set. They could bypass mentioning the name. Up to now, she hadn't even met the Allegro rep. He always dropped in when she was gone. Of course, the rep could be a woman too. She picked up the scrawled note that came with the coffee.

To N. M. Bradley,

Enjoy the coffee and the catalog. Both pack robust charm and character, which should 'suit' your discerning taste.

T. Dante

The note told her exactly nothing. It was a useful note, similar to something she might write. The sales rep combined humor, plug his product, and did enough research to know she loved coffee. It could have been a safe guess too. The digital clock glowed five-fifteen, which meant most of her junior executives had left the building, pleading t-ball games, scouts, and dance lessons for their little princes or princesses. She didn't begrudge them family time, but she often wondered how much of it was actually t-ball lessons or wind-down time at the local sports bar around the corner.

The few times she decided to nip out for a bite at Sammy's Bar and Grill, she found a handful of her employees who'd muttered various excuses for their early departure. The place's reputation was for their breaded tenderloin and scantily clad waitresses. Sometimes it embarrassed her to stop in for a burger, but not as much as it should embarrass Hector, who claimed to leave early on Wednesdays for prayer meeting. Did they lie to her face about their plans because she was female? It really didn't matter since she mentally noted who kept showing up at the sports bar. A smart man would know enough to go somewhere else once caught by the boss. Apparently, she had a few who weren't too sharp.

Her female employees actually did manage to make it home, fix dinner, and help with homework as they said they were. If not, she never caught them at Sammy's or in the mall as she walked to the parking lot. Since she had no home life per se, she stayed late. Ellie, her best friend, pointed out she had no social life because she spent most of her waking hours at her job. It was rather a Catch-22 situation. She could have married, was even asked twice, but it didn't feel right.

She expected something more than the routine proposals she received. The men who rendered the proposals were good, decent men, as her mother liked to remind her. Now they were married with children. Her mother always tacked on the additional info, in case she'd somehow forgotten. Sometimes she saw them in town, often with the family in tow. At best, she nodded when she saw them, aware a wife would not appreciate an enthusiastic greeting. Often, she watched them before they saw her, trying to decide if the men looked happy. For the most part, they looked harried and tired. Still, they were probably happier without her by their side.

Neither Trenton nor Paul had confessed to great passion in their proposals. Nope, it was more like if you don't have any plans for the rest of our life, then why don't we marry. She wondered if they ran the same proposal past their current wives. If they did, apparently the women weren't doing anything with the rest of their lives. They could have fallen madly, passionately in love. Thinking of the two earnest men, she snorted with laughter, glanced at her door to see it was open. It wasn't.

The clock now glowed five-thirty-one. She might as well head home and start her ginger diet. Tucking the coffee under her arm, she prepared to leave. Glancing in the mirror on her office wall, she reapplied her lipstick and corralled some wayward strands of hair back in her French twist hairstyle. The small twelve by twelve-inch mirror reflected a woman in a dark suit with a bright fuchsia silk blouse. Her makeup and hair reflected her place on the corporate ladder. Her index finger smoothed her foundation. When it came to makeup, she was her own worst enemy, often scratching her face or rubbing her eyes. Well, she was good to go now.

Striding through the showroom, she called out goodbyes to the remaining associates. A client came out of the dressing room, looking unsure in their top of the line suit. The slightly pudgy man was not the type to attract women's eyes, she knew. Feeling playful, she eyed him good, before whistling, and calling out, "Looking good."

No doubt, the man regarded her curiously along with her three sales reps. She was out to find her true love. It was about time too. She walked with a bit of a bounce in her step, watching the reflective store windows for a sign of Mr. Wonderful. Nothing yet. At least she had her coffee. Bending her head slightly, she inhaled the delicious aroma.